LADY OF MYSTERY

THE UNCONVENTIONAL LADIES
BOOK ONE

ELLIE ST. CLAIR

CONTENTS

Facebook: Ellie St. Clair

Cover by AJF Designs

Do you love historical romance? Receive access to a free ebook, as well as exclusive content such as giveaways, contests, freebies and advance notice of pre-orders through my mailing list!

Sign up here!

The Unconventional Ladies
Lady of Mystery
Lady of Fortune
Lady of Providence
Lady of Charade

The Unconventional Ladies Box Set

For a full list of all of Ellie's books, please see
www.elliestclair.com/books.

CHAPTER 1

MARCH 1814

"'Women have no ideas, except personal ones,'" Lady Phoebe Winters recited, leaning forward in indignant earnestness. "And *then*, the article continues. I will not force you to sit through the entirety of it, but will summarize to tell you that it does admit that, in fact, women do have more *tenderness* than men — oh yes."

She snorted and continued as her friends looked on, allowing her tirade to continue. "But then — and I have committed this to memory, so impactful the words were — 'Women admire in men those qualities which are necessary to their own deficiencies — courage, the power of taking the lead, activity, strength, everything in short which may be called the sexual distinction of man's mind, and which flatters the tenderness and wraps a guiding arm around the weakness of his associate.'

"Can you believe such drivel? If only I could respond with the truth. For the *truth* is that women are stronger than

1

men could ever be. We must endure while always maintaining the facade that everything is perfect, that there is nothing of which we are concerned. And all of this while looking immaculate, maintaining perfect manners, and hiding all of our true feelings. I wish I could show him a true demonstration of strength and courage, that is for certain."

Phoebe finished her recounting and sat back against the soft green silk cushions of the sofa, her chest heaving as anger flowed through her veins anew. After retelling what she had read that morning with her breakfast, incredulity seeped out of every pore as she seethed and her ire began festering anew.

When she had first read the words, while she was certainly not completely surprised, she had nearly spit her coffee all over the paper. She had at first shoved the paper away but could not help herself from picking it up once more to continue.

Now she looked around at the faces of her friends, women she had been so sure would wholeheartedly agree with her, but they stared back at her with sympathy more than anything. Her stomach began to sink as disappointment crept in.

"You agree with me — do you not?" she demanded, raising an eyebrow as she looked at them all, challenging them to refute her.

"We do agree with you, Phoebe," Elizabeth reassured her, leaning forward from her place next to her on the corner of the sofa, placing a hand on her knee. "Of course we do, you know that. It is only that articles such as that you quoted are not particularly *un*believable. In fact, I would be surprised were anything ever written to the contrary."

Phoebe loved Elizabeth, truly she did, but damn her endless practicality.

"How can you say that?" she demanded, as the fire next to her flashing, accentuating her words as if it agreed with her.

"How can I not?" Elizabeth replied, waving an elegant hand in the air. Elizabeth's strength was her steadiness, and she held an air of refinement that was unmatched by nearly any other woman Phoebe had ever met. "It is the way of the world, Phoebe. It is set in place by men. It is how they see women, and they write their own viewpoints without fear of retribution."

Phoebe crossed her arms over her chest and took in the rest of them. Julia, sitting in the chair across from her, sent a sweet smile her way, while Sarah leaned forward in the seat beside Julia.

"It is galling, Phoebe, truly it is," Sarah said, a long tendril of her soft, cinnamon brown hair brushing the side of her temple as she leaned forward slightly. "The ways of the nobility ... well, they have certainly been a surprise to me since I arrived in London, to say the least. But these are the rules of society, are they not? You have to play amongst them, or you risk getting hurt."

Phoebe worried her bottom lip, a habit that was becoming all too familiar as at times it left her lips painfully dry.

"But who made the rules?" she asked.

"What do you mean?" responded Elizabeth.

"These rules you speak of, that we must conform to — how did they come about? They are not *rules*, so much as conventions that have become part of our lives because we all agree to follow them, because no one speaks otherwise. And why do we not? Because we are afraid."

Phoebe pushed away from the mahogany sofa and started pacing the Aubusson carpet lining the floor of their current meeting place, one of the Earl of Torrington's drawing rooms. Phoebe and the three women who convened together had found themselves seated amongst the wallflowers one time too many. But unlike the other women who bordered the dance floors with them, they were not cast aside due to their unattractiveness, nor their shyness or unsuitability.

No, it was rather that none of them had much interest in the games of the *ton*, the whispers, the flirtations, the giggles behind the fans. One night over a glass or two of sherry, they found that their very disdain for what was considered to be attractive and desirable by most was, in fact, what drew them together.

They far preferred their lively conversations and debates to watching others make fools of themselves, and so at events such as these, balls and parties and the like, they would often ensconce themselves in a nearby room where they could speak without fear of social derision.

Tonight, however, went far beyond simple conversation for Phoebe. If these three women, who she now counted as the closest people in the entire world to her, did not understand, then who would?

"It was not always this way, was it?" she ventured to her friends. "Men have always been the leaders, the warriors, it is true, but there have been times when women held much more power than we do now. In the Roman era, women possessed great influence over the decisions of men. Only three hundred years ago, some women held fortresses, fought on battlefields alongside their husbands and brothers."

Phoebe was now waving her hands emphatically, needing them to understand the importance of what she spoke. "Half the world is composed of women. However, men seem to be able to say whatever they want, whenever they want, in whatever form they choose. Men — of the nobility, at least — receive education, the power of a title, the financial independence to do whatever they seek. And yet women are bred only to please men. We sit and listen to the drivel such as that in the article, and we are expected to not only believe it but to follow it. Why?"

Julia looked up at her, chin in hand, a riot of blonde curls cascading from the top of her head about her pixie face. She was tiny, almost childlike and angelic, yet she held an inner strength that Phoebe knew few could rival.

"I suppose," Julia began slowly, "we follow it because it is what we know. Because no one is doing any different. Because no other woman is challenging it."

Looking at the nods of the other two, Phoebe stopped her pacing and simply stared at them, a niggling thought tugging at the corner of her brain. What Julia said was true. No one questioned such opinions. No one presented any other way of thinking. The newspapers may employ writers of a wide variety of opinions, true, but besides a different political stance, what else truly separated one writer from the other? They all held the same ignorant opinions — when it came to women, at any rate. The wife of a Whig was held to the very same expectations as the wife of a Tory.

"Exactly," Sarah agreed with Julia, a grin covering her freckled face. "No one has ever spoken out otherwise. So why would any hold an opinion to the contrary? Your thoughts are very opposed to most others, Phoebe, truly, you must know that. I know your parents raised you to be a woman who creates her own opinions, but you are an exception, as you well know."

Phoebe nodded slowly, the words of her friends causing an idea to form in her mind. Another public voice was required to provide a different way of thinking, to give women the opportunity to receive knowledge outside of what had been instilled in them since childhood.

"You are right," she said, pointing a finger in their general direction with some flourish. "A new viewpoint needs to be shared. It is time."

She strode back to the sofa, taking a seat with a flounce of her skirts. She picked up the glass in front of her, containing some type of punch that was altogether too sweet. She reached into the folds of her skirt to find the flask within a deeply hidden pocket, adding the rum to her drink before offering it to her friends.

"A toast," she said, holding up her glass. "To the future."

Confusion reigned on their faces at her words, but they raised their glasses anyway.

"To the future," they chorused, and Phoebe shared a grin of triumph with them.

"Now," Elizabeth said, rising gracefully. "We must return to the party, or my mother will never allow me to hear the end of it upon our return."

"I suppose we must," said Phoebe, standing herself, and, being in closest proximity to the door, she began to lead them out. She brought her hand to the doorknob, but gasped when it turned of its own accord, and, off balance, she fell forward through what was now open space, until she collided into something very hard, very immobile, and very unforgiving.

She looked up. And up further. A very strong jaw, one currently clenched quite tightly, entered her view. Phoebe took a step back, tilting her head so she could better see the face of the statue in front of her — for it seemed the man was incapable of moving.

His cheekbones were harsh, his nose pronounced. The only soft feature about him was the lock of sandy blond hair swooping down low over his forehead. His eyes were a deep chocolate brown. And they were currently looking down at her with an icy hard frigidness that nearly made her shiver. Not that she would. She refused to show him any indication of weakness, nor any sign of backing down. For she knew very well who this man was.

"Lord Berkley," she finally greeted him. "May I be of assistance?"

If it were possible, he looked even further down his nose at her.

"Excuse me?" His voice was low and gravely, sending a wave of shivers down her spine. Not of fear, no — it was something else, something peculiar that she couldn't quite place.

"I asked you," she drawled slowly, as if he couldn't understand the words coming out of her mouth, "if you required assistance. For I can think of no other reason that you would be standing so immobile in the path of a lady when she is trying to exit a room."

She heard one of her friends gasp behind her, and she started a bit, having completely forgotten they were still there for a moment.

"Lady Phoebe, isn't it?" the man asked, not moving an inch — and neither did she, as they seemed to be locked in a battle of wills, neither prepared to provide the other any glimpse of weakness or retreat.

"It is," she said, holding her head high. She was of average height, but still this man towered above her. It annoyed her, but it wasn't as though there were anything she could do to change that.

Finally his lips turned, in what might be considered a smile on another man, but on him simply made it look as though he were mocking her. He inclined his head slightly, and took a step backward, waving his hand in front of him, as though he were permitting them to leave.

"Ladies," he said, his facade softening slightly as he looked past Phoebe to the three women standing behind her. "Forgive me. If you please."

Phoebe made to walk around him, but he held up a finger.

"Lady Phoebe, would you be inclined to stay a moment? I am actually interested in speaking with you."

Phoebe narrowed her eyes as she tilted her head back to look at him, wondering what he was about. She had met him a time or two, as she was slightly acquainted with his sister. The marquess being a favorite among polite society, however, meant he had likely hardly ever looked at her, and she had certainly never sought him out. He seemed a serious sort, the type of man typical to the *ton,* with outdated opinions and interests only for those who were like himself. He often had one young lady or another on his arm, the simpering type with their coquettish grins and flirtatious giggles. Phoebe avoided men who seemed to prefer that mold of woman, as to them, she would certainly prove to be a disappointment.

She looked past him at her friends. Elizabeth was shaking her head in warning, Julia shrugging her shoulders, and Sarah attempting to smother a grin.

"Very well, Lord Berkley," she said, her curiosity overcoming her disdain for the man. "A moment."

CHAPTER 2

*J*effrey Worthington, Marquess of Berkley, casually strolled past Lady Phoebe into the drawing room, hands behind his back as he made a show of studying the military paintings lining the walls, the intricate carvings in the marble of the hearth, and the time upon the ormolu clock set upon the mantle. The gold walls were bright and cheerful, the carpet a cream that he estimated would likely require much upkeep.

Finally he turned, seeing the woman was still standing in the doorway, her hands on her hips as she tapped her foot on the floor impatiently.

"Ah yes, Lady Phoebe," he said as though he had forgotten she was there, and he saw the cross look on her face deepen, her vivid green eyes narrow in consternation. He wished she would open them further, as they seemed particularly striking. As a whole, she was actually quite attractive, he considered, looking her up and down. Her hair, such a dark brown it was near black, was tied back in a chignon but was held loosely away from her head, with wavy, soft tendrils of hair framing her face.

He couldn't help but notice the way her dress – which matched her eyes – skimmed curves that were … the perfect shape, he realized with a start, an image of his hands upon her hips, caressing her backside overwhelming him.

His face must have belied his thoughts, for suddenly her hands moved from her hips to cross over her body as though she were hiding something from him. So perhaps the woman was a bit shyer than she came across, he thought with a flare of interest.

She bit her lip as she stared at him, and his eyes dipped down from her surprisingly delicate nose to her rosy, plush bottom lip. Which was not a particularly smart idea, for it did nothing to remove his mind from her generous curves or the swell of her bosom.

"Are you done, Lord Berkley?" she finally asked, breaking the silence, and he smiled thinly at her. "Is there anything you would like to actually speak about, or did you simply request that I remain so that you may determine whether any of my attributes are particularly pleasing?"

He raised his eyebrows. Of course, he expected nothing less from a woman such as this one, who seemed to disregard all propriety and determine for herself what was proper and polite.

He chuckled to throw her off balance, but she ignored him as she moved to the door, placing a hand on the knob.

"If you have nothing to say, then I will be going," she said, beginning to turn the handle.

"Actually, Lady Phoebe, there is something else," he said, and when she turned to him expectantly, he continued. "You see, I opened the door of this drawing room some minutes ago to avail myself of its privacy, however within I found the four of you, deep in conversation. I was about to leave when I heard your words. I must tell you, Lady Phoebe, I was appalled."

"Oh?" she asked, coming toward him now, her eyes now wide, fury lurking within them. "And what aspect of our *private* conversation did you not approve of, Lord Berkley? For I must tell you that what *I* do not approve of is gentlemen — or ladies, for that matter — lurking around doorways, listening to matters which do not concern them."

"On that, I must disagree," he said, standing tall in front of her, attempting to intimidate her but wondering if anything ever could. "For when a woman begins to question the order of our society, I find that such views do concern me, as a man with responsibility to uphold our way of life. You reject the opinions of men toward women, Lady Phoebe, but you must realize that there are reasons our society is shaped as it is. You speak of women warriors, of women who have influenced the decisions of men. But what you declined to note in your tirade was that it is still *men* who have always made decisions. It is *men* who have the ability to make change. Women have influenced men, yes, but has that been a good thing? I would argue that when emotion becomes involved, decisions are swayed in a way that removes all practicality, all rational argument. And women, Lady Phoebe, are composed of emotion, so how are they supposed to make any decision logically, the way a man does? Emotion leads only to weakness. To allow a woman such control and responsibility would be a detriment to all society — you must understand this. On that note, I implore you to keep such opinions to yourself, to not affect other young women. In fact, it was why I decided to return and seek you out. For all you will do is keep them from making the matches required of them. Women have an important role to play as well. They birth children and raise them, so of course, they are contributing to society in a very important manner. Now, you would not want to harm your closet friends with your foolish notions, would you?"

Pleased with his speech, he crossed his arms over his chest and leaned back against the wall, studying Phoebe to determine her reaction. As he had spoken, she had remained in one place, her expression stoic, her body frozen. Only her fists, which had tightened into balls, belied any sort of emotion. She opened her mouth once, twice, three times. Jeffrey stood, smiling, pleased that he had gotten through to her. He strode forward, nodded, and was about to walk around her and out of the room.

Until she slapped him in the face.

* * *

WELL, that captured his attention.

She hadn't meant to do it. She really hadn't. He had just been so smug standing there, figuring he had taught her some lesson. When he tried to brush by her, she had acted before thinking.

Violence was never the answer – she knew that as well as anyone.

But she couldn't give him the satisfaction of apologizing now.

It was his turn to stand in shocked silence as he stared at her, and finally Phoebe found her words. Her anger had been so great, her frustration so pronounced, that it had taken her a moment to register what he had said to her. It was not such a shock that he believed what he said, or that he actually thought he was correct in his assumption, but it was that he had no qualms in sharing such opinions and felt completely within his rights to say such things to her.

"You arrogant, impossible man!" she ground out, pointing a finger at him, striding forward until it was buried in his chest. "Do you honestly believe that you are so important, so far above me, that you can come in here and berate me for words that were not even said in your presence, but in a private conversation? You speak of politeness, but *you* sir, are at the height of rudeness! And let me ask you this. Do you truly believe that most men are incapable of emotion? While *you*, Lord Berkley, certainly might be, I truly believe that most men feel as much love, as much emotion, as any woman. It is simply that they do not have the strength to accept it, as women do, and therefore most choose to hide it instead. I can tell you that I am capable of making decisions much better than a man *because* I use both my heart and my head. Love is real, Lord Berkley, and so is hatred, which at the moment, I am feeling in *spades*."

"You slapped me," he said in wonderment, and she stomped her foot on the floor, frustration coursing through her, made worse by what she knew was a childish response. After all she had said to him, he didn't hear a word of it, as he was still caught off guard. She knew, belatedly, she had made a mistake in taking such an action, but her hand had moved of its own accord before she even knew what she was doing. She didn't exactly regret it, though she was unsure what repercussions might come of it.

"I did," she said, her head held high. "And I am glad of it. You, Lord Berkley, epitomize everything that is wrong with our entire society. Now, if you will excuse me, I have far more important things to do with my time than explain myself to you."

And with that, she brushed by him with a flounce of her emerald green skirts. As her shoulder knocked into his, a jolt of heat raced through her, and she was disgusted with herself that part of her found this man attractive, that she had actually appreciated his rugged handsomeness when he had first walked into the room. She simply reminded herself of his words, however, and all thoughts of him as anything other than a stubborn, frustrating, idiotic man fled.

She pushed open the door, the din of the great room echoing down the hall, breaking the silent tension that had been present between the two of them in the drawing room. She slammed the door behind her and continued down the corridor toward the noise, for once welcoming it and the people it held.

* * *

JEFFREY RUBBED his cheek where it still slightly stung, and he could imagine a hand imprinted within its folds. A sleek, slender hand, that looked as though it was fair, feminine, and altogether lovely, but in fact held a fierce temper of a different kind. What was wrong with the woman? Who did she think she was, that she could *slap* him, a marquess, for speaking the truth, one she needed to understand? He was trying to help her. For if she shared her opinion within larger society, it would only be of detriment to herself.

He shook his head as he pushed open the door she had slammed behind her, his face set in a grim line as he followed her likely path to the ballroom. He needed a drink — badly.

He found his way across the wide, cavernous room, filled with color this evening from the multitudes of hues of women's dresses to a table on the side, which held an assortment of drinks, pastries, and all sorts of epicurean delights. The only thing he had any interest in, however, was the brandy. He took the glass with relish, letting the amber liquid burn down his throat. Women.

"I say, Berkley, what sort of beast has a hold of you?"

Jeffrey turned, his frustration abating somewhat upon finding his old friend, the Duke of Clarence, at his elbow.

"Nothing that cannot be tamed," he said, covering his unease with a grin, and the Duke laughed, holding his glass up to his own in a salute.

"Troubles of the female persuasion, then?"

"You could say that," Jeffrey muttered, his eyes perusing the room for a glimpse of the vixen. When he found no sign of her, he wasn't sure whether it was relief or dismay churning within his belly. Though why he would want to see a woman such as her, with her viperish tongue and threatening hands again, he had no idea.

"When one disappoints, there is always another," Clarence said with a shrug, and Jeffrey nodded, though he was sure Lady Phoebe was one of a kind — a kind he should avoid. He looked around the room at the young women and their mothers sending admiring glances and inviting smiles toward the two of them — both eligible, unattached, powerful men of the *ton*. There were many who would hold no issue with his views nor his presumptions of how a young woman should behave. Yet none of them, despite their attractiveness and their equally lovely shapes, lit a fire in him as did the lady of the drawing room. Lady Phoebe Winters was trouble, and he needed to do all he could to keep from furthering any acquaintance with her.

He shook his head, not realizing that he had spoken her name aloud until Clarence questioned him.

"Lady Phoebe? I know of her. Is it she who is vexing you so?"

Jeffrey came back to the present moment, turning his gaze upon his friend.

"I suppose you could say that. We had an interesting ... exchange a few moments ago. She has a wicked tongue, but there is something rather intriguing about her."

"Hers is an interesting story," the Duke began as he drained his glass. "Her parents died of illnesses within months of one another, though romantics would say her father died of a broken heart. He was a viscount, and his title went to the next in line, of course — some cousin — but he had amassed a plentiful fortune through his lifetime, and ensured the unentailed portion of his inheritance was bestowed upon his only child — the Lady Phoebe."

"Indeed?" Jeffrey had heard some of this, of course — of her parents' untimely passing, but not of the inheritance. He supposed he should pay more attention to the gossips.

"Indeed," Clarence confirmed. "She has a chaperone — an aunt, I believe — who lives with her here in London, who attends events such as these so all is proper. As far as I am aware, however, for the most part the Lady Phoebe lives as she pleases, acting upon her own whims."

"That's a dangerous thing, a woman on her own in the world," Jeffrey muttered.

"I suppose," returned the Duke with a shrug. "Though it has been near a couple of years now, and she seems to do well enough on her own. It's not my business, I suppose, but that's the story."

"Interesting," Jeffrey said, his eyes scanning the room for her once more. "Very interesting indeed."

CHAPTER 3

"*T*he *nerve* of that man!"

Phoebe was describing to her aunt in great detail her entire conversation with the Marquess of Berkley. Her aunt, Lady Aurelia, was somewhat sympathetic to her plight, although her expression changed from one of understanding to horror when Phoebe told her of striking the marquess.

"Oh, Phoebe!" she exclaimed, her gloved hand coming up to cover her mouth, which was lined with deep wrinkles. She had never married, choosing to live as a spinster her entire life. Phoebe's father, much younger than Aurelia, had loved his sister immensely and ensured she lived a comfortable life. One of the stipulations of Phoebe's inheritance had been that she take her aunt in to live with her, a requirement with which Phoebe had no reservations.

After her encounter with the marquess, Phoebe had found Aurelia amongst the crowd and feigned a headache, requesting that they return home. She no longer had any desire for company — polite or otherwise. Seeing the look upon her face, her aunt had quickly agreed, bidding farewell to her acquaintances.

Now, sitting in the carriage together, Phoebe let all of the anger that had been building within steam out of her, and her aunt, silent for the most part, allowed her to vent.

Finished, Phoebe crossed her arms over her chest and leaned back into the squabs. Her aunt reached out a hand and pushed back a strand of hair that had fallen out of her chignon and over her face.

"Phoebe, dear," Aurelia began. "I am sorry that you had to listen to that, truly I am. I understand how you feel, you must know that. The marquess, however, is a powerful man, with many friends in high places, and he only speaks the truth of which he knows, the truth that most live within. I am not sure that he is a man of whom you should be making an enemy."

Phoebe shrugged. "Does it really matter? It is not as though I am exactly beloved in social circles."

"No, and I am not saying that you have to be," her aunt said, shaking her head. "I am only saying to be careful, darling. And, while he is terribly wrong on much of what he said, there are some aspects of which he has the right of it."

Phoebe opened her mouth to retort, aghast that her aunt, a woman who had shared many of the same thoughts regarding the female role in their world, would say such a thing.

Aurelia held up a hand before Phoebe could say anything further.

"Let me explain," she said in a soft, but stern voice and Phoebe respectfully sat back to listen.

"He is correct in that this is the society in which we live. You can voice your displeasure to a few friends, but if you speak any louder, you will only be ostracized. Is that what you truly want?"

Phoebe waited a moment before responding. She had an idea — one that had begun to form when Sarah questioned whether anything would change if no one did anything about such views, if no one presented another option. Her thought was outrageous, now that she had time to consider it further, but ... perhaps ... an outrageous act was required.

"Aunt Aurelia," she began, needing her aunt to understand, for in order for this to work, she would need her cooperation. "You read the newsletters and journals every day, just as I do, do you not?"

"Most of them," her aunt said, the feather on the top of her velvet maroon hat bobbing as she nodded her head at Phoebe. "Though not nearly as many as you. I do not believe anyone in all of London reads as much as you do, my dear."

"And of all that you read, who writes such publications?"

"A wide assortment of people I should say," said Aurelia, looking at Phoebe quizzically. "We read the papers of the Whigs and the Tories, the gossips and the reformers. It is the only way to truly understand all that is happening in the world."

"We do not read the words of an assortment of *people*," Phoebe said, holding a finger up to note one clear, particular distinction. "We read the words of an assortment of *men*. Men who use the power of the written word to portray their opinions, to shape the thoughts of those who read them. Men who are friends, or acquaintances, with those who influence their way of thinking. We are guided by the very people who want women to stay within their particular role. That is the problem, Aunt Aurelia."

Aurelia cocked her head to the side, considering Phoebe's words. "You are correct, darling, as you always are. And that's all very well and good, but whatever are we supposed to do about it?"

"I'm so glad you asked," said Phoebe with a triumphant

smile. "For I actually have a solution. *I* have an opinion on the world as well. And I am going to share it."

* * *

SHADOWED BY HIS LARGE, unruly mutt, Maxwell, Jeffrey marched down the stairs of his London townhome the next morning with a weight in his chest. Last night had been a disaster. The woman had gotten into his head, and she wouldn't leave it, no matter how hard he tried to shove her out of it. After his conversation with Clarence the previous night, Jeffrey had lost all interest in anything occurring around him at the party. In fact, he had found himself completely tired of the affair, as well as any others to come.

Suddenly all he could focus on was the fact that he repeated the same actions night after night. He spoke to the same people, had the same coy words whispered in his ear, was approached by the same women, none of whom seemed to have an original thought in their heads. What was the use of it all?

He sighed as he rounded the newel post at the bottom of the stairs, pushing his hair back off of his forehead. He was being ridiculous. He had never had thoughts like this before. Why one conversation with *her* would make a difference, he had no idea whatsoever.

Well, it was a new day. A day in which he was sure, he thought with a wry grin crossing his face, that he would face many new challenges.

He was not disappointed, for when he entered the breakfast room, four beautiful, luminous, yet mischievous faces were grinning up at him, as though they had been waiting for him to appear. His mother — equally as beautiful and luminous, in his opinion — also looked on, contemplating her children.

"Jeffrey!" shouted Annie, the youngest, now sixteen. "We have been waiting for you."

"So it would seem," he said wryly. He loved his family — truly he did — but sometimes he wished they would allow him at least a few minutes to drink his coffee and clear his head in the mornings before they began shouting questions and making demands at him.

He smiled gratefully at the footman, who poured a steaming cup of the bitter drink for him, and he closed his eyes as he swallowed it, for just a moment turning out the cacophony of voices that resonated in his ears.

He opened his eyes to find four pairs of expectant eyes upon him as Maxwell placed his shaggy head upon Jeffrey's knee, the dog's droopy ears and chin settling upon Jeffrey's leg.

"I'm sorry, what was that?"

"Oh, Jeffrey." Penny rolled her eyes. At eighteen, she felt she was already a woman, and she shook her head at him, her blonde curls swinging around her face. "Why do you never listen?"

"I do," he said gruffly, looking around the table, finding only his mother had any ounce of sympathy on her face. The rest were simply looking at him as though he had told them he was going to marry each of them off right that moment. Not that they would ever allow him to choose their husbands without their opinions.

"Fine," he sighed. "What is it?"

"We heard a rather interesting tale about you last night," said Rebecca, looking at him with her chin on her fist and a gleam in her eye. "About you ensconced in a drawing room with an unmarried woman."

"That is ridiculous," he said, shaking his head and returning his focus to the eggs and ham on the plate in front of him. How in the world had anyone even known the two of them had been there? As far as he was aware, no one had been the wiser but for Lady Phoebe's friends.

"*And* she did not look particularly pleased when she left," Rebecca continued, leaning toward him now. "In fact, after your conversation, she found her aunt and left the party completely."

"I didn't realize you were all so inclined to believe everything the gossips tell you," he muttered, looking up to see that his sisters had all cleared their plates, obviously having remained at the table only to pester him about this story, which truly was of no particular consequence. "Do you not all have things to do? Lessons to see to? Friends to visit?"

"We are not leaving until you tell us more about this liaison," Penny said primly, and Jeffrey slammed his coffee cup on the table much harder than he intended to, but nevertheless it made his sisters and his mother jump. Maxwell even left him to explore the plates of his sisters instead.

"There was *no* liaison," he said in a tone to make them understand that he would not speak any further on the subject. "I simply had a conversation with a woman that turned into a slight disagreement. It is of no consequence and I am sure I will not be speaking with her again. It has nothing to do with any of you, and I would be pleased if you would simply leave it be. Do you understand?"

He looked round at each of them individually, the youngest blinking at the bite to his words. He typically was soft with his sisters — he knew it was a failing, but since he had taken responsibility of them five years ago when his father passed, he had never had the heart to be particularly stern with them, and now, perhaps, he was beginning to pay the consequences.

"Very well," Penny finally said, and she led Annie away from the table, Rebecca following, although not before she turned to send him a venomous look, and while he wanted them to understand his consternation, he had to hide his smile.

His mother leaned over, covering his fist with her hand as she looked at him imploringly.

"It is not like you to be so upset over something so minor," she said softly. "Is everything all right?"

"Of course, Mother," he said, bestowing a smile upon her as he turned his palm to grip her hand in his. She was still beautiful, her blonde hair, so like his own, just beginning to show signs of grey woven through it when the light hit it just right. Somehow, it suited her.

"What did you think of Lady Phoebe?" His sister, Viola, finally spoke from across the table. Unlike her sisters, she was a serious sort, and she was able to ascertain his feelings better than anyone.

"That she is rude and I should be glad not to speak to her again," he said, waving his hand in the air.

"I would think otherwise, the way you have responded," said Viola, her smile as gentle as her mother's. "In fact, this is the first woman that has caused *any* sort of reaction from you in quite some time."

"Are you interested in her?" his mother asked hopefully, light coming into her eyes. Jeffrey knew she had been wishing he would soon find a woman he cared for, but he dissuaded her hopefulness by shaking his head vehemently.

"Not at all."

"Nor any woman?"

"Mother, we have discussed this," he said patiently. "I have enough women to look after without having to worry about a wife."

"Jeffrey, you know we are the ones who take care of you," Viola joked, and he shook his head at her with a laugh.

"Maybe so," he said. "But I have not yet met a young woman who is appealing enough to spend the rest of my life with. I should like to a meet a woman who, for once, has a mind of her own, who does not simply mutter what she believes I would like to hear."

"Perhaps you have simply not given these ladies a chance to be themselves around you," his mother said practically. "You can be an imposing man to some."

To some. Not his family, nor to Lady Phoebe Winters, apparently.

His mother rose from the table, coming around behind him to place her hands on his shoulders. She leaned down to kiss him quickly but softly on the cheek.

"Whoever you choose to marry one day — hopefully soon — I'm sure she will be lovely."

With that, she patted him on the shoulders and left, leaving Jeffrey sitting with only Viola across from him at the table, arms crossed as she leaned back and stared at him contemplatively.

"So tell me the truth," she said. "What really happened?"

Jeffrey sighed. Viola was as soft and gentle as she appeared, but she could be relentless when she wanted something.

"Her name is Lady Phoebe Winters and her father was a viscount," he began, and Viola's eyes lit up from behind her spectacles.

"Of course, Jeffrey. I am acquainted with Lady Phoebe, and have, in fact, introduced the two of you in the past. Do you not recall her? She is striking."

Striking — that was the word for her. Not beautiful, but there was something about her that captivated him like no other woman had as of yet.

"I overheard a conversation between the lady and her friends. She—"

"You were *eavesdropping*?"

"It was an accident," he defended himself. "Anyway, she

was going on about women, and men and women's place in our society. She seems to think women should be equal to men, that anyone who says they do not have the ability to make the same decisions or also hold power is in error, that they are preposterous. Can you believe it? She thinks that we should all change so that women's opinions can be heard. I can hardly imagine it."

He snorted, picking up a bit of toast, but when Viola was silent, he looked back up at her to judge her reaction.

"Let me guess," she said, leaning onto the table, her brown eyes intent upon him. "You argued with her."

"I did not *argue*," he said indignantly. "I simply suggested that it would be best if she no longer spread such ideas to other young women. She could impede her own friends' ability to find a match if they begin to share such ideas. Lady Phoebe herself had best be careful, or she will find that she no longer has any prospects at all, if she did to begin with. She is lucky that I did not widely share her words."

Viola was shaking her head at him, pieces of light brown hair escaping the knot at the back of her head.

"What?"

"Do you really believe so strongly that you are right?"

"Of course I do," he retorted. "What other answer could there be?"

"Well," she said slowly. "Perhaps Lady Phoebe has a point."

Jeffrey looked up at her in shock. "You agree with her? You cannot, you —"

"Why not?" Viola asked, widening her hands in front of her. "Because I am your sister? That doesn't mean I do not have my own beliefs. Think of it like this. If you could choose to trust one of your siblings with your entire life — God forbid you became ill, and you could no longer look after your estate, your investments — who would you trust?"

Jeffrey was silent for a moment. Of course, if anything did

happen to him, the title and all it entailed would fall to his brother, Ambrose. But Ambrose was not exactly the most... responsible man he knew.

"You," he finally said begrudgingly.

"You see?" she asked, a smile brightening her face. "You would trust me, a woman."

"That's different," he finally said, unwilling to meet her eyes.

"How so?"

"You are practical — rational. You are intelligent and would not make decisions on a whim."

"So you think I am an anomaly, then?" she asked. "That no other woman is like me? It does not matter whether a person is a man or a woman, Jeffrey. What matters is the person."

And with that, she simply shook her head at him — in regret? Or dismay? He wasn't altogether sure — and rose from the table, striding out the door with her head held high and no returning look his way, though she did stop to quickly pet Maxwell before continuing on.

Jeffrey sighed as he rubbed his temple. This was going to be a long day.

CHAPTER 4

*P*hoebe picked up her teacup, absently adding in more sugar as she read the papers in front of her. Her breakfast table was set for one, as her aunt always preferred to spend her mornings in her room, particularly if she had been out the night before. Phoebe didn't overly mind. It gave her time to read, to become caught up on the day's news. Not that there was anything of particular interest today.

She was about to skip over the gossip pages — none of it was ever true anyway — when initials jumped off the page toward her, and she leaned in for a better look.

Lady P.W. was seen leaving the drawing room at the home of the Earl of T. with a look of consternation on her face. Minutes later, the Marquess of B. was seen departing the very same room. What were the two of them doing within — alone?

Phoebe threw the paper back down on top of the pile in disgust. Well, perhaps some of it was true. It was bad enough that the marquess had listened to her private conversation. At the very least, however, he had the courage to admit to it. Not like this particular coward, whoever it was, who spied upon people and then fed it to the gossip columns — and for what purpose?

She closed her eyes and resolved to push the entire issue — the words of the marquess, the reporting of their meeting — completely from her mind. She had more important things to see to.

She forced down two more bites of toast before pushing back from her circular rosewood breakfast table. She loved this quaint room, a little nook in the corner of the house off of the main dining room. She ate many of her meals here, alone or with her aunt, as it seemed silly to use the larger, more formal dining room, which was often cold and rather drafty.

She continued down the hall toward the study. It had once been her father's, and while she had kept many of the paintings in the same style he had preferred, she had added her own touch to the room, making it slightly softer, a little more feminine. There was now an ornate brass mirror on the wall where an elk's head — a hunting trophy — had once been showcased, and the portrait of her grandfather had been moved from its previous place of prominence to another wall in order to make room for a portrait of her parents within an oval frame. She looked up at them now, wondering what they would think of her latest scheme. Would they be proud of her, or would they frown upon her thoughts, and her resulting actions?

They had raised her to have her own mind, to believe that she could create possibilities for herself. Even if they would not have completely approved of her plans, she felt that they would understand it was something she had to do. Aunt Aurelia had been concerned over Phoebe's safety, more than anything, when she explained to her the idea running through her mind.

But in the end, Aurelia had offered her support, for which Phoebe was particularly grateful.

She sat down now in front of the satinwood desk, running her hands over the gilded edges. When she closed her eyes, she could still see her father sitting here, bent over his ledgers and papers, his quill pen scribbling furiously. She missed him — she missed both of her parents. It had been the three of them for so long, and then everything changed when her mother became ill, her father soon following. Phoebe had always thought that if he had fought harder, perhaps he could have beaten it. Her mother had always been so frail, and she went quickly, but her father... his heart had gone with her mother.

Phoebe wondered if she would ever find a love such as that of her parents, with a man who would support her, who would love her for the outspoken woman she was. If not... well, she shrugged, she would create a good life for herself. Her parents had ensured she had the means to do so, at any rate.

Phoebe opened the top drawer of the desk, pulling out a piece of paper and laying it on the flat surface in front of her. She dipped her pen into the ink and then began making a list of everything she needed. The ideas beginning to flow, she found a new sheet of paper, beginning to organize her thoughts into sections, columns, and headlines. She wasn't sure how long she sat there, scribbling away on multiple pieces of paper until the desktop in front of her was scattered with sheets full of notes in her untidy handwriting. Despite the disorder, a swell of purpose coursed through her, unlike anything she had felt in a long while. This was it. Now, she only had to put her plan into action.

She stood to find her butler, to tell him to have the groom ready her carriage, but was startled when he appeared in the doorway before she could take a step forward.

"My lady? Lady Julia Stone here to visit you. Shall I tell her this is not a good time?"

"Oh, no, of course not," she said with a wave of her hand. "I will greet her in the upstairs drawing room. Could we have some tea sent in?"

"Of course, my lady," he said, and was gone as silently as he had arrived. Phoebe looked down at herself. She had a morning gown on still, though it wasn't her best — an old navy dress that was comfortable more than anything. Her hands were stained with ink, and she didn't even want to know what her hair looked like at the moment. Oh well. Julia would understand.

She gathered her papers, binding them together with a strand of twine as she made her way down the corridor to the drawing room. This had been her mother's domain, but again Phoebe had simply put her own touch on it. The gold walls gave the room a feeling of grandeur, with the wainscoting, intricate ceiling roses, and gilded cornices providing a touch of extravagance. The delicate furniture was feminine, setting off the expensive pianoforte and musical instruments along the wall — instruments she never played, but that her mother had so loved.

"Julia, how lovely of you to visit!" Phoebe said with a true grin, bending to greet her longtime friend with an embrace. Julia looked as lovely as ever, of course, her blonde hair pulled back away from her face, with the slightest corkscrew curls round her forehead, her blue eyes wide.

"Of course," Julia said with a smile as she took a seat upon the pink floral motif of the stenciled and gilt settee. Phoebe took the matching one across from Julia. Phoebe noted as she did so that, somehow, the tea had already arrived and was centered in the middle of the table in front of them.

"I had to speak with you about last night," Julia continued. "You left so quickly, I was sure something untoward must have occurred with the marquess. Whatever could he have wished to speak with you about?"

"Oh that," said Phoebe with a sigh. "Just another belligerent man making his opinions known."

She no longer felt like discussing the entire conversation, now having something much more exciting of which to speak.

"But oh, Julia, following our discussion last night, I've made a decision. One that will change things — forever, I hope."

Julia raised her eyebrows, leaning forward slightly at Phoebe's exuberance.

"This sounds particularly consequential," she remarked. "Do tell."

"Very well," said Phoebe with a grin, appreciating Julia's interest. "Last night we were discussing one newspaper article in particular, but the truth is, that is only one of many. Even worse, most times women are not even discussed except in the columns of the gossip pages."

"Oh yes, speaking of that, I saw —"

"That matters not," Phoebe cut in, tired of any discussions regarding the marquess. "But this does. What became rather apparent is that nothing is ever going to change, because all discourse is created by men. Well, it's time to take action. I am going to begin a paper, Julia. A newspaper that only includes the opinions of women, written for women. It will include everything they may be interested in. News articles — from a women's point of view. Opinion pieces. Some articles on various pastimes of women — many of which I am not particularly fond, but I understand that many women are. Fashion. Advice. It will be brilliant."

Julia's eyes widened the more Phoebe spoke, and now her mouth opened in surprise.

"Oh, Phoebe," she said, her voice just over a whisper. "I

must say … that sounds magnificent!" Phoebe grinned at Julia's support. "I would read it, to be sure, and not just because I'm your friend. I often become bored by the newspapers and journals available. If you can do it right, this would be of interest to so many ladies. You would be the talk of London! Though," Julia mused for a moment, "you would be met by those who would not be supportive. You would be considered scandalous. Besides that, it would be quite the undertaking. How would you even propose to go about it? To fund it?"

"I have my inheritance," said Phoebe, holding up a hand when Julia looked as though she was going to protest. "When — *if* — I ever marry, it would only go to my husband. This allows me to do something with it that would make a difference, that would have meaning. I will be sure there is always enough to manage the household, my everyday living, and provide for Aunt Aurelia, of course. Besides that, the idea is only to use it to begin, and then sales would take over. I will find a building, hire staff, acquire a printer. I actually just finished making notes of all there would be to do when you arrived."

Julia was nodding at her words, though she began to tap her foot on the floor, a sure sign that she had thoughts to share. "I must say, Phoebe, when you are determined about something, there is no stopping you. Though you must be careful. If word emerged that this is of your doing, you would be shunned. I'm not sure that any gentleman would want to tie himself to a woman who is making such statements. You would not attach your name, would you?"

"I have thought of that," Phoebe said and, remembering the tea tray, picked up the pot and poured a cup for Julia. "I will keep my name anonymous. I will hire an editor and writers, though I will write a column myself. And if, for any reason, my name should come out, then so be it. I would rather do this than do nothing but complain about the way things are."

"You are brave, Phoebe," Julia said in an awed tone. "I admire you for it. I must ask one thing of you, however."

"Of course."

"Do you have room for a column on horse racing?"

"It is certainly a topic we could try," she said, looking at Julia with interest. "And why do you ask?"

"Would you consider me as a writer?"

"Of course!" Phoebe exclaimed, clapping her hands together. "I welcome you as the first employee of *The Women's Weekly*."

"I love it," said Julia with a small smile of her own. "And I thank you. What you are doing, Phoebe, it is extremely admirable."

"Someone has to do it," Phoebe said with conviction. "So why not me?"

CHAPTER 5

*P*hoebe had dressed with care in a modest cream gown, a simple matching cloth bonnet over her black waves. She was determined that she be taken seriously today, woman or not. Finding her aunt awake, but still in a state of undress despite the fact it was well past noon, Phoebe had bid her a quick farewell. Aurelia was, for propriety's sake, her chaperone, true, but Phoebe was certainly no debutante. After Phoebe's parents passed, naming Aurelia her guardian, she and Aurelia had a frank discussion regarding their arrangement. They came to the mutual understanding that while they enjoyed spending time together, they each could continue to enjoy the freedom they so treasured.

Now as the publisher of a periodical, Phoebe would have others relying upon her. She did not see the need to disrupt Aurelia's life by requiring her to follow Phoebe around during her business pursuits.

For her first task, Phoebe knew exactly where to go — Fleet Street, where all of the printers and publishers were known to operate. She began by stopping to meet with her banker to determine exactly what funds were available to her, and then she began her second mission — to find an office.

She had perused the papers that morning to locate available properties, and with a list of addresses in hand, she conversed with her driver and then they were on their way. The first building on her list was a few streets away from her desired location, but the rent was low. It did not take long to determine why, as she could smell the interior before she even walked in the door, and with a quick shake of her head she was onto the next. When that one proved equally dismal, its floorboards rotting and some indiscriminate liquid dripping from the ceiling, her heart began to sink. Perhaps this was a futile effort. There must be a better way. Her aunt had suggested she hire someone to find a place for her, but this was important, and Phoebe was determined to find exactly what she was looking for on her own.

The third property was slightly more expensive than she would have liked, but it was a small office tucked between two larger buildings on Fleet Street, and she walked in to find a jovial man sitting behind a desk waiting for her.

"Hello, there," he said with a smile. "Are you lost? May I help you find where you are going?"

Phoebe suppressed a sigh at the man's assumption but smiled, for he seemed kind and genuinely interested in helping her.

"Are you renting out this property?" she asked instead, walking over to the desk.

"I am," he acquiesced with a nod.

"I'm interested in it," she said with a smile. "What can you tell me about it? Can you show me around?"

The man looked her over for a moment, as though assessing her sincerity and whether or not she was jesting with him. Finally it seemed he determined she was serious, as she stared right back at him, her jaw set and a very slight curve to the edge of her lips.

"Very well," he said, standing himself. "Come with me."

An hour later, satisfaction filled her as she strode down the busy street, filled with all manner of businesses, hers soon to be one of them. After a thorough tour of the building as well as a careful review of the rental contract, Phoebe had decided that it would suit her needs. A property in place, now she needed people to fill it. That she would do through an advertisement in some of the current newspapers, but in the meantime, she needed to find a printer. Someday, she thought wistfully, she would have her own press, but that would prove far too expensive for her current budget. In the meantime she would have to hire the work out, so it was imperative she find a printer she could trust. She was looking into shop windows, deep in thought, when she crashed into something so hard she nearly fell backward, saved only when a long, strong arm reached out and caught her.

She gasped, looking up to find herself staring into the dark, searching eyes of none other than the Marquess of Berkley — the very man she had spent far too many hours pushing from her thoughts.

"We have to stop meeting like this," she said sardonically, to which he nodded his head. At least there was one thing they were in agreement upon. After what seemed like minutes though was likely simply a few seconds, he wrenched his gaze from hers to look over her head behind her.

"Where is your chaperone?"

She nearly jumped. It had been only an evening prior that she had last heard his voice, and yet she had forgotten how deep and husky it was.

"She does not accompany me today," she responded, not

seeing the need to provide him any further answer. What business of his was it whether or not she was alone?

His frown deepened, his thick eyebrows sinking low.

"You should not be wandering London unaccompanied," he said, showing his clear disapproval of her actions.

"I am not unaccompanied," she said with a sniff. "My driver follows behind in the carriage. I simply decided it would be easier to walk from one appointment to the next. Now if you will excuse me."

She made to brush past him, but a strong gloved hand reached out to take her arm in a firm grip.

"I will escort you wherever it is you wish to go," he commanded, and she bristled.

"Thank you, but I am fine without you," she said, wresting her arm away. "If I had need of an escort, I would have found one of my own choosing."

"I cannot allow you to continue on alone," he said, and some of the hardness of his face lifted slightly. "I am only doing what I would ask another to do for one of my sisters."

Her frustration melted slightly then as she thought of Viola, who was a sweet girl, though it was difficult to believe she was related to the hard marquess. Somehow it was a challenge to imagine him holding any emotions besides disdain and derision.

"Very well," she said, realizing that the best way to be rid of him would be to simply allow him to think he had done his duty, then he would be on his way. "I am simply walking to Madame Boudreau's around the corner to have a dress tailored. But do not allow me to keep you from your business, Lord Berkley."

"I have time," he said simply and took her arm in his once more. Phoebe held herself stiffly away from him, and yet she cursed herself for feeling the burn of his hand upon her, for noticing every time his body came into even the slightest contact with hers. When they rounded the corner and the dressmaker's shop came into sight, she couldn't extricate herself fast enough.

She turned, and with the slightest dip of her head, offered, "Farewell, Lord Berkley. Until we meet again."

And with that she practically flew into the dress shop, where she waited by the window, watching him depart as she determined just how long she would have to wait until she could emerge once more.

He had been generous with his time, chivalrous even, for which she certainly could not fault him. And yet it irked her that it would be so untoward for her to walk through the streets alone. Really, what could happen to her in a street filled with businesses in the middle of the day? she wondered as she politely thanked Madame Boudreau for her offer of assistance, but told her she would have to return another day when she had more time to browse. It wasn't as though she were strolling along the streets of the Seven Dials without a care. Why, the marquess could have just as easily taken advantage of her as any other man.

She frowned when the thought of his body against hers in a way altogether improper caused not the consternation she would have hoped, but rather a warm flush to begin to flood through her. *Stop it, Phoebe. You're being ridiculous.*

Men such as the marquess were the very reason it was better to become a spinster unless one found true love. Aunt Aurelia had never married and enjoyed life just fine — just as Phoebe likely would.

A grin took over her face, however, when she thought of just what the marquess would think if he knew what she was truly doing here near Fleet Street. Not shopping for dresses — the riot of color around her was beautiful, to be sure, but did not captivate her attention as it did many women. Oh no, it was the thought of printing presses now that made her blood rush quickly through her veins. The marquess would be scandalized. Which was exactly the point.

* * *

JEFFREY TOOK one last long look at the dress shop, shaking his head as he continued on his way. Lady Phoebe. Just when he had successfully omitted her from his thoughts, there she was, rushing back in again. He couldn't determine exactly what it was about her that caused such turmoil to arise within him, but she was like a storm — majestic and astonishing, yet so tumultuous and destructive.

She needed someone to watch out for her. He pitied her for the loss of her parents, but it wasn't right for a woman — particularly a young woman such as she — to be alone in the world without a man to protect her. Despite her protestations, it wasn't natural, as was apparent by her wandering Fleet Street completely alone, save for her driver a fair distance away. What kind of chaperone was her aunt, allowing Lady Phoebe the freedom to act completely as she pleased?

But this lady wasn't his problem, he reminded himself as he continued on a few streets off of Fleet to meet his brother at the address provided to him on the note he had sent. Jeffrey had enough to deal with himself, including four sisters, as well as a brother who seemed intent on destroying him.

What Ambrose was up to now, he had no idea. His note had been cryptic, but Jeffrey feared it was another scheme of his, trying to make himself quick coin. By his own choosing, Ambrose lacked any sort of purpose, and the majority of his time was occupied spending his entire allowance, using most of it in a fool's quest to become independently wealthy. The more Jeffrey tried to convince him that it would never work and that he should make himself an honest living, the more determined Ambrose was to prove his brother wrong. Jeffrey continually found himself thrust into situations in which he had to save his brother, and he was tired of it.

Finding the correct address to be a small, rather unkept building crammed between two others, he knocked, only for the door to swing open at his touch.

"Jeffrey, there you are!"

Wary, Jeffrey took a slow step inside, allowing his eyes to adjust to the dim light. Despite the fact that the sun was shining, the windows were smoky, the floorboards scuffed and dirty, and the odd assortment of furniture was scattered around the room in various states of disarray. Finally he found his brother perched on one such rickety wooden chair, a hefty man sitting in the shadows across the table between them.

"Meet Hector," Ambrose said, sweeping his arm across the table with a flourish. "He's about to make us rich."

"Hector," Jeffrey nodded toward him before returning his attention back to his brother, ignoring the chair to which Ambrose gestured. "Make us rich, will he? How so?" he asked with sarcasm.

"Well, all we need to do is to give him a small sum of money, and then within a year, he will more than double it. Perhaps even triple it!" Enthusiasm lit up Ambrose's face as Jeffrey rubbed his brow. He had cleared his afternoon for *this*?

"Come, Ambrose, let's go," he said, gesturing to the door. "Excuse me, Hector. Our apologies."

Ambrose stood but refused to move, stubbornness setting in. "Can you not even listen to his plan?"

"No."

"He lends money, Jeffrey, then charges interest back. It's a sure thing, for if people do not pay, then—"

"I said, no." Not wanting to argue with his family in front of a stranger, Jeffrey strode over to the door without looking back, wrenching it open as he stepped outside, allowing it to slam behind him. He was pulling his gloves back over his fingers, breathing deeply to find a sense of calm, when Ambrose finally joined him.

"That was terribly rude, Jeffrey. Hector didn't do anything wrong, and you hardly even acknowledged him."

"Hector is making his money off of people's misfortune. That is not the way I do business, Ambrose, and I should hope that neither do you."

"He's helping people, really," Ambrose attempted to reason as Jeffrey began walking down the street to where his carriage awaited. Ambrose's charming, handsome face, which he had used to extricate himself from more than one scrape, was beaming up at Jeffrey now, but he would certainly not be fooled by his brother. Oh, no, he knew him far too well, had allowed him too much leniency in the past.

"It's time you began acting like an adult, Ambrose," he said as a father would, though he was only two years his brother's senior. "You have a choice."

Ambrose looked at him warily but said nothing.

"You have the small estate near Peterborough. You could actually take some responsibility for it, grow it to the point where it is much more profitable."

"But it's so far from London! I—"

"Or, I would purchase you a commission."

"The military?" Ambrose looked horrified. "Do you really think I would be fit for the *military*, Jeffrey?"

No, he certainly did not, though it would teach Ambrose some required life lessons.

"Or, you could continue your education and become a barrister."

"A barrister? Jeffrey, do you know how much work that would entail?"

Jeffrey continued his straightforward march back toward the busy Fleet Street, pausing to look at his brother only when he reached the carriage.

"Three options, Ambrose. Choose wisely."

"And if I do not wish to take any of the paths you suggest?"

"Do you fancy the church?"

Ambrose snorted.

"Continue as you are and your allowance will be cut off. Now, are you getting in, or not?"

CHAPTER 6

 *ne month later*

JEFFREY SMILED TRIUMPHANTLY as he entered the breakfast room. For once, he was alone. He had finally risen early enough that he had a few moments before the herd of women stampeded in to greet him. He could read his papers in silence, enjoy his coffee, and start the day on a pleasant note.

He nodded to Harper, his ever-efficient butler, who stood in the doorway overseeing the staff. Jeffrey took his seat at the table, and Maxwell, never one to miss accompanying Jeffrey to a meal, settled in beside him, well behaved for the moment, as he knew he could perhaps be fortunate enough for a crumb to drop from the table. A stack of papers was folded at Jeffrey's elbow, ready for him to peruse as he ate his eggs and toast.

The first was the typical news of the day in the *Morning Post*. A review of the most current performance at the

Theatre Royal, discussions that had occurred within Parliament, a list of the officers killed and wounded in battle, a mix of information from the very same battlefields. Everything contradicted itself, and Jeffrey was looking forward to receiving a more noteworthy report, hopefully in due time.

Setting that paper aside, he picked up the next, frowning as he did, for he didn't recognize the typeset nor the size and structure of it. "What's this?" he murmured as he read the heading. "The Women's Weekly."

What in the...

He began reading, his eyes widening as he did. It was apparently the debut issue, for the first column spoke of what a reader could come to expect from the publication going forward.

Common sense and reason remain two of the most revered attributes of a man. A woman? Far be it for one to say the same. For that would be at odds with what is expected of women. Beauty, decorum, and modesty are appreciated in the female species, while if a woman displays her wisdom or idealism, she becomes a scandal. Let it not be so. Women, it is true that our education is often lacking, as we are hardly provided with learning environments that are even half as vast as those of men. Therefore, we must become learned in our own right. Never fear a witty conversation, nor telling a scandalous joke in proper company. What am I suggesting? Simply be the woman you truly are.

So often, women gossip and envy one another, particularly if another is more attractive or possesses attributes she is told are desirable. I urge you to put this aside. Strive to help one another rise up, to display the strength we each hold together. Only then will we be seen as equals.

On these pages, we will inform, advise, and ask questions about what we know to be true. Politics, travel, fashion, advice, and even a little bit of (truthful) gossip will provide you all you need in one publication. Welcome.

The next article included texts and publications that might be of particular interest to women looking to better educate themselves, followed by a piece about marriage. It claimed that marriage was necessary for most women in order to look after themselves, but it went on to describe what qualities to search out in a man who would become a lifetime companion.

Jeffrey could hardly believe what he was reading. He looked at the heading to find the name of an author, and seeing nothing but "By a Lady", he turned the paper to its back, desperately searching.

He looked up, surprised to see that three of his sisters, excluding Viola, were now at the table. He had been so intent on the pages in front of him that he hadn't even noticed them arrive.

He nodded at them absently before returning to the sheet in front of him. He was about to continue reading when he felt a hand on his shoulder, and before he knew what was happening, the paper was lifted from his hands.

He turned to find a flustered Viola, who was now holding the paper behind her back, out of his sight.

"Viola," he said sharply, his words clipped, and she flinched slightly. "What is that outrageous thing?"

"It's nothing, Jeffrey. It should never have become entangled within your morning reading. My apologies. I will advise Harper to ensure that it is held for me next time."

She attempted a smile and began to walk away, but his voice held her within the room.

"You never answered my question. What is that piece of drivel?"

"It is simply a periodical, Jeffrey, much like *Ackermann's Repository*. You know, fashions of the day, some gossip, general news, how women can help in the war effort, that type of thing. Nothing to be overly concerned about."

"Yes, Jeffrey, there really are some lovely fashion plates within," Rebecca chimed in. "You should take a look! They are on page four. Perhaps then you will see the need to send us for new gowns."

"I believe half the earnings of the estate went to outfitting the lot of you, and that was but a few months ago," Jeffrey said sternly, before returning to the matter at hand. "I read some of the pieces, Viola, and it contained much more content than you described. I will *not* have this type of nonsense within my home. You will dispose of it immediately."

The room had gone silent, the fork that dropped from Annie's hand clattering to her plate as they all stared wide-eyed at their brother. Jeffrey knew he was far too lenient with his sisters, proven by the fact that such an order had shocked them.

"You simply read the first page, Jeffrey!" Viola protested. "There is much more within it, I assure you. It is not untoward, either. All of the young ladies have a copy. It was on the lips of women in all the drawing rooms yesterday — or so I'm told — so I had to find a copy of one myself. Well. Good day, then."

"Are you not taking breakfast?" he asked, taking in her red cheeks, her eagerness to escape his presence as soon as he would allow it.

"I-I'm not hungry at the moment," she said with a forced smile. "I will return later on."

And with that, she was gone. Jeffrey no longer had an appetite, nor a wish to read anything further. He thought of Lady Phoebe's ideas on the subject, of his own sister's conviction and belief in the changing role for women. This was what he had been concerned about when he heard Lady Phoebe speaking to her friends of such matters. Now, to have a publication spreading this same type of useless ideals that would come to nothing but trouble? It was certainly not acceptable, particularly now that he had seen its effects within his own home. But what was he going to do about it?

* * *

NOT FINDING AN ANSWER, Jeffrey took some advice from the column of the very paper he was battling. Sometimes, it was better to find strength in numbers. While he was unable to find Viola's copy of the publication, he picked one up from a boy who had one copy left in his hand. As much as Jeffrey hated the thought of supporting the damned journal, he bought the thing to take with him. If there was one place where he knew he could find others who would be equally as appalled as he was, it was White's.

He strode down St. James with purpose, then strolled through White's front doors, where he was greeted by the footmen. Ease settled over his soul as he walked through the marble-columned hall. Here, he could always find himself a moment of peace, away from the many females who were constantly ordering him about, telling him how to live his life or asking him for one thing or another.

He was surprised to find the club was rather empty, with the exception of the morning room, where every gentleman seemed to have congregated, gathered around a small table, chairs filled, while many were standing.

No sooner had he stepped into the circle when he was noticed and gathered in.

"Ah, Lord Berkley!" the rotund Earl of Totnes greeted him. "I'm glad you have arrived. Tell me, have you seen this rot yet?"

So it would seem that he had not needed to stop for a copy of his own. The publication was already spread out on the table below, men staring at it in consternation, as though it was about to grow claws and rise up to attack them.

"I have, unfortunately," he said dryly. "In fact, it was on my very own breakfast table."

Some began nodding in understanding, apparently having found themselves in similar circumstances in their own homes. Heated words began to form, and soon enough there were shouts and arguments echoing around walls of the typically reserved club.

Finally the Duke of Clarence, who Jeffrey hadn't seen until this moment as he had been sitting behind the rest, reclining in one of the wide leather chairs, stood and raised his hands.

"Silence!" he shouted with all of his ducal authority, before lowering his voice once he had their attention. "We will get nowhere by bickering amongst ourselves. There is only one thing we can do at the moment, and that is to investigate this further and to encourage the proprietors to discontinue operations. In the meantime, if we are divided, it will only provide credence to ideals such as those contained within this publication. What we must do is create a plan and to take this down immediately, before any further traction is gained. What do you say?"

The Duke smiled at their resounding "Aye." Jeffrey felt a momentary twinge of unease at the thought of this "lady" being hunted down by a vast number of powerful men, but it was to be expected, was it not?

"And what, pray tell, is this plan of yours?" someone asked.

Clarence turned a wicked smile toward Jeffrey and the swirling unease increased.

"I believe Lord Berkley can help us in that regard."

"I can?" he raised an eyebrow as he studied his friend. Now was not the time to jest. What was Clarence doing?

"You can," he confirmed with a nod, then turned back to the rest of the throng. "It looks as though Berkley has already informed himself of the matter, as he holds in his hand the very publication we are discussing. Not only that, but he has four sisters he must protect, and therefore will be particularly motivated to resolve the matter. Is that not true, Berkley?"

He nodded slowly. That, he couldn't deny.

"Very well," Clarence said, clapping his hands together. "The matter is settled, then, gentlemen. Berkley will find the owner, explain our position, and shut this down. Now, let us clear this publication off the table and move to the billiards' room. Who challenges?"

Jeffrey backed away. Well, this was a fine predicament. He had come here for a solution, not for additional reasons to pursue the matter. A storm cloud began to build within him, which began to pour out when Clarence came over to speak with him away from the other gentlemen.

"What were you thinking?" he ground out, his ire growing as Clarence simply laughed.

"I know you, Berkley. You were not particularly thrilled when you read this little paper, now were you?"

"No," he said begrudgingly.

"Well, I thought it would put your talents to good use. Your task will not be altogether difficult."

Jeffrey looked at him with some chagrin. "You do not overly care about this drivel, do you?"

Clarence shrugged and began walking toward the exit as Jeffrey followed. "Not really. It's a harmless little paper for women. They have arisen before, and they never last longer than a few months before they go out of print. What harm is it for ladies to have their fun? Besides that, they are not saying anything particularly blasphemous. So they discuss ladies having a brain in their heads? That is not exactly news.

Tell me you have never spoken with an intelligent woman, Berkley, one willing to share her true thoughts?"

Jeffrey thought of Lady Phoebe and her forwardness, of his own sisters and their willingness to say whatever entered their minds.

"I suppose I have," he said begrudgingly.

"If you find the owner, you get what you want. If not," Clarence took his hat from one of the porters, fitting it neatly on his head. "There is no harm done, Berkley. Women are mystical creatures. Hell, if you ask me, the world might be better off with a little more injection of their thoughts to be heard. And it will be great fun watching you take this on. Good day, Berkley."

And with his charismatic grin, he was off, Jeffrey staring after him, left wondering what had just happened.

CHAPTER 7

"*D*o you have the fashion column, Rhoda?" Phoebe called across the room to the woman who was sketching out the order of this week's final list of articles before they would send it to the press for printing.

"I do, it's here!" the woman called back, her dark head, dusted with grey, bent over her work. Phoebe could not have asked for a better editor of the paper. The woman was efficient, dependable, and had a knack for knowing what would be of interest to readers. A widow, she had aided her husband in his own small publication before he passed, and when she had seen Phoebe's advertisement, she had replied immediately. She was the first potential editor Phoebe had interviewed, as well as the last. She was perfect.

Phoebe spent as much time in the office as she could. She was drawn to the work, thrived on it really, but she had other engagements to see to as well, and so could not be exclusively here. Their team, however, was talented — frightfully so. And even better, their first publication had been widely read, judging by the reaction of other young ladies of her station. While Phoebe hoped women of all classes would benefit from the words of *The Women's Weekly*, she was well aware that the cost alone would prohibit many from reading. Not only that, but the unfortunate way of it was many women simply couldn't read, or had no time for leisure.

She hoped she could help change some of that. She didn't know how, but perhaps in time she could do more. They could, at the very least, write of such issues to bring more awareness of the plights of many women to the noble and middle classes.

"We sold all of the copies last week, Rhoda?" she asked the woman, coming around to sit in front of the table where she currently worked, looking around at the drab brick walls to which she hoped to soon bring life.

"We did," Rhoda answered with a returning smile. "All one-thousand of them. I hate to admit it, but I can hardly believe it. Do you suppose we should print more this next issue?"

Phoebe tilted her head, considering.

"No," she finally said. "Let's ensure it continues to remain in demand, and then we'll print more the following week."

"Very well," she said with a nod. "And as for next week's deadline—"

"Miss Phoebe!" Rhoda was interrupted by the young lad who raced through the doorway so fast he nearly collided with another of her writers.

"Slow down, Ned," she admonished, but with a smile. "And do come in."

He was one of her delivery boys. She paid them more than most young ones of their station would make, but she wanted them to remain loyal to her and continue to return, to not steal any of her profits.

"Now," she said briskly once he was seated in front of her. "What is the matter?"

"There was a man asking after you, Miss," he said, his blue

eyes wide in his dirt-splattered face. Phoebe wished she could do more for these children, but at the very least they were taking home money to their families. They should be in school, really, but if they weren't working for her, they would be working for someone else, picking pockets or worse.

"A man?" she asked carefully, not wanting to rush the information, to ensure he imparted it thoroughly. "Was he asking for me specifically?"

"No, ma'am," the boy said with a shake of his head. "He was asking about the publication. He wanted to know who the owner is, and the editor. He wanted to know where I receive my pay, but I wouldn't tell him. He offered me decent money for it, he did, but I told him that I didna know anymore."

"I see," Phoebe said, standing, pulling a coin out of her small reticule, and the boy's eyes gleamed. "Here you are, Ned, for the trouble and for your loyalty. Now, tell me, what did this man look like?"

"He was dressed fancy, he was, a nob to be sure," Ned said with a nod. "He had the neckcloth choking him like fancy men do, and a fine jacket. Light hair. Dark eyes. His face was kind of… craggy. And hard."

That's all Ned seemed to remember as he then shrugged. Phoebe's heart flipped in her chest as she listened to the boy's description. Was she simply picturing the marquess as the man Ned described because he continued to infiltrate her mind? He *had* been so against her own words at the party. But would he truly go so far as to come after her newspaper?

"Did he give you anything, Ned? Any way to try to contact him?"

His eyes lit up. "He did! He gave me his card, said to call on him if I wanted to talk about anything further."

He handed her over the slim white card.

"The Marquess of Berkley," she read the embossed words aloud as unease and disappointment filled her in equal measure. "Just as I thought. Thank you again, Ned. You have been more than helpful. I shall not forget it."

He blushed a bright crimson and nodded at her, then was out of the door and gone just as fast as he came in. Phoebe walked over to Rhoda, who had been listening intently.

"I know this man," she said in hushed tones. She hadn't told her staff of her particular status, though they were smart enough to know that she was of a fairly high station. "He is relentless, and stubborn. I will do my best to stay apprised of his actions so that we are not surprised. But if he does come here, we cannot tell him anything."

"Of course not, Miss Winters," Rhoda agreed. "I knew when I came to work for you that this type of publication wouldn't be accepted by all. But I believe in what we're doing, and we'll continue it."

"Thank you, Rhoda," she said, before turning to speak with the other two women who currently occupied desks in the large room, and were attempting to look as though they were not listening to the conversation. "None of us have done anything wrong. This is simply men trying to prove their dominance over us. We will continue to carry on. If they are scared, well, that means we are doing something right."

The paper ready, her staff in understanding, Phoebe threw her cloak around her shoulders and left. So the marquess was coming after her. She refused to go down without a fight. And she had an idea of just what weapon she should use against him.

* * *

"LORD BERKLEY, how lovely to see you here tonight."

The marquess slowly turned toward her voice, drink in hand, his brown eyes hard as they raked over her, from the bottom of her toes in their cream kid slippers peeking out of her patterned hemline, up the skirts of her royal blue silk gown, over the embroidered waistband and up the gathered bodice, where they rested for a moment on her skin peeking out the top before finishing at her face.

He had done it on purpose, she knew, to disarm her, but she refused to allow him to notice he had caused any sort of reaction within her. She smiled at him in the sultry manner of a woman interested in a man for more than his conversation.

He raised his eyebrows, and she wondered if she had begun too strong, if he would become suspicious following the tone of their previous encounters. She sucked in a breath as it was her turn to now take him in. She had forgotten how tall he was, how imposing his figure could be.

But she would not be cowed.

"Lady Phoebe," he said after sending a nod of dismissal the way of his companion. Perhaps she had intrigued him after all. "I must say I am surprised to find you seeking out my company after our past … meetings."

She was prepared for this.

"I simply wanted to apologize, Lord Berkley," she said with what she hoped was a disarming smile. Should she try to bat her eyelashes at him? No, that would be going too far. He wasn't a fool. "I have not seen you again following that day on Fleet Street, and I have since realized that you were simply looking out for my best interests, and I was altogether boorish toward you. As for our previous meeting … well, we remain in disagreement, but I must tell you how interesting it was engaging in such a clash of wills with you."

One thing she could not do was to veer from her beliefs, to agree with his ridiculous notions. Best to not speak of it with him for now. He said nothing for a moment, studying her as he took a slow sip of his drink.

"Very well," he finally responded. "I am pleased, if somewhat surprised, you feel that way. But, Lady Phoebe, I would happily challenge you to another test of wills. Would you care for a dance?"

"Pardon me?" Phoebe gaped at him, her mouth hanging open. He wanted to dance with her after one simple apology? She hadn't expected this, wasn't prepared for it. She didn't dance. But — wasn't this what she wanted? She hastily closed her jaw and nodded at him mutely. A wicked gleam came into his eye as he set his drink down and lifted her hand, placing it upon his arm.

The cacophony of noise around her, voices, music, booted feet, and laughter, blended together to become a chorus of sound that she hardly registered as she allowed him to lead her to the dance floor. Phoebe could feel each of the curious stares sent her way — that she, Lady Phoebe, a woman who lived on the outskirts of the *ton*, had captured the eye of Lord Berkley, enough for one dance at least.

She didn't care for the thoughts of others, she reminded herself as she held her head high, ignoring the stares. She had come tonight to the party of Lord and Lady Holderness with one purpose, and she was achieving it. She should be pleased with herself.

Phoebe was startled for a moment when the marquess abruptly stopped, then jumped when his hand curled around her waist and was nearly floored when he took her other hand in his, heat pouring into her from where they were connected, even through the thin layer of her white glove.

This is just a game, Phoebe. She felt his gaze upon her, but instead of looking up at him, she allowed her eyes to wander around the top of the ballroom, at the mural of angels on clouds painted on the ceiling above them, the crimson red of the backdrop and walls below providing a feeling of decadence. The Holderness family lived in grandeur, and they were pleased to show it off.

"Did you find a new gown?"

Phoebe whipped her head toward her dance partner, her eyes colliding with his. Damn, he was an attractive man. Not traditionally so, but there was something about him … what was he saying? A gown? Why was a man asking her about a gown? Oh yes — the dress shop.

"I did, Lord Berkley, thank you," she said, avoiding the need to add details. "And your business the day we met?"

His jaw tightened. "All remains in order," he said cryptically.

She nodded, and as she did so, she tripped slightly. She had never been a particularly adept dancer, and it seemed lack of practice had not increased her skill.

"Damn," she muttered under her breath, then stiffened when she heard the marquess snort.

"How ladylike of you," he said, the traces of a smile gracing his lips.

"I never purported to be ladylike," she said with an edge of steel to her voice, and he shook his head.

"I am not disparaging you, Lady Phoebe," he replied. "I was taken aback, that is all. I have heard such words on the tongues of my own sisters, though I believe they do it only to torture me, and I continually advise them to keep from uttering them amongst polite company."

"I would hardly consider you to be *polite company*, Lord Berkley, considering our history with one another."

The words were out before she even thought them through, and Phoebe bit her lip to keep from saying anything further. She was supposed to be attracting the man, for goodness sake, not pushing him further away.

But to her surprise, after a moment of stunned silence,

the marquess laughed. A deep, low chuckle, it came rolling out of him, and Phoebe could only watch him in astonishment as she felt the rumble in his chest from where they were connected. Gone for a moment were the harsh lines of his face, the cold eyes, the intimidating bearing. Somehow he became … just a man, and she couldn't help the true smile that spread across her face in response.

She looked down for a moment before meeting his eyes once more.

"Tell me of your sisters. I have had the pleasure of meeting Viola, but not yet the rest of them."

And so he did. He described his sisters, his face retaining its soft look as he did so, and Phoebe could read how much he cared for them — not just because they were his responsibility, but because he loved them, nearly more as a father than a brother.

"How long since you became the marquess and have been looking after them?" she asked softly.

"Five years now," he said with a shrug. "It is trying some days, but they keep life interesting, I suppose. Thank you for the dance, Lady Phoebe."

Phoebe looked around, realizing the dance had ended, and she felt a fool as she noted she had continued to move. She stopped, nodded, and smiled once more.

"Thank you, Lord Berkley. I hope to see you again soon."

CHAPTER 8

"*P*hoebe!"

She heard her name being hissed from the shadows, and she smiled, knowing exactly what was coming. She picked up a glass of champagne to celebrate the first successful step of her plan, then stepped over into the dim light where the voice originated, finding three women standing around the other side of the bronze statue, waiting for her.

"There you are!" she exclaimed. "I was looking for you."

"And we," said Sarah, "were looking at *you*. Phoebe, you were dancing with Lord *Berkley*."

"I was," she affirmed. "I am well aware of his identity."

"But why?" Julia asked, her head tilted as she studied her. "Last time we spoke you seemed to want nothing to do with him."

"Nothing has changed in my feelings toward him. He remains a disagreeable man of outdated opinions," Phoebe said, though she felt a niggling of doubt at her own words. She pushed it aside and continued. "But something else has changed, and becoming close with him is the best possible solution."

She told her friends, who were as rapt an audience as one could ask for, about learning the marquess had been asking about her, and her publication. On one of the weekly walks with the three women, she had finally told them the full story of their encounter in the drawing room, of which they were all suitably shocked, though just as much at Phoebe's own behavior as at the fact that the marquess had spied upon them. They were less surprised about his reaction or his words. Now they stared at Phoebe wide-eyed at her current plan of attack.

"The only reason he could be so interested in finding the publisher of *The Women's Weekly* is that he wants us to cease operations," she finished. "It is what I expected, though I didn't think it would be so soon, nor that he would be the man to lead the charge. As I learned this information through one of my delivery boys, I couldn't very well walk up to the marquess and ask him why he is persecuting us. I do not want him to be aware that I have any involvement. And so, I decided the best way to determine what he has planned and what his actions may be was to become close with him myself."

She finished triumphantly, looking around to see her friends staring at her. Sarah wore a shocked expression, Elizabeth looked rather worried, and Julia grinned.

"Brilliant!" she said, leaning forward toward Phoebe, but her exuberance was cut short when Elizabeth held up a hand to protest.

"I am not so sure about this," she warned. "Clearly you are not keen for anything more than a flirtation in order to ascertain the marquess' movements. How long do you plan on maintaining this charade? At some point you will have to break things off. He is a marquess, Phoebe, a respectable man, and he will not associate with a young lady for an overly acceptably long period of time for anything more than what might potentially lead to courtship, and then marriage. Yes, marriage," she said at Phoebe's shocked expression. "It would lead to scandal. I understand what you are doing, Phoebe, and I support you, I do, but I simply do not want to see you hurt. I do not see this ending well — for either of you."

Phoebe took a breath. Elizabeth was looking out for her best interests, she knew that. And yet, her friend was pointing out the issues with her plan that she herself was unsure of, but had determined were not nearly as important as saving *The Women's Weekly.*

"I understand that Elizabeth, I do," she said. "But I promise you that I will not allow this to get out of hand. It's a mild flirtation, that is all. Besides that, I am clearly not the type of woman in whom the marquess would ever have a serious interest. Look around this ballroom — or any ball-room, for that matter. Do you see many other outspoken women who are not afraid to speak their ideals, who can hardly dance a step, who spend their inheritance instead of saving it for a dowry? No. It's because those types of women are not the ones who will marry gentlemen of title. In fact, they will likely not marry at all."

Seeing Sarah study at her with her head tilted, one side of her lips curved in a look of sympathy, Phoebe shook her head with a smile. "Do not pity me. This is what I choose. This is what I would far rather do with my life. Now, a glass of rum punch, anyone?"

* * *

JEFFREY LEANED back against a sculpted marble column, shifting positions when the corner of a carved angel wing dug into his back. He was itchy, but not for any reason he could easily identify. He was brooding, he knew, as he kept his eye on Lady Phoebe, ensconced in a corner with three other ladies — the very same ones he had found her speaking with upon the occasion of their meeting at the Earl of Torrington's. Their heads were together, Lady Phoebe gesturing animatedly. They reminded him of his sisters, the way they spoke without reserve, assured in unwavering friendship.

What was she up to? One moment she was arguing with him, slapping him without reservation, the next she was prettily flirting with him like every other young miss who approached him. Though none, he knew, would be so bold as to approach him without introduction nor cause for conversation.

His view of her was momentarily obstructed by a face — one rather like his own, but covered in a perpetual — though disingenuous — smile.

"Jeffrey," Ambrose said with a nod, his grin increasing as he knew very well his brother preferred to be called by his title when out in a public setting.

"Ambrose," Jeffrey responded, as he attempted to peer around his brother's head when he noticed Lady Phoebe and her friends were departing from their station in the shadows.

"Something — or *someone* — catch your interest over there, brother? A certain heiress, perhaps?"

"What are you on about?" Jeffrey muttered.

"Why, it's on everyone's lips," said Ambrose before his words took on a mocking tone. "Lord Berkley, who waltzes with no one, who avoids showing interest in any one particular young woman, on the dance floor and during a waltz, no less! And with none other than Lady Phoebe Winters, a wallflower who looks as though she has never danced a set before in her life within polite society. Why, Jeffrey, why?"

He asked the question in mock interest, holding a hand to his breast, and Jeffrey rolled his eyes at him. "Go away, Ambrose."

Ambrose only laughed, and it was then that Viola passed by, inserting herself between the two of them, knowing their propensity for disagreement, clearly not wanting them to make a scene in the Holderness ballroom.

"Is everything all right?" she asked, looking from one of them to the other, and Jeffrey couldn't help but smile at his sister. She was so calm, so gentle, and he knew that it bothered her when he and his brother found themselves in conflict in her presence.

"Everything is fine, Vi," he said reassuringly. "Ambrose here is shocked that I was able to locate the dance floor of the ballroom, that is all." He sent a glare his brother's way. "And he was just leaving."

Ambrose bowed mockingly to his brother, kissed his sister on the cheek, and, thankfully, continued on his way, likely to find a woman who would believe his charming words were genuine.

"What was that about?" Viola asked, and Jeffrey waved a hand in response.

"You know Ambrose."

"That's not what I meant," she said, looking up at him meaningfully through her spectacles. "Lady Phoebe. I had thought that the two of you did not get on particularly well, and yet there you were together, looking as though you might actually be having a nice time."

"It was just a dance, Viola," he said with a sigh. Had everyone been watching him, or did his family not have their own affairs to see to? "I thought you enjoyed your acquaintance with Lady Phoebe."

"I do, but that has nothing to do with this conversation. Now you, Jeffrey, are not one to ask just any young woman to waltz in front of all the *ton*," she said, an eyebrow raised as she studied him for a few seconds before continuing on her way.

A moment alone, in silence, Jeffrey thought. *That is all I need. Then I will—*

"Berkley."

So much for that.

"Clarence," he replied, pushing himself away from the pillar. At least the Duke wouldn't question his dance. His friend would understand that one waltz meant nothing at all, was as regular an occurrence as any other.

"I hear you were dancing with the Lady Phoebe."

Or not.

"Yes," Jeffrey said, gritting his teeth. "That I was. One dance. As every other gentleman dances with every other young lady. It is nothing to be particularly shocked about, nor to make any note of."

"True," Clarence said, standing beside him to peruse the scene in front of them. He took a sip of his drink before tilting his head toward Jeffrey. "Unless the one dancing is a marquess who avoids waltzes with young ladies of the *ton*. And his partner is a woman who, as far as I am aware, is not particularly enamored by said marquess and is not typically found on the dance floor."

Jeffrey snorted at that. Clarence had a point.

"She apologized," he said by way of explanation, and now Clarence actually turned to look at him, disbelief on his face.

"One apology and you are in one another's arms? How do you do it, Berkley? I wish I had such a way with women. You will have to teach me your skill. But tell me — you could dance with any woman in this ballroom. Most are desperate for you to even look at them. Why choose a woman who vexes you so?"

Jeffrey contemplated his words for a moment. They were true, but the issue was he himself didn't quite know the answer. Clarence was patient, and finally Jeffrey spoke words that were as true as he could gather.

"There is something about Lady Phoebe that I cannot exactly explain," he said. "But the very reason she captures my attention is that she is not at all like most other young women with whom I am acquainted. From what I have gathered, she is unpredictable, it is true, she holds opinions that are rather unpopular, and she is not afraid to speak of them. And yet, I find myself intrigued."

Incredulity only grew on Clarence's face as Jeffrey spoke, and finally the Duke shook his head.

"I cannot say I completely understand you, Berkley, but it is good to see you interested in a woman, at the very least. It has been far too long for you — at least, as far as I am aware. Nevertheless," he tipped his drink toward him. "I myself like to know what to expect when it comes to women. I believe I will go find myself one of the young ladies whom you so despair and engage her in a dance. I will leave you to your lady of mystery."

Unwilling to have to explain himself to yet another friend or family member, Jeffrey passed his drink to a waiting footman and perused the ballroom for a means of escape. The expansive garden doors beckoned, and he climbed the stairs before lighting his cheroot on a wall sconce and pushing open the door, the slight wind pushing at the glass door as he did so.

The fresh air, however, was cool against his skin, refreshing after the close heat of the ballroom. The early spring air nipped at him, but it would mean there would be far less possibility of running into anyone out here. He took a deep breath of the misty air, which held a hint of the rain that had been threatening all evening. Meandering down the garden path, he took a puff of his cheroot. He slowly blew out the smoke in front of him, seeing it curl through the evening air.

"I would really prefer you didn't do that."

CHAPTER 9

"*L*ady Phoebe," he drawled as he slowly turned to her, seeming to know who was in the shadows before seeing her face. "If I didn't know any better, I would think you were following me."

Phoebe smiled as she stood from the bench where she had been taking a moment alone, away from the people and the prying eyes of the ballroom, and stepped out into the light of the moon and that from the house above them.

"Would that not be my line, Lord Berkley, as I was out here first?"

He tapped his cheroot against his leg.

"I am sorry to intrude," he managed.

She shrugged, ignoring his words as she took in the offensive instrument swirling between his fingers.

"I do not understand the appeal."

"Pardon me?"

"The appeal of those things," she said, gesturing to the cheroot. "They smell disgusting, and while you may like them, everyone else has to breathe in your smoke as well. It is quite a selfish hobby."

He lifted an eyebrow at her words before he glanced down at his hand. He seemed about to drop the cheroot but then paused for a moment. He smiled wickedly at her, then purposefully brought it to his lips, taking a deep inhale without breaking eye contact with her.

She narrowed her eyes at him, knowing he was purposefully continuing to smoke it in order to spite her, but decided that to say anything further would only give him additional pleasure. Instead she crossed her arms and waited for an answer to her question, and he finally acquiesced with a sigh.

"It's just as you said — a hobby. I do not partake often, and nor do I typically do so unless I am with others who express a similar interest. I must say, however, Lady Phoebe, that many women enjoy the scent, or so I am told."

"Have your sisters told you that?"

"No," he said slowly.

"Well, I would ask them how they feel, as they are the young ladies who are most likely to be truthful and straightforward with you," she said, waving a hand. "The rest, well, they say what you want to hear."

"Not all the rest," he said, stepping closer to her. "There is one in particular who does not seem inclined to hide her thoughts from me."

Despite her bravado, when he stepped toward her, a headiness came over her. Perhaps she was simply overwhelmed by the dizzying array of scents surrounding her — the brandy on his breath through the smoke of the cheroot, which he had yet to bring to his lips once more, the spice of the scent that seemed to be emanating from his very body, all mixed within the rain-scented air. Or perhaps it was simply him. She was going about this all wrong. She was supposed to be flirting with him, to become closer with him, and yet here she was, vexing him all over again. "Forgive me, Lord Berkley, if I have offended you."

"No offense taken," he said, and she thought his eyes crinkled a bit as he grinned at her. Or perhaps that was simply a trick of the shadows. For he wouldn't be actually pleased with her about this, now would he?

"I-I'm glad to hear it," she responded, frowning when she heard the hitch in her voice. No man had ever made her cower before, and Lord Berkley was not going to be the first.

"Lady Phoebe," he said slowly as he inched toward her once more, now dropping the cheroot on the stones of the garden path and grinding it out with his heel. "Would you mind if I called on you?"

"Called on me?" she echoed, sounding like a dim-witted idiot.

"Yes," he said with a slight laugh. "As in, came to your home for a visit. A short visit. With your aunt present, of course — all aboveboard."

She chuckled herself now. "I think you may have come to realize by now, Lord Berkley, that I am not particularly 'aboveboard,' as you say, when it comes to much."

He smiled then, and Phoebe was shocked by how it changed his countenance. The ruggedness of his face, his prominent features, lost their edge, and he seemed actually … charming. Friendly, even. Certainly attractive.

"No, Lady Phoebe," he said, his face descending dangerously close to hers. "You certainly are not."

Before she could even contemplate his words or his actions any further, she let out a gasp, the sound lost when his lips descended on hers. He kissed her with some hesitation at first, as though he was questioning whether he should be doing so. But, Lord help her, as much as she knew she should resist, it was as though her body became disconnected from her mind, and not only did she return his kiss, but she pressed herself closer against him, feeling his warmth through the thin material of her silk dress.

This man thinks nothing of the value of women, she attempted to remind herself, but then his arms came around her back, and she let herself go with him. *He believes your role should be to marry and to bear children — that's all you're good for.* Oh, but now he was kissing her neck.

And, a small unwelcome voice told her from deep within the recesses of her mind, *he also has four sisters whom he loves and respects. Clearly, he can't be all bad?*

And then she stopped thinking completely as his mouth returned to her lips, and his tongue teased against her seam and she opened to him. He was tasting her, teasing her, one hand still at her back, the other in her hair, his strong fingers kneading into her scalp as he ravaged her mouth with the abandon of a man who was starving for her touch.

Phoebe didn't know how long they would have continued, practically making love in the gardens of the Holderness estate, but suddenly a drop of moisture hit the back of her neck and she shivered involuntarily. It was but the first warning, however, as a deluge of rain descended from the sky, the clouds having collected the water throughout the day, now opening up and sending it down upon them, seemingly all at once.

They broke apart, staring at one another in astonishment for one crazed moment before he took her hand in his, and, fingers intertwined, he led her racing back toward the house. Instead of returning to the ballroom, however, he pulled her under the balcony so that they were hugging the wall, though he didn't pull her up against him once more, leaving her confusingly bereft.

"We cannot go in there like this," he murmured, his voice husky as his brown eyes analyzed her, and she brought a hand to her hair, finding that it was now all hanging in clumps around her head, soaked right through. Suddenly a horrid thought rushed through her, and she looked down to see what effect the rain had upon her dress. As she feared, the silk gown was now plastered to her skin, the material of the dress hugging her to reveal far more than she would have cared to show.

The marquess apparently noticed as well, as he swallowed and cleared his throat before removing his jacket and throwing it around her shoulders.

"I cannot wear this!" she protested.

"It's much better that you do," he responded, staring off into the distance, refusing to look back down at her. Was he really so repulsed by what he saw? "Now, come," he said. "We'd best get you straight to your carriage."

He led her around the side of the building, an arm around her back as they slowly navigated the slippery steps and pebbly path that led around the side of the house toward the Mayfair street. Eventually Phoebe found her own carriage, and as she climbed the steps inside, she began to remove his jacket to return it.

He held a hand out, stalling her. "I'll have the butler find your aunt before I return home myself," he said. "I will collect the jacket tomorrow when I come to call. Which, I do not remember you agreeing to. So tell me, Lady Phoebe," he said, leaning further into the carriage, which made it suddenly feel much smaller than it was. "Do you permit me to call upon you tomorrow?"

Yes, she had specifically avoided the question. She had wanted this, a short flirtation, but had never imagined it would become so … heated … so soon. It was moving altogether too fast for her, and yet to say no now would not only push him away but would also force a blockade between them.

"Very well," she finally said. "I shall see you tomorrow."

At that he only nodded before shutting the carriage door, leaving her to her musings within.

Phoebe forced herself to remember their first encounter and all he had said to her. This was not the kind of man she needed in her life. She was only entertaining this charade to keep apprised of his movements.

Yet that kiss… perhaps Elizabeth was right. Perhaps she was getting far too ahead of herself.

Whatever was she going to do about this man?

* * *

IT WAS a question she was still mulling over in her mind the next day as she waited anxiously in her drawing room. It seemed silly, to be here waiting for a man when she had much to do at the office, in addition to the tasks of looking after her own household, but there was nothing to be done about it. This was why she had hired an editor, she reminded herself. But the truth was that she enjoyed the actual running of the publication, liked the hubbub of people working around her.

But this was more important. Today, without the distraction of his arms and lips — oh, those lips — she would determine exactly what he was up to.

And in the meantime, she would write her column. She was going to write it on the fact that one could not pinpoint the very nature of women because women, in fact, were as different from one another as men.

She was having a hard time concentrating, however, and she blamed *him* for it. He had made her forget everything that was important, and she didn't like it — not one bit.

Aunt Aurelia had been full of questions when she had joined Phoebe in the carriage, of course, but Phoebe hadn't felt inclined to share much about her time with Lord Berkeley. She told Aurelia instead that she had been out for a walk in the gardens and been caught in the rain. The marquess had happened upon her and had graciously walked her back to the carriage. That was, after all, the truth. For the most part, anyway. She wasn't sure if Aunt Aurelia had entirely believed her but she had, eventually, let the matter go.

Despite the fact that she was waiting for it, when the knock came on the door, Phoebe stood abruptly, startled, nodding at the butler when he introduced Lord Berkley, as well as Lady Viola. Wait... Lady Viola? She had no time to contemplate the implications of Lord Berkley bringing his sister along when the two of them were shown into the parlor.

CHAPTER 10

"What, exactly, are your intentions toward Lady Phoebe?" Viola asked as they pulled up to the modest yet stately home on the other side of Oxford Street, near Cavendish Square, within the neighborhood of Marylebone.

"You sound as though you are her father, Vi, or her mother at the very least."

"I am neither of those things," she responded hotly, her head held high. "I am a *friend*."

"I am aware," he responded dryly.

"I am not altogether sure why you brought me here today, for that matter," she continued, pushing her spectacles back up her nose. "Are *you* not the one courting her?"

"I am not courting her," he said patiently. "Not yet, anyway. I am simply calling upon her. And you are here because I would like your opinion of her."

"I already know her, and would be pleased to share with you what I think of her. She is quite—"

"I would like your opinion of her... countenance toward me."

"You are not able to ascertain that yourself? Come, Jeffrey, I thought you were more astute than that."

He took a deep breath as he tried to maintain his patience, then turned to Viola and gave her his full attention.

"Lady Phoebe puzzles me. In one moment, she is contrary and outspoken, and then in the next, she is pleasant and complimentary. I do not know what to think of her."

Viola narrowed her eyes at him.

"It is not like you to take such interest in a woman, especially one that vexes you so. I like Lady Phoebe, but why do you not find another young woman who would better suit?"

Jeffrey ground his teeth together.

"Will you help me or not?"

"Fine," she said, sitting up straighter as she looked out the window at the white brick of the townhome, assessing it. "But only because I am altogether interested in why this woman has so caught your attention."

"I am eternally grateful," he said sarcastically, then softened somewhat. "You must know, Vi, that you are the only one I would trust with this."

She rolled her eyes but allowed him to help her out of the carriage. Apparently, his compliment regarding her opinion meant enough to open her up a little bit.

A middle-aged butler let them in and led them into the first room, which Jeffrey assumed was a parlor of sorts, though it didn't look like a typical London parlor. He studied the interior of the house as they walked. It was small, quaint, and decorated in rich colors. Paintings of far-off lands decorated the crimson walls, while the carpets were certainly not Aubusson — they looked quite exotic, and he wondered where they had come from.

As they entered the parlor, he was taken aback by the large number of curiosities that littered the room — tropical shells, magic lanterns, and paintings that seemed to have been completed with primitive instruments, yet were somehow oddly captivating. Magnifying glasses and a wide variety of timekeeping instruments hung on the walls amongst the more common draperies and English-made furniture. And in the midst of it, the most exotic of everything in the room stood and walked toward them — Lady Phoebe.

Once they found her, Jeffrey's eyes were arrested upon her, unable to look away, and she blushed under his scrutiny of both herself and the room.

"My father was somewhat of an eccentric," she said by way of explanation. "This was his drawing room, though if you prefer, we can meet in my mother's. My father was always much more interested in what lay beyond England, out in the rest of the world. He loved to travel, and when his health failed him, others satisfied his love for the strange with gifts. I have not yet brought myself to put anything away."

"Nor should you," came a voice from the door, and Jeffrey turned and took a few quick steps forward to offer an arm to the woman who, while slightly elderly, held a twinkle in her eye that bespoke of the same spirit as her niece. "Your father is to be celebrated, Phoebe, not hidden away."

"Of course," Phoebe said with a smile. "Aunt Aurelia, may I introduce you to Lord Berkley. And Lady Viola," she crossed over and took Viola's hands within her own in a welcoming gesture. "I am so happy to see you again."

Viola's eyes widened as she looked toward Jeffrey and then back at Phoebe.

"Did you know I would be accompanying Jeffrey?"

"Not at all. Though on the brief occasion I have had to converse with Lord Berkley, he has specifically mentioned you, which leads me to believe that you are the sister he would choose to bring with him to call."

Viola brightened at that, and even gifted Jeffrey with a small smile as Lady Phoebe led her to sit next to her on the coral cushions of the intricately carved rosewood settee. He and Lady Aurelia each took a seat in one of the matching rosewood armchairs across from them.

And now that the four of them were sitting here staring at one another in somewhat awkward silence, Jeffrey wished he had left Viola at home, so that perhaps Phoebe's aunt and chaperone would not have felt the need to greet them. For he longed for another opportunity to have Lady Phoebe alone, to feel her lips under his once more. He wasn't sure what had come over him yesterday. Never before had he acted in such a manner with a young woman. It seemed that Lady Phoebe caused him to lose his mind – or, at least, his reservations.

He glanced at her, sitting across from him in her fine forest green muslin dress that hugged her bosom and then dropped away to loosely gather around her. He caught her vivid emerald eyes when she looked over at him, noticing him scrutinizing her. He dropped his gaze, but not before the thought crossed his mind of just how much he would like to let down the pile of midnight locks upon her head, to run his fingers through their silky strands.

He shook his head to clear it. This would not do. He could not be practically undressing Lady Phoebe in the middle of a drawing room with her aunt and his own sister present.

"Your father was a scholar of sorts, was he not?" Viola asked, prompting conversation, and Jeffrey thanked the heavens that at the very least his sister was astute.

Lady Phoebe smiled and shrugged slightly. "I do not think he could be called a scholar," she said, a wistful look crossing her face as she remembered her parents. "But he was certainly a curious man."

"And your mother, what was she like?"

"Viola," Jeffrey cut in. "Perhaps Lady Phoebe—"

"It's fine," she said with a quick wave of her hand. "It is lovely to speak of them. My mother was an intelligent woman in her own right, though not in the same vein as my father. She did help him, however. She loved to write, and while he would concentrate on his studies, she would take notes for him. Somewhere in this house we have journals full of his thoughts, written in her hand."

"How fascinating!" Viola said, leaning forward slightly. "I would love to see them sometime."

At that, Phoebe's smile dropped so slightly that Jeffrey wasn't sure anyone else noticed. But clearly, those works were private.

Viola's gaze continued to wander around the room, before finally coming to rest on the table in front of them. Phoebe was apparently taking note as well, for suddenly she leaped into action.

"I am so sorry! Would anyone like tea? I completely forgot to pour."

At their nods, she began to fill the cups and paused momentarily when Viola made another observation.

"Oh! You have a copy of *The Women's Weekly*," she said, pulling on a paper from the bottom of a stack of journals and newspapers. Somehow she must have seen the corner of it peeking out.

Jeffrey attempted to stifle the direction of the conversation. "Viola, I really do not think—"

"It *is* wonderful, isn't it?" Lady Aurelia asked, her face more animated than it had been since their arrival. Jeffrey had never actually read a copy of the publication besides the initial two articles, and nor did he intend to. No, his intention was to shut down the bloody thing, not discuss it over tea with Lady Phoebe, her aunt, and his sister.

"It is smart," Lady Aurelia continued, "and witty, and is

written for ladies of every station. I think it should be in the home of every woman, although that would be altogether impossible at the moment. But yes, I believe these women should be commended for having the courage to write what they believe in, to embolden women to speak for themselves and to have a voice."

She paused to take a breath, and Phoebe cut in, "Aunt Aurelia, it is a wonderful publication, to be sure, but you are far too complimentary."

"I must say," Viola said with a cautious look at Jeffrey. "I *am* enjoying it. And it's true, it does appeal to all women. Why, I enjoy the fashion column as much as I love the column discussing a woman's role in a marriage. And the advice columnist is so fun and witty. I do hope it continues."

"Is there any reason why it wouldn't?" Phoebe asked as she took a sip of tea.

Curiously, she hadn't expressed her opinion. This was just the type of publication a woman with her ideals would celebrate. Perhaps after their previous conversation, she didn't want to raise the matter.

"The reason it *shouldn't* continue is that it contains articles which will disrupt the order of our society," Jeffrey said, bringing his steepled index fingers to his chin.

"How so?" Phoebe asked, cocking her head, and all three women turned to look at him, discomforting him as they awaited his response.

"Well, if a woman is to wait to marry for love, or to pursue her own interests, then what will happen to families? Who will look after the households and all that reside within them?"

Phoebe's lips twitched.

"You have never actually read an issue, have you?" she asked, her face emotionless.

"He read the first page of the first one," Viola said, rolling her eyes. "But do not try to convince him that his opinion is incorrect. He is quite stubborn when it comes to issues such as this."

Phoebe contemplated the both of them, looking from sister to brother and back again.

"Lady Viola," she began. "You strike me as an intelligent woman, a practical one with a good head on her shoulders. Now, Lord Berkley. Would you force a woman such as your sister to marry against her will, to someone in whom she has no interest?"

"Of course not," he said gruffly. "That is different."

"How so?" Phoebe asked. "It is the very same. How you would wish for your sisters to be treated is how all women want to be treated. The only difference between the newspaper and others you might see or purchase is that this one is written with a woman reader in mind. It still reports on the news, on sporting events that women have the opportunity to attend. You should read a copy sometime."

"Yes," Viola chimed in, looking over at him with a gleam in her eye. "You should."

Jeffrey sighed. He was defeated, with the three women intent upon him. He nodded and resigned himself to the fact that they would always think him wrong, no matter what he said. Seeing they were waiting for an answer, he finally told them what they wanted to hear.

"Very well," he said. "I will."

They spoke a while longer on other matters — Viola's interest in books, social events of the season, that type of thing. Lady Phoebe and her aunt were well informed, despite not being overly involved in *ton* matters.

Finally he rose to take his leave, Viola standing as well. But first, she had one more invitation to make.

"Lady Phoebe, Lady Aurelia, it was so lovely to meet you

both today. Why do you not come for dinner tomorrow night?"

Jeffrey choked slightly, but of course to say anything contrary now would be the height of rudeness. But Lady Phoebe in his house, with his family? It was too much — at least, at the moment. He was still attempting to determine if they would suit, beyond the physical attraction that clearly drew them together.

"Oh," Lady Phoebe said, looking from Viola toward Jeffrey. Apparently correctly interpreting his look of dismay, she began to shake her head. "Thank you for the invitation, but we really would not want to impose."

"Please come," Jeffrey heard himself say, and Phoebe looked over at him in surprise. Finally, after sharing a glance with Lady Aurelia, Phoebe slowly nodded her head.

"We would be honored, then. Thank you very much for the invitation."

It seemed he could not stay away from the lady, and he wasn't altogether sure what to do about it.

CHAPTER 11

"$\mathcal{A}$re you sure this is the address?" Aurelia asked as she peered out the window of the carriage at the massive brick building that stretched out in front of them. It sat in the middle of Grosvenor Square, the center building that spoke of prestige and wealth. It even had wings — slight as they were, but they bracketed the fountain in the front of the house.

"This is it," Phoebe responded. "Berkley House. It is rather extravagant, is it not?"

"I suppose we shall see when we enter," Aurelia responded with all of her practicality as she took the footman's hand to descend the carriage steps.

Their assumptions proved to be correct as they entered the foyer, which clearly meant to impose with its grandeur, a white marble statue at the bottom of the steps, high, expansive ceilings upon which murals of cherubs and clouds were painted, and gilded cornices and lavish landscapes of what Phoebe was sure were the Berkley country estates and grounds surrounding them.

Aurelia looked over at her with a slight nod of her head

and a wink, telling her that yes, this was very much what was expected, the grandiose residence of the marquess.

Phoebe bit her lip, as she suddenly wished they had never come. She had wanted to become close with the marquess, yes, but to be invited to his house for dinner? Of course, it would have been the height of rudeness to refuse, but now their families were involved in this charade. And she was no closer than she had been at the start of this in determining what the marquess was planning in regards to her publication.

But they were here now, so she supposed she would just have to make the most of it. They were about to follow the butler up the stairs when a huge, furry body came flying down them.

"Maxwell!" came a cry from up above. "Come back!"

But it was too late, as Maxwell found a welcome audience in Phoebe and Aurelia, who stopped to greet him, and he returned their affections by pressing his wriggling body into their legs while he licked their hands and faces.

"He's lovely!" Phoebe exclaimed, to which Aurelia nodded in agreement.

"Maxwell, come!" repeated the bark from above, and Phoebe thought she caught the butler rolling his eyes. She suppressed a smile as Maxwell went bounding back up the stairs, and they followed him up, entering the first door, which proved to be into a drawing room. No sooner had Phoebe stepped through the doorway when she was surrounded by a chorus of voices, all belonging to young women of varying heights and shades of the same blond locks that she had come to appreciate upon the marquess.

"You're here!"

"We are so glad you came!"

"You are as pretty as Viola said!"

"Penny, that's enough!" came a voice from behind the

three women in front of her, and Phoebe smiled, knowing it was Viola admonishing them. Apparently, she was altogether unlike her sisters.

Viola pushed through her sisters now, taking Phoebe's hand.

"My apologies for my sisters," she said, looking at each girl with some reproach. "They can be... slightly overwhelming at times."

Phoebe had to laugh at that. Not only was Viola correct, of course, but Phoebe was also enjoying the fact that these were Lord Berkley's sisters. Somehow she had pictured prim and proper young ladies who would be waiting for her, sitting in a line on the sofa, with the same reserve that he possessed. But no. She looked around the room, finally finding him leaning against the mantle of the fireplace, and he raised a shoulder helplessly. She shook her head. How could a man who, at the very least, allowed his sisters to be women of character, have opinions so annoyingly old-fashioned?

She looked down when she caught motion at his feet and saw that Maxwell, friendly yet unkempt, was sitting next to him, with one of Lord Berkley's hands on his head. Phoebe was drawn to the dog — not the man, she assured herself — and was about to approach him when an elegant older woman, streaks of grey running through the same light hair as her son, entered through the doorway, shooing away her daughters as she took Phoebe's hand.

"Good evening, my dear, and welcome. I am Lady Berkley, Jeffrey's— that is, Lord Berkley's— mother, and the crowd that greeted you when you arrived is made up of my children. My apologies if they are slightly overbearing. And Lady Aurelia! How lovely it is to see you again."

Phoebe raised her eyebrows as she looked at her aunt, who had never mentioned that she was acquainted with the

Berkley family. Her aunt winked at her before turning to greet Lady Berkley.

"I am Rebecca," said the girl who looked to be eldest after Viola, as the three light-haired young women once again crept closer to Phoebe, studying her as though she were one of the curiosities on the walls of her home.

"And I am Penny."

"Annie," said the youngest.

"It's lovely to meet you all," Phoebe said, nodding to each of them in turn. "And thank you so much for hosting me."

She included Lord Berkley in that statement, and he finally pushed himself off the mantel, sauntering over toward her, a half-smile on his face.

"Are you allowing her to breathe, children?"

"We are not *children*, Jeffrey," Penny said with a dramatic roll of her eyes.

"Yes, Jeffrey, we are young women," said Rebecca with a sniff. "I am 20 years old for goodness sake, and have been out already for a season. You cannot call us girls any longer."

"Act like girls, and I shall call you girls," he said nonchalantly, but his eyes were on Phoebe. "Lady Phoebe," he said with a nod, as though he had happened upon her in a ballroom and not invited her into his home.

Although she supposed he actually hadn't invited her. His sister had, and he had simply done the polite thing and agreed with her request.

"Lord Berkley," she said with equal stiltedness. "Your dog is lovely."

"That is the first time I have heard Maxwell referred to as such, but thank you."

It was their only conversation before they went into supper, for his sisters did not allow anyone else to say a word, as they questioned Phoebe about everything from how long she had been "out" in society, to when she had met their brother. She couldn't exactly tell the truth of that. Somehow she didn't think the marquess would be pleased with her sharing the fact that the two of them had argued to the point of her slapping him in the middle of one of the Earl of Torrington's drawing rooms.

The women were equally curious of who in society Phoebe was particularly close with, and what her plans were for events this season. She tried to appease them as best she could, but they weren't exactly enthralled with the fact that she only attended the odd event, and solely when she knew her friends would be in attendance. When she thought about it, she wasn't entirely sure why they went out in society, though now it was helpful in order to review the fashion and gossip columns of her newspaper. Not that she would call it a gossip column. No, it was more of a who's who in order to entice new readers, who would then hopefully continue on reading the rest of the paper.

She certainly couldn't explain all of that to the eager young ladies, however — nor especially their brother.

They were going in to dinner — Maxwell was sent to the kitchens for his own supper — when they heard a voice within the foyer, and soon a smiling face greeted them at the bottom of the stairs.

"Ah, I'm just in time!"

"Ambrose!" the girls shouted in chorus.

"You're late," Lady Berkley admonished, though she still placed a gentle hand on his cheek as she strode by.

"My brother, Lord Ambrose," Lord Berkley said to Phoebe with a wave of his hand, not even looking at the man as he walked by. Phoebe looked from him to Ambrose with some consternation at the animosity between them, but before she could ask anything, Lord Ambrose took her hand and bowed low over it.

"Ah, the Lady Phoebe Winters," he said with a charming

smile. He looked like Lord Berkley, except that his smile seemed much easier, his features slightly softer. "You have been on the lips of my family ever since my brother was found with you on the gossip pages and the Holderness dance floor. I am pleased to finally have the opportunity to make your acquaintance."

Lord Berkley apparently re-thought his dismissal of his brother as he returned to the foyer, taking Phoebe's hand from his brother's and placing it on his own arm.

"If you were so eager, Ambrose, then perhaps you should have been here on time," was all he said, and as he led her away, Phoebe looked over her shoulder with a smile. "A pleasure!" she called, to irritate Lord Berkley more than anything else.

Phoebe could not recall ever being part of a livelier dinner, particularly one with so prestigious a family. She glanced over at Aunt Aurelia, who was laughing at Ambrose beside her. Apparently the man did not reserve his charm for young ladies.

"Tell me, Lady Berkley," she said to the woman seated next to her, who, for the most part, watched her family's banter with a smile on her face, "Did you happen to know my parents? The Viscount and Viscountess of Keith?"

"But of course," she said, her smile warm yet confused. "Did your aunt not tell you? My late husband was a great friend of your father's in their youth."

"Truly?" she asked, sitting back in her chair, slightly stunned. Why would her aunt not say anything on their travels? And was the marquess aware of their relationship?

"Their family homes were but a mile from one another when they were boys," Lady Berkley continued. "We always enjoyed your parents' company when we saw them in the city."

"Interesting," Phoebe murmured. "I had no idea."

"Oh, yes," said Lady Berkley whimsically. "Why, I can remember many times spent together. We would have dinner parties, sometimes just the four of us, sometimes with others invited as well. Or we would attend parties that would last long into the night, so late that the hours would turn into early mornings. Your father always told the most wonderful stories, and your mother was such a gentle soul. Your father fell in love with her the moment he saw her, and that love never waned."

She continued on, remembering parties and balls from their first days in London, as Phoebe listened with rapt attention and wide eyes.

"Thank you for sharing such wonderful stories," she said, leaning toward Lady Berkley. "I do not mean to pry but why … why did I never know you?"

"Oh, well, I suppose we drifted apart at some point," she said, with some regret in her tone. "John, my husband, and your father had a bit of a falling out as it were, and unfortunately never did reconcile. It's been years…" her face turned wistful. "Anyway, I am so glad to have you here, to make amends with you if not your parents."

Phoebe simply smiled, her mind full of thoughts, curious at all Lady Berkley had told her.

She had hardly paid any attention to the rest of the table, and she looked around now, her gaze stopping suddenly when she felt the marquess' eyes upon her. They were slightly hooded, and yet nothing could hide the intensity of the deep brown that stared at her.

She managed a slight smile and a nod of her head. She reminded herself why she was here and determined that before this night was over, she must discover what the marquess was up to.

When they rose to leave the dinner table and return to the drawing room — the entire lot of them, as the men were composed only of the marquess and his brother — Lord Berkley appeared at her elbow, holding her back as the rest of the party drifted out of the room.

"A moment of your time, Lady Phoebe?" he asked, to which she nodded. Perfect. Time to ask her questions.

He drew her down the corridor, but stopped at a door before the stairs, pushing it open to reveal what must be his study. An ornate mahogany desk sat in the corner, while three of the walls were lined with filled bookshelves. A huge globe dominated one corner, while a portrait of a man who must have been his father hung in prominence between shelves behind the desk. The fire crackled merrily in the grate, and the marquess led her over to a pair of brown leather mahogany chairs sitting in front of it.

"I realize it is not altogether done for you and me to be alone, but I do not believe, Lady Phoebe, that you are particularly concerned about propriety."

"Not really," she laughed. "Now, what can I do for you?"

CHAPTER 12

*W*ell, she certainly got to the point quickly. He had hoped to draw her out slowly, to ask his questions with more tact. But that, apparently, was not to be done with Lady Phoebe.

He didn't want her to think that the only reason he had invited her to dinner was to question her — but after Viola had asked, he had realized what an opportunity it could be. He was, however, enjoying her company more than he cared to admit.

After he and his sister had visited her yesterday, Viola had spent the entire carriage ride home entertaining him with the many wonderful attributes of Lady Phoebe, and how perfectly she would fit in with their family — "Just you see!" she told him, when she explained that was the very reason she had invited her for supper. She seemed to think that the woman was exactly what — or who — Jeffrey needed. Jeffrey wasn't so sure.

He tapped his finger now against the arm of the chair.

"I do not wish to cause discord between us once again, Lady Phoebe," he began. "However, as you may know, this publication we have previously discussed continues to come to my attention. As you share ... similar beliefs as the publisher, I was hoping that, perhaps, you might be of some assistance to me."

She said nothing, hardly showing any reaction. She nodded slightly for him to continue. He cleared his throat.

"I have been tasked, so to speak, with determining the identity of the publisher, though it is proving rather difficult. Anyone holding any apparent association with *The Women's Weekly* remains tight-lipped on the subject. I thought that perhaps others within your circle might have some information in regards to who I might be looking for."

Lady Phoebe remained silent, stoic, staring at him with her hands folded in her lap. The only sign of any response regarding his request was the slight nibbling of her bottom lip. She looked down at her fingers for a moment, and he was distracted by her long, dark eyelashes.

She looked back up at him, meeting his eyes.

"I cannot say whether or not I would be able to help you unless I know how the information would be used," she said. "If you do unveil the identity of this publisher — what exactly would you plan to do?"

"Speak to him or her," he explained, though that was not entirely true. His ultimate goal was to encourage — or threaten or bribe if needed — the publisher to quit operations entirely, though a cease to the contrary articles would be agreeable. "Perhaps it might be possible to find a solution that would allow the publisher to continue without putting our entire society at risk."

"At risk of what?" she challenged, sitting forward in her chair now, her eyes flashing. "At risk of change? And what would be so wrong about that?"

"It could mean turmoil," he countered. "There has been enough conflict in our world in recent years — why do we need to add to it? I am told this publication suggests that women should receive more education. Can you imagine if women spent the same amount of time as men at school? What would happen to our homes? Who would learn how to raise a family?"

Her stoic countenance changed as he spoke. What had been a face of serenity grew more tumultuous at every word, until now her fingers were grasping the arms of her chair, biting into the bronze floral mounts at the curve of the arms.

"Thank you, Lord Berkley," she said, her tone clearly not at all grateful, "for reminding me of all of the reasons that I should want nothing to do with you."

"I did not mean to upset you. I am simply stating facts," he said, maintaining his control on his temper. "And I believe *you* sought me out, initially."

"Tell me," she said, not moving, though not relenting. "Do you believe men to be smarter than women?"

He thought on that for a moment. They were certainly more educated. Did that make them smarter? He compared Viola to Ambrose and knew with certainty that she was much more intelligent. But were all women like his sister? He stole a glance at Lady Phoebe. This one assuredly was. But when he compared her to the many other women of the *ton,* or, at least, how they presented themselves…

"I'm not entirely sure," he said at last. "Some are, some aren't."

She nodded, apparently content with his assessment. "And when a woman marries," she continued, "do you believe that her husband should receive all of her property, all of her funds, everything she owns?"

He shrugged, his brow furrowing. "That is the way of it. Then he can care for all of the financial matters. Often the husband needs those funds for his own estate."

"Because he has mismanaged it himself."

He sighed and stood, hands behind his back as he wandered over to the room's sole window, pushing back the curtains to look out at the dark night beyond.

"Neither one of us is ever going to win this battle of wills."

"On that, I agree," she said, her voice just behind his ear, and he jumped slightly, not having realized she had moved from the chair.

"I must tell you one thing, however," she said, leaning close enough for him to smell the slight hint of perfume she must be wearing. It was sweet, akin to orange blossom, with a hint of spice. Cinnamon, perhaps? A mix of the unexpected — just like its wearer. "Even if I could, I would never, ever help you in your quest."

He turned to her and narrowed his eyes. This conversation had followed the course he had assumed it was likely to take, but nonetheless, he had to try.

"I do not understand it," he muttered, shaking his head slightly.

"What's that?"

He had thought the words had remained inside his head, but apparently, he had spoken aloud.

"Everything about you is altogether wrong for me," he continued, his hands coming to her elbows so gently he wasn't even sure she noticed. He traced the lines of her face with his eyes — the delicate nose, defined cheekbones, plump bottom lip. "When the time comes for me to find a wife, I require a woman who is demure, gentle, agreeable, and, of course, attractive. You are none of those things."

She brought a hand up, and for a moment he feared she would slap him again, but instead she put it on his chest and began to push away. "You know exactly how to charm a woman," she said sarcastically, though he could hear the hurt in her tone. "I agree with you on all you say, but that is not exactly something you actually tell a lady, despite how you may feel about her."

"You are not attractive," he said, ignoring her and not letting go. "You are enchantingly breathtaking. You are so contrary and yet…"

With that, he crushed his lips onto hers, taking what he had been desiring since he had first kissed her in the Holderness gardens. She was as delicious as he remembered, and he could still taste the cream on her lips from the dessert the family and guests had just shared.

He tugged her against him, felt the lusciousness of her bosom press against his chest, and he groaned into her mouth, which she had already opened to him. The passionate barbs they had hurled at one another became ardor of another sort as they poured everything out into one another. All the anger, the frustration, the longing they could not ignore flowed between them, and his arms wrapped around her in an effort to pull her even closer.

This was a woman. Not those silly, flippant girls who said what he wanted to hear, who fluttered their fans in the air ever so prettily. No, Lady Phoebe Winters was none of those things, nor was she the type of woman he should seriously consider as a wife. But none of those other women who fit the list of attributes of a future marchioness called to him like Phoebe. His body was betraying him, he told himself. That was all. But as her arms snaked around his neck and her fiery passion overwhelmed him, he had to admit to himself that it was not just his body. It was his soul.

They were in the middle of his study, and he slowly began to move her backward toward the settee across from the chairs. It wasn't exactly built for comfort — and not at all for romantic trysts — but it would do. For what, however, he had no idea.

He laid her down upon it, and she grasped the lapels of

his jacket as she tugged him toward her. Her hands became lost as they roved over him, and as she dissembled his no longer immaculate cravat. His hand, which until now had simply been framing her head, dug into those silky tresses that so called to him. Her hair was fine, yet there were masses of it, now trailing over her shoulders, her collarbones, and the bosom that was straining at the lace of her bodice.

It was only fair that he free it.

He loosened her gown down her shoulder, one of her breasts falling out of the satin material and into his hand. This was better than he could have ever imagined. He brushed his thumb over her nipple and she arched up into him, her breath coming in short pants now in his ear as he kissed his way down her neck, over her delicate, soft skin, searching for her other breast, which he now released from its confines. As his mouth came over it, she moaned deeply in his ear.

When he heard her murmur, "Lord Berkley," he shook his head.

He came up for a moment to whisper, "Jeffrey."

She repeated his name, and when he heard it slide from her lips, a sense of satisfaction overcame him. He reached down a hand between them, hunting for the hem of her skirts, but he stilled when a knock came at the door.

"My lord?" came the muffled voice of his butler.

"One moment!" he called out, willing his voice to steady as he jumped off Lady Phoebe and began to straighten his clothing.

"Your mother is asking of your whereabouts, my lord," Harper continued through the door. "The party is in the first drawing room when you are available to rejoin them."

"Thank you, Harper," he said. "I am seeing to some urgent business, but I will return shortly."

"Very well, my lord," Harper replied, and Jeffrey sighed when he heard his footsteps retreating down the corridor.

He wiped his brow on his sleeve, as he turned back to Lady Phoebe.

"Phoebe, I—"

He cut off short as he found that in the few moments his attention had wavered, she had replaced her bodice in its proper position and was now re-arranging that beautiful hair as best she could, angrily sticking pins back in to secure it.

"Lady Phoebe," he said cautiously, clearing his throat. "My apologies if I became … caught up in the moment."

"You have nothing to apologize for," she retorted, standing, though she certainly seemed perturbed. "I was as 'caught up in the moment,' as you say, as you were."

"Very well," he said, finding his cravat on the floor, and he clumsily attempted to arrange it in its proper place. She was much more adept at dressing herself than he, who had become far too reliant on his valet. But he couldn't exactly call the man to his study to re-dress him after this.

"Here," she said, rolling her eyes at his clumsy attempts. "Allow me."

She swiftly pleated the cravat, folding down the creases as expertly as his own valet. He looked at her, astonished.

"How did you know to do that?"

"My father often became caught up in his hobbies and neglected his personal care," she explained. "My mother and I became accustomed to ensuring he was respectable enough for polite company, as it were."

She turned away from him, running her hands over her dress once more to ensure all was proper. When she spun back around, he had to say she had recovered remarkably well, though nothing could hide her plump, thoroughly kissed lips, nor the pink stain that covered her cheeks.

Apparently the unflappable Lady Phoebe could be flustered, after all.

"Well," she asked, "shall we go?"

He simply nodded and escorted her out the door. She had better not think they were finished here. Far from it.

CHAPTER 13

*P*hoebe attempted to concentrate on the tasks ahead of her the next morning as her maid pulled her hair back to pin it atop her head. She had chosen a lavender muslin gown, which she would wear with her navy cloak overtop. Very practical for the publisher of a newspaper. Which, she reminded herself, was currently her focus. Her only focus.

She stared at herself in the mirror, studying her face. Her lips, far too large. Her eyes, wide and green, not the beautiful blue, like Julia's, that enticed gentlemen. There was certainly nothing staring back at her that most men would be drawn to. Which led to only one conclusion. She and the marquess had found themselves in a very … *improper* embrace last evening not because he had wanted anything about her in particular, but simply because they had a clash of wills that became extremely heated, which led to their liaison.

She dropped her head into her hands. Thank God the butler had knocked the door when he had, or she wasn't sure what would have happened on that blasted uncomfortable settee in the middle of the study. Lord Berkley must think her some kind of harlot for the way she had acted — though he was equally as responsible for their actions, so what did that make him?

"My lady?" her maid asked, bending toward her. "Are you all right?"

"Fine, Nancy, just fine," she said with a smile, attempting to regain a hold of herself. "I'd best be downstairs for a quick breakfast before I must leave."

If nothing else, at the very least she had determined that while the marquess was attempting to find her — the publisher of *The Women's Weekly* — he was getting nowhere if he was asking her — Lady Phoebe Winters — for help. He should have been very aware that she would do nothing to aid him in that regard.

Though it was advantageous to know that, if required, she could provide him with information that would lead him away from her. She would have to think carefully on the best way to redirect him without raising his suspicions.

She contemplated *The Women's Weekly* as she went downstairs to her seat at the breakfast table, buttering her toast and pouring her tea. She was actually shocked at just how successful it was after the first two issues. They would be printing more copies of their third installment. It seemed that it had worked to draw in many women with gossip columns — as much as she abhorred them — as well as fashion and advice columns. Whether or not they read her articles on the need for reforms to acts regarding marriage, property, and children, she had no idea, but she hoped they at least read the headlines.

She smiled when she thought of the response they had received so far to Julia's column. Apparently more women were interested in horse racing than one would think. In fact, they had already received requests for a column on cricket as well. Who would have guessed?

She was still smiling when she opened the front door of her townhouse to leave for the office on Fleet Street and was so wrapped up in her thoughts that she didn't notice the presence at the bottom of her steps until she nearly ran into him.

"Oh, Lord Berkley!" she exclaimed, holding a hand to her chest. "You frightened me. What — what are you doing here?"

"I came to call upon you," he answered, his face stoic and unmovable.

"It's rather early," she said, looking up and down the street, seeing not many had arisen for the day.

"I realize that," he said, finally showing slight chagrin. "However I — damn it, Phoebe, I needed to see you."

She raised her eyebrows, shocked at his forthright admission. Color had heightened in his cheeks, and blast it if her own heart didn't begin a rapid beating in her chest at the thought that he — the Marquess of Berkley — was disquieted by the very presence of her — Phoebe Winters, daughter of an eccentric viscount. It was all rather confusing, if she was honest. For she didn't want to feel anything but frustration and annoyance toward Lord Berkley. Her turmoil was because of last night. He was the first man she had ever truly kissed — besides the odd peck when she was first coming out — and as for her actions in his study, well, they were truly a first. Oh, what had she been thinking?

Apparently he came to his own conclusions regarding her silence.

"I apologize," he said straightening, looking into the distance. "I should not have used such language in front of you. And this is all very untoward, I realize. Clearly, you have a prior engagement, from which I should not keep you."

And in that moment, she could only laugh at the apparent distress she was causing the powerful marquess.

He stared at her in astonishment as the first giggles bubbled out of her throat, and then when it became a full-on chuckle of amusement, finally his lips spread into a smile of abashment.

"While I am unsure what I have done to cause you such mirth, Lady Phoebe, your laugh is contagious."

Her laughter slowly abated as she realized he must think she was poking fun at him.

"It is not the most ladylike, as I have been told," she admitted. "But I am not laughing *at* you, Lord Berkley. You need not worry about such language in front of me. My father was very vocal in his emotions, to be sure. As for acting in an untoward manner … I thought you knew me better than that by now?"

She cocked an eyebrow at him, and he grinned at her. Oh, Lord, when he smiled, it did something to her stomach. It was as though there were tiny birds fluttering around within it. *Take a hold of yourself, Phoebe.* She realized she was frowning now, but just then a sharp noise from within his carriage, stationed behind him, captured her attention.

"What was that?" she asked, peering around him. Was there someone else within the carriage? "Did Lady Viola accompany you once more?"

He let out a bark of laughter at her question.

"Ah, no. I did all I could to keep him from coming, truly I did, but the brute hadn't yet run today, and—"

"My goodness!" Phoebe exclaimed as a very hairy, very shaggy head appeared in the window of the carriage. "You've brought Maxwell!"

"I didn't *bring* him," he emphasized. "He climbed in and he wouldn't get out. Somehow he seemed to understand we were off to Hyde Park. Or maybe he knew my intention was to see you. I do not know exactly."

Phoebe could only laugh and shake her head. For a man who seemed so interested in maintaining order, everything in his own life seemed to be completely out of his control.

"At any rate," he said, turning from the carriage back toward her. "Maxwell and I were going to go walking near the Serpentine, and we were wondering if you would be at all interested in joining us."

"Oh, I am not sure..." she said, torn. She should say no. She had work to do at the office. But then she looked at Maxwell's hopeful face, his tongue lolling out one side of his mouth, and she just couldn't resist.

"All right," she conceded. "A quick walk, and then I really must be going."

"Very well," he said with a nod. "Is there a maid, perhaps, who you are waiting for?"

"Oh!" she exclaimed. No, she hadn't planned on bringing her maid with her to the newspaper offices, but she supposed that walking across Hyde Park alone with the marquess may be crossing the line farther than even she dared. "One moment, I shall see what is keeping her."

After a hasty conversation with the butler to find Nancy and have her meet them outside, Lord Berkley took her elbow to lead her to his rather magnificent carriage, with its family crest painted in gold on the door of the shiny black vehicle. She noted Nancy scurrying out the door and receiving a hand from the footman as he helped her atop the seat.

"Careful," Lord Berkley warned as he provided Phoebe with a hand up the stairs. Initially, she thought he was referring to the steps. But as soon as she ducked her head to enter the carriage, she realized that it was not the steps he was warning her of, but rather the ball of fur that came hurtling toward her, shaking in excitement.

Maxwell launched her back against the seat, and she laughed as he bathed her face in his excitement.

"Maxwell, off!" Lord Berkley called as he followed in behind her, and the dog reluctantly removed his paws from her shoulders to sit dutifully beside his master as the carriage began to move. "He's a menace," he said by way of apology, but Phoebe waved away his words.

"He's friendly, "she supplied instead. "I love it. How long have you had him?"

"Three years," he said, and a change came over his face as he spoke of his dog. No longer was he serious and stoic, but he seemed …. almost animated, excited. "One of my neighbor's dogs had pups, and he was one of them. He found his way over to our yard once he was big enough to roam and he's been with me ever since."

"What type of dog is he?" she asked him, though her attention was focused on Maxwell.

"The mother was a bloodhound, actually," he said, and once he told her, she could see it within him. "But whatever the father was, it seems to have overcome any bloodhound attributes or instincts. I've tried to take him hunting, but a tomcat would be more useful."

"Well, he certainly is intriguing looking," she said diplomatically, and he laughed.

"Intriguing is a very polite word for Maxwell," he agreed.

She took the opportunity to do a perusal of the man now, instead of his dog. He wore a forest green jacket that was quite becoming on him, expertly fitted to his tall frame. He wasn't thin or even lean like many men she knew, but had a broad chest and shoulders that filled out his clothing. She had felt that chest beneath her hands when they had kissed in his study. She remembered slipping her fingers under his waistcoat, feeling the hard muscle of him beneath his linen shirt.

Her face warmed as she thought of it, and she hastily looked away when she caught his gaze upon her.

"Are you all right, Lady Phoebe?" he asked.

"Never better, Lord Berkley," she said airily. "Never better."

She fanned herself slightly but dropped her hand as she saw the crinkles form in the corner of his eyes and lips.

"I will feel fine once we are out in the fresh air," she continued. "I have a bit of sickness from the motion of the carriage, that is all."

Actually, for once she hadn't noticed it, but she wasn't about to tell him that.

"You're in luck, Lady Phoebe, for here we are," he said as the carriage came to a halt.

The footman opened the door and Maxwell bounded out, a startled shriek quickly reaching them as he apparently caught someone unaware.

"Maxwell, come!" Lord Berkley called, and the dog returned after a few moments, tail wagging exuberantly. "Stay with me now," he commanded, pointing a finger at Maxwell, who dropped his tongue out of his mouth in response.

"Do you fancy a walk near the lake?" he asked Phoebe, and she nodded with a smile on her lips. Nancy stepped down from the top of the carriage to follow along behind them.

Most of their attention was consumed by Maxwell, which was fine with Phoebe. He was a joy to watch, and she wished they could all live their lives with such exuberance. When they reached the Serpentine, Lord Berkley picked up a stick, throwing it as far as it could into the lake, and Maxwell jumped in recklessly with a splash, swimming with all his might.

"He's amazing," she said with a laugh as she looked up at Lord Berkley. "He made the right choice, Lord Berkley, in choosing a master who would allow him to be the dog he truly is, to not force his incredible spirit out of him."

Lord Berkley shifted from one foot to the other at that and finally shrugged.

"I didn't have much choice," he said. "And, Lady Phoebe, perhaps... you might call me by my given name. It seems only appropriate since we ... well, it makes sense."

She dimly recalled him suggesting it to her the prior evening, but she had been within such a dreamy haze she could scarcely remember it. Besides that, she had thought anything he said at the time were just the words of a man consumed by desire. What did he mean by asking her this?

"I, um, suppose I could. In private," she said. "And there is no need to call me Lady Phoebe. Phoebe is just fine. It is what most people I know well call me anyway."

She was rambling a bit now, but she was taken off guard by his request.

"Very well," he said, a smile spreading over his face. "Phoebe."

As she watched, his smile slowly dropped, his gaze becoming much more intense as he focused on her face. His brow furrowed, his eyes narrowed, and his lips stretched into a line as he moved in ever so much closer to her. Was he going to kiss her again? Was she going to let him?

She closed her eyes — apparently they were going to do this once more, here in the open, where anyone could see them — but then a scream rent through the air, and they jumped back in surprise.

"What in the hell — Maxwell!" he called, and he started

after his dog, who was busy shaking out his wet fur all over a group of ladies.

Phoebe picked up her skirts and chased after them, curious to see exactly how the marquess was going to handle this situation.

This was turning into an interesting outing, after all.

CHAPTER 14

*A*fter innumerable apologies to a trio of very angry, now somewhat wet, women, Jeffrey snapped his fingers at Maxwell and pointed at the ground by his side. Hanging his head, Maxwell followed his instructions faithfully, and Jeffrey sighed as he couldn't help but give the dog a pat on the head.

"Poor Maxwell," said Phoebe with a look of pity toward the dog. "So misunderstood."

"And misbehaved," he added, looking over in her direction.

She was something else. She now held her bonnet in her hand, as it had gone flying when she chased after him and Maxwell. Her hair was half down around her shoulders, the rest still restrained within pins on the top of her head. Her forest green eyes seemed to practically sparkle in the sun, and there was quite a becoming flush covering her cheeks from their exertions.

Most women would have left him and his errant dog. Most women would have told him to wrest control of the animal or they would have nothing further to do with him. But Phoebe Winters was not most women. She was forthright in her opinions, that much was for certain. She was outspoken. Self-assured. But more than anything — she was honest. She said what she thought, not holding anything back. She didn't hide any of her past. She had freely told him that her father had been eccentric, that she herself enjoyed pursuits that most would frown upon. Her parents had instilled in her a love of reading and writing, and an appreciation of continual learning, particularly of other cultures, other people, the world beyond London and its surrounding counties. When she hadn't wanted to help him in his investigation, as it were, she had simply told him so. And that, he admired.

Jeffrey sighed as she bent over his dog, patting his head as though to soothe him from the harsh words of the ladies he had so disturbed.

Heaven help him. He was falling for her.

"We should go," he said gruffly and placed a hand at her back, though she suddenly turned around, surprising him.

"Nancy!" she called, seeing her maid in the distance, scrambling to keep up with them. "We must wait," she told him, tugging his hand off the path, just as another trio was entering.

"Phoebe!" one of the women called, and Phoebe turned, gasping in surprise. "Sarah, Elizabeth, Julia! How wonderful to see you."

She embraced them warmly, and Jeffrey inclined his head toward them. Maxwell, of course, rushed to make their acquaintance as well. Jeffrey attempted to call him back, but it was of no use. These ladies, however, did not seem to take issue with his dog's over-exuberance.

"How charming you are," said the woman with light-brown hair, crouching down to take Maxwell's head in her hands.

"Lord Berkley," Phoebe said, remembering him, "May I please introduce my very closest friends, Lady Julia, Lady Elizabeth, and Miss Jones."

"A pleasure," he remarked.

"What are you doing here?" Phoebe asked them, and the same woman who spoke before — Miss Jones, he believed she was called — widened her eyes in surprise.

"It's *Wednesday*," she said as though that explained everything.

"Oh dear," Phoebe murmured, worrying her lip. "It is, isn't it? I'm ever so sorry." Apparently, Wednesday held some significance.

"It's all right," Miss Jones continued. "We understand. You've been so busy ever since… ever since…."

It was now Miss Jones who looked flustered, and Jeffrey was impatiently waiting to hear the rest of that sentence.

"Ever since you began to redesign part of your house, you have been incredibly busy," Lady Elizabeth said in a rush, and Jeffrey turned to look sharply at Phoebe.

"You told me you enjoyed the way your parents had left the home."

"Yes, I do," she said, her cheeks reddening. "Of course. I am making no changes to any of the main areas of the house, but rather my … private chambers." She flushed even deeper, were it possible, and a small smile played around his lips at her shyness in that regard.

Unless… he nearly missed it, but he could have sworn he saw Phoebe send a glare of warning toward her friend. He shook his head. He was reading too much into this conversation.

"What significance does Wednesday hold?" he asked instead.

"Oh, we typically meet for a walk every Wednesday morning," she responded before turning back to her friends. "Please forgive me. I completely—"

"I believe I am the one to blame here," he cut in, holding a finger in the air. "Lady Phoebe clearly had prior arrangements when I called upon her, but I'm afraid I convinced her to accompany me by utilizing my dog as bribery. Accept my apologies, ladies."

They nodded agreeably.

"'Tis understandable," Miss Jones said. "It would be impossible to resist that face."

"It was lovely to see the both of you," Lady Elizabeth said politely. He recognized her from many events, her family being one of the most respected of the nobility, her grandfather the senior partner of Clarke & Co., where many of the *ton* housed their riches — or their pennies, as the case may be. "We should continue on. Have a wonderful day, and Phoebe, I hope to see you soon."

"Very soon," Phoebe promised before following Maxwell out of the park, with Jeffrey at her side and Nancy trailing behind them before she climbed into the seat upon the carriage once more.

"You should have told me I was interrupting a visit with your friends this morning," he said as he helped her into the carriage.

"I see them quite often," she said with a wave of her hand. "They understand."

They took their places on opposite sides of the carriage, Maxwell on the floor between them.

"What is it?" Phoebe asked, feeling his gaze upon her, looking down at her clothing before reaching up to pat at her hair. Finding most of it now down upon her shoulders, she let out a muffled curse, just loud enough that he could hear.

She began to shove pins back into it as she tried to wrest some control of the silky black strands. "I must look a fright," she added, not able to meet his eyes.

"I apologize if you feel I was staring because of anything amiss," he said, leaning in slightly toward her. "You are mistaken if that is what you assume. For I was only looking at you because I am, Phoebe, inexplicably attracted to you."

Her hands drifted down to her lap, her eyes rising to finally meet his. "Oh?" was all she said.

"Oh yes," he added, leaning even closer. "You captivate me. You know how to find the fun in life, you are forthright, you are striking, and you are honest. I had never thought of settling down anytime soon. Lord knows I have enough to take care of as it is. But when I think of letting you go, that upsets me even more."

She stared back at him, her face blank and unreadable, unsettling him. With most women, he would have no fear of expressing his emotions, but Phoebe was not a woman who would be easily swayed by title and prestige.

"I—"

Before he could say anything further, however, she closed the remaining space between them and kissed him.

* * *

SHE HAD to make him stop talking. The moment he had told her how much he appreciated her honesty, she knew she could no longer hear any more of his praises. What would he say if he knew the true reason she was here with him? That this entire courtship was based on a charade, due to her desire to discover his motives regarding her newspaper? That *she* was the publisher of the newspaper of which he so despaired?

So she had taken the only action possible — the one that, was she actually being honest, had been on her mind since the moment he had appeared at her doorstep. She silenced him with her own mouth.

Initially, she had planned for this kiss to be something sweet and chaste, a kiss that could never lead to the same result as last night. But what she continually underestimated was her own attraction to him and the power he so unfortunately held over her.

For when her lips met his, he took that sweet, chaste kiss, and turned it into something that spoke to much more than the kiss of a sweet, budding courtship. No, his kiss was one that solidified the words he spoke to her, that told her that he admired the woman she was and would meet her strength with his own. Oh, why was it so easy to communicate through their actions and yet not through their words?

She groaned as he picked her up and placed her on his lap as though she weighed nothing, which was far from the truth. Unlike her own dismay at her somewhat full figure, however, he was apparently interested in the feel of her body, as his hands ran down over her sides to stroke her hips before cupping her bottom.

As for her breasts, well, he had been quite clear the night before of what he thought of them. Would he do the same today, she wondered, in the middle of his carriage in broad daylight?

Her imaginings, however, would remain that just that. For when his hand came up to fist in her hair — which she had rearranged but moments before — she let out a moan of desire, and Maxwell, apparently, did not like the sound of her in what he must have considered was immediate distress. For soon his huge, shaking body was in front of them, his head inserted into the smallest of spaces between them, breaking them apart. Apparently he wasn't going to be pleased until they were back in their own seats, far from each other.

Jeffrey let out a curse — certainly not muffled this time — before setting her back down across from him, and she began to rearrange herself once more.

Maxwell sat back down on the floor, thumping his tail enthusiastically against the wood at his success.

"You are supposed to be *my* dog," Jeffrey muttered, shaking his head, and Phoebe could only laugh.

"You are a fine protector, Maxwell," she said, giving him a quick rub under the chin. "I shall never forget your bravery."

Jeffrey rolled his eyes, though he couldn't help but give a bark of laughter himself at her words.

The carriage rolled to a stop in front of Phoebe's townhouse. She looked up at it through the window, considering what it must look like through the eyes of the marquess. It was certainly nothing of which to be ashamed. It was well built, facing a beautiful square, and was a decently sized home, especially since it was only Phoebe and Aunt Aurelia who lived within it, though at one point in time, of course, her parents had called it home within London.

Yet in comparison to Jeffrey's own fine, majestic manor, it was fairly nondescript, the white facade so similar to many of the others that lined it on either side. It was the only home she now knew, for the country estate had been entailed, of course. The fact she owned a home, however, was more than most women could say.

"Thank you for the lovely walk," she said, petting Maxwell's ears, and Jeffrey raised an eyebrow at her before he helped her down the steps of the carriage.

"I am beginning to think that you had more fun with Maxwell."

Phoebe laughed. "That is up to you to ascertain," she said,

pausing before the front entrance of her house. "Farewell, Lord Berkley."

"Jeffrey."

"Jeffrey," she repeated. "Farewell, Jeffrey."

And at his slight bow, she trotted down the stairs, to resume her other life — the one he knew absolutely nothing about.

CHAPTER 15

"*I*f we write this in next week's issue, we are sure to attract many additional readers!" Collette, her gossip columnist argued, but Phoebe adamantly shook her head.

"We will not sully the girl's reputation."

"But it is done all the time!" Collette's voice rang around the open space where all of the writers worked. Eventually Phoebe hoped to have some separation, but for now, the building's original layout remained. Only she and Rhoda had their own private offices down the corridor, though to call them offices was, perhaps, rather generous.

"It's an exclusive! I am the only one who saw their embrace. Why, people will be lining up to buy our paper. How could I not run it, Miss Winters?"

Phoebe sighed, placing a hand on her hip. This was the trouble with a gossip column. She understood the draw, and she appreciated Collette's efforts, but at the same time, her purpose was not to go around ruining the lives of young girls.

"We do not know enough details, Collette. Perhaps she

simply fell and the Duke caught her to prevent her from injuring herself."

Collette scoffed, knowing as well as Phoebe that was certainly *not* the case.

"Fine," Phoebe finally compromised. "How about this? Run the piece, but ensure none will know the identities of those you write about. And not just the Duke of M. and Lady F.N. or any of that nonsense. Understand?"

The girl finally nodded and returned to her desk, though she continued to look up at Phoebe moodily. This was one aspect of running the newspaper that Phoebe didn't particularly enjoy. Typically she would have Rhoda deal with such matters, but when she was in the building and it was so close to the publishing deadline, she liked to have the final word.

She heard the door open behind her, smelled the air of the London street — a strange mix of smoke, spice, and, oddly, freshness — fill the room, and she turned.

"Julia!" she greeted her friend with delight. Julia smiled widely as she was followed in by a maid, who sat dutifully by the door. "I was hoping you would come yourself today."

Depending on her prior engagements, Julia sometimes sent in her column through a messenger, though at times she came herself.

"I love seeing everyone at work," she said wistfully, looking around at all of the writers. "How lovely it would be to actually do my writing here amongst the other women."

"You are more than welcome to," Phoebe offered, but Julia shook her head, her curls dancing.

"I would never be able to make my excuses to my parents for such a time. And as much as I love them, somehow I think this would be a bit much for them."

Phoebe nodded in understanding.

"But I am so grateful for the opportunity," Julia continued, placing a gloved hand on Phoebe's arm. "I have always enjoyed watching the races, but never with such purpose as I do now!"

After ensuring Rhoda received Julia's piece, Phoebe led the way to her office. She hadn't changed much in the small room since they had begun publishing — there simply hadn't been time. It was rather horrid, she knew, with its nearly broken chair and scarred desk, but it filled her purpose for now. Julia took one look at the chair and instead perched on the corner of the desk, a cat-like smile on her lips as she contemplated Phoebe, who took a breath, as she knew very well what was coming next.

"So," Julia said, swinging a leg back and forth, her skirts sailing around her as she did. "You looked awfully chummy with the marquess this morning."

Phoebe picked up her quill pen and twirled it between her fingers.

"He called upon me while I was about to leave to come here," she said with a wave of the pen. "Unfortunately, I could not think of an excuse in time, and then my resolve was weakened by that dog of his. I did have a lovely time with Maxwell."

"The way he looked at you – the marquess, not the dog – was magical," Julia said with a wistful smile. "Why, I would give anything for a man to contemplate me like that. The question is, how do *you* feel about *him*?"

"I feel that he is a nuisance," Phoebe said brusquely, dipping her pen in the ink. She loved Julia, and any other time would welcome conversation, but she didn't particularly feel like speaking of this, and she hoped Julia would pick up on her signal of just how busy she was.

She was to be disappointed.

Julia hopped off the desk but now leaned into it with her hip, lowering her voice so no one else could hear.

"Phoebe," she murmured. "I know why you initially began

this... flirtation with him, or whatever you would like to call it. By now you must have made enough progress, have you not? Should you not be ending things soon?"

"I have determined that he knows nothing, that is true," she said with a nod, her stomach oddly sinking when she considered her time with Jeffrey coming to an end. "Yet. I cannot be certain it will remain that way."

"So what will you do?" Julia asked, spreading her hands wide, "Are you going to simply continue courting the man? Will you marry him eventually?"

"Of course not," Phoebe said, looking up at Julia sharply.

"Where else do you think this will lead?" she asked, now looking at Phoebe with an expression akin to pity.

"The marquess would never marry a woman like me," Phoebe said matter-of-factly. "He enjoys my company, true, but to make me his wife? Surely not. I am far too outspoken, and even if he is not aware of my current occupation, he does know my opinion on such matters. And I will never give this up for a man. It is far too important."

"You never completely answered my question," Julia persisted. "You say he is a nuisance, true, but you can still feel something for a nuisance. Do you truly have no emotions toward him, no attraction?"

"I do not," Phoebe said with more emphasis than neces-sary, and Julia started a bit, causing Phoebe to soften and place a hand on her arm. "I am sorry, Julia. The truth is, perhaps — physically — I am attracted to him, but that is no reason for anything to change. Now, if you would like to stay, you are more than welcome to, but I have some work to do if we are going to manage to get this thing to the printing press in time."

"Very well," said Julia, though she eyed Phoebe knowingly. "If you ever need to speak of this, however, you know where to find me."

Phoebe nodded, smiled, and tried to concentrate on the work in front of her.

* * *

PHOEBE MULLED over Julia's words — as well as Jeffrey's — as she traveled home in the carriage. Some of what he had said to her had been rather concerning. Not only because it expressed a seriousness in his pursuit of her, but, more than that, because it turned something within her, made her feel some sort of hope that shouldn't be present.

For she and the Marquess of Berkley could never be. She knew that. Perhaps she must discontinue speaking with him at functions. Try to distance herself from him, avoid places he typically liked to frequent. Yes, she thought as she entered the front door of the house, her butler nodding at her in welcome. That's what she would do.

"Phoebe!" Aurelia called as she entered the door of the drawing room before preparing for dinner. "You will never guess what came."

"What is it?"

"Guess."

"But you said I would never – fine. An invitation to dine with the Prince Regent?"

Her aunt swatted her with the paper she held in her hand.

"Of course not, why would you guess that?"

Phoebe chuckled and allowed her aunt to continue.

"We are to attend the theatre tomorrow night with Lord Berkley and his family! Oh Phoebe, how wonderful! You have found love with a marquess. I know you are not inter-ested in a title, but he does seem to be a polite gentleman, and you could find no better family of which to become a part."

"But I don't love— you didn't accept already, did you,

Aunt Aurelia?" Phoebe asked as a mixture of dread and excitement began to flow through her veins.

"Of course I did!" she exclaimed. "Now, what shall we wear?"

* * *

AURELIA WAS SO excited about the potential match between Phoebe and not only a marquess, but also an old family friend, that Phoebe didn't even have to worry about what she would wear the next evening. The moment she entered her bedchamber to prepare, her aunt was right there behind her, bustling about as she opened Phoebe's wardrobe and began to rapidly review the contents.

"The silver satin?" she mused. "No, no, not appropriate for the theatre. The yellow taffeta?" Phoebe made a sound of disgust. Taffeta was ever so uncomfortable and made her feel like a young girl. She wasn't even sure why she still owned the dress, and she resolved to be rid of it the moment she had time to go through her things. Aurelia continued to mutter to herself as she browsed the gowns, commenting that perhaps Phoebe should take a morning and visit the modiste's shop to replace a few of the outdated garments.

The wardrobe itself was tucked away in the corner of the room. Phoebe quite enjoyed the relaxed feel of her bedroom, which had been hers since she was a girl but had certainly grown up with her. The white paneled walls remained bare with the exception of the fleur-de-lis carved into them, and a canopy of crimson poppies on pink and cream stripes flowed from the ceiling down to the head of her bed, the top of which matched the curtains covering the sash windows. A settee of gold, green, and cream sat in front of it, upon which Aurelia was now laying out all manner of gowns. Phoebe's vanity table, with the small ornate mirror in the center, sat in one corner, her wardrobe in the other. Above it hung a portrait of her parents, the only decoration she wished upon the walls.

A chaise lounge rested near the door, but Phoebe hardly ever set her bottom upon it. Instead, the writing table across from it was where she often found herself in the middle of the night lately, when she was haunted by ideas for the paper that wouldn't leave her mind or allow her any rest until she had them listed.

"This! This is perfect," Aurelia exclaimed as she finally decided on a gown, laying out the red silk with its black lace trim on the bed while Phoebe's maid Nancy waited patiently, a smile on her face. All of the servants loved Aunt Aurelia despite her eccentricities, for she treated them all with kindness. "It gives you such an air of mystery. I'm sure you agree, Nancy, do you not?"

Nancy nodded while Phoebe smiled and she brushed a hand over the gown. She did love this one, it was true, but it was not as though she were trying to trap Jeffrey into anything — rather the opposite, as it were. Though she hadn't yet shared that with Aunt Aurelia. A small niggling worry had tugged at her, one that told her Aurelia most likely wouldn't approve of her methods. She had never guessed that they would be invited to socialize with the Worthington family, or that there had been a prior connection between them.

Now, seeing Aurelia's hopeful gaze, she could hardly say anything to disappoint her at the moment.

"It's lovely, Aunt Aurelia, and of course I will wear it this evening," she said, and Aurelia broke into a wide grin. "Now, tell me, what have you selected for yourself?"

Her question brokered the response she had wished for as Aurelia launched into a debate — with herself — over what would be most fitting. Five minutes later, having decided, she nodded her head and sailed out of the room, leaving Phoebe and Nancy to share a smile of both amusement and affection.

Once she had dressed and prepared for the evening, wrapping a black shawl around her shoulders, Phoebe had to admit, however, that Aurelia was right. This dress *was* appropriate for the occasion — and the circumstances that accompanied it.

CHAPTER 16

"You wouldn't be trying to play matchmaker, now would you, Mother?" Jeffrey asked, leaning back into the squabs of his carriage as he eyed his mother with raised eyebrows and the slightest curve to his lips.

"I would never dream of such a thing," she responded, looking away from him out the window, though he didn't miss the rapid blinking of her eyes, a sure tell. "You are a marquess, after all. Surely you can handle something as simple as finding an appropriate wife. Though…"

"Yes?"

"I cannot say you have been doing a particularly admirable job of it so far."

"Mother!" he exclaimed as Viola stifled a choked laugh, while Rebecca did not even attempt to hide her chortle of glee from the corner of the carriage. Thankfully it would just be the four of them this evening. He could do without his *entire* family in the theatre box with him. It would be difficult enough to control Rebecca's tongue with Phoebe around; he didn't want to have to worry about his other two sisters.

Unfortunately, Ambrose had also promised to meet them there. Where he was at the moment, Jeffrey had no idea and no wish to know, but he secretly hoped that his brother would forget to attend. Ambrose had never been particularly fond of the theatre, after all, and Jeffrey knew he would only be in attendance to witness his brother attempt to woo Lady Phoebe Winters.

Which he seemed to be doing, although whether or not he was proving successful was yet to be seen. Phoebe was open with her thoughts, that was true, but as of yet, she had said nothing regarding their relationship, though her actions proved she was, at the very least, certainly attracted to him.

"Do you truly believe Lady Phoebe would make for an appropriate marchioness?" he asked Lady Berkley, and his mother seemed somewhat startled when she realized that he was interested in her honest opinion of the woman. It humbled him to ask her, but this was an altogether important decision, and his mother was an intelligent woman who was an expert on what would make a suitable marchioness.

"I believe," she said slowly, "that the proper wife is one who makes you happy. Who you would feel grateful to wake up with every morning. Who you can laugh with, and will allow you to be yourself. From my short acquaintance with her, it seems that Lady Phoebe may not be the most reserved, demure woman, it is true. But she has a zest for life that, I think, would be most fitting for you, Jeffrey. Do you admire her, respect her?"

"I do."

"What do you feel when you look at her?"

He simply smiled and shook his head. *That* was not a discussion he would have with his mother.

"Your silence speaks for you, and tells me all that I need to know," she said with a satisfied grin. "And does she feel the same toward you?"

Jeffrey frowned, rubbing his forehead to hide any emotion that might show on his face. The truth of the matter was that he had no idea. Phoebe returned his caresses, true, and she had accepted his invitations — or those of his family — but she had never actually said anything regarding her feelings toward him.

"I do not know," he said honestly, and his mother gave him a look of consternation, though her attention wavered as the carriage slowed, and she leaned forward to peer out the window as they trundled down Bow Street and pulled up to the front of the Theatre Royal at Covent Garden.

"It matters not the number of times I have seen it. This new building remains as dramatic as the plays themselves," Rebecca sighed as she looked out at the four fluted columns upon which the portico sat.

"It is rather ostentatious, isn't it?" Viola remarked practically as they exited the carriage.

Jeffrey had no thought for the white marble building at the moment, but rather the night that lay ahead of them.

His mother had invited Phoebe and her aunt to join them in their private box, and Jeffrey found himself eagerly looking one way and the next for Phoebe as they ascended the grand staircase. When they rounded the top of the steps to the anteroom, he was arrested for a moment by the sight before him.

For there, standing next to the statue of Shakespeare, was a vision more animated, more alive, than any carving or actress on stage could ever do justice. She wore a long red gown that perfectly set off her midnight tresses, some of which were pulled back away from her face, but most were left to cascade down her shoulders in artful, loose curls. It was a scandalous look, and altogether not the style of the day, and yet he knew that she would not care, that she had simply styled it how she pleased. The color of her dress brought out the bright green of her eyes with their striking brows overtop and complemented the lush redness of her lips.

She was a siren. She was drama and mystery and comedy all rolled into one. He hadn't even realized he had stopped moving until he felt a bony finger poke into his spine.

"Stop staring," Viola whispered in his ear. "You're making a fool of yourself."

Phoebe's eyes were locked on his, and he allowed them to pull him forward toward her. By the time he reached her side, his family alongside him, he had at least found the words to greet her, as well as her aunt, who he finally noticed. She looked at him now with a smug grin, as though she knew the effect her niece had upon him.

"Lady Aurelia, Lady Phoebe, we are very pleased you could join us this evening," he said with a smart bow, as the women made their pleasantries.

"We are in for a treat tonight," his mother said with a smile. "Both J.P. and Charles Kemble are performing, as is Mrs. Siddons. It should be fantastic."

"Yet dreary," Rebecca added with a dramatic sigh. "*Henry VIII*. I should have preferred a comedy."

"Hush, Rebecca," Viola said with a glower, and Lady Berkley chose to subtly march her daughters toward their box rather than admonish them in such a public place.

Jeffrey had not even considered the play. He had been told by his mother when and where he would be in attendance. His refusal had been upon his lips until she told him who she had invited to accompany them.

Phoebe trailed behind the rest of their party, who had left the two of them to bring up the rear. Jeffrey was sure it was not an accident, particularly when he noticed the calculating, self-congratulatory smile between his mother and Lady Aurelia. He wanted to be upset with them and their well-meaning manipulations, but when he looked at Phoebe standing beside him, attempting to hide her uncertainty, he couldn't help but be pleased to have a moment alone with her.

"You do look lovely tonight," he said, and when her head turned to his, her profile in the light of the patent lamp, he couldn't help but add, "though that is not altogether the truth. In actuality, you are beautiful."

"Thank you, Lord Berkley."

"Jeffrey."

"Jeffrey," she said with a smile. "And thank you for the invitation tonight."

"For that, you will have to thank my mother," he returned, "though I was pleased when I heard of your acceptance. Have you been keeping well?"

"Since yesterday?" she asked with a teasing laugh. "Yes, I have, as a matter of fact. And you?"

"I have," he said with a nod. "Though I have been rather distracted as of late."

"By your investigation?" she queried, and it took him a moment to discern of what she spoke.

"Oh, into the women's paper? I can hardly recall its title."

"*The Women's Weekly*," she supplied. "And yes, that is to what I am referring."

That, in fact, was one quest he had been quite remiss of pursuing lately, which was entirely her fault. He should have been chasing many more lines of inquiry. It would not be altogether difficult to find the publisher. He simply had to pretend to be an advertiser, perhaps, or come to the paper with a story. But, no, all he had done was ask a few questions of people who may have a connection, and at their refusal to provide further information, he had let it be.

And he knew exactly why he had done so. Because to shut down this paper would displease his sisters, and, most of all,

Phoebe Winters. And all he wanted to do at the moment was to make her happy.

His eyes dipped below where was proper, to the lace that teased him as it covered just enough of the top of her creamy breasts to be appropriate. He longed to reach out a finger and trail it along the edge of the lace, to dip it low to feel how soft her skin was underneath it.

"Phoebe," he said, clearing his throat — and his head. "Follow me."

He took her hand then, somewhat surprised when she allowed it, as she didn't seem the type of woman to typically follow the lead of a man anywhere. He ducked around the corner, peering through the doorway of a row of private boxes. Finding one empty, he drew her in quickly enough to elicit a sharp gasp and pressed her back against the wall within the shadows, where he brought his head down to hers and took those plush, enticing lips in his.

He wasted no time in beginning softly or gently, but rather crushed his mouth upon hers, licking the seam of her lips, though she needed hardly any encouragement to open them to him. He tasted the mixture of mint and berries on her tongue, and when her fingers dug into the backs of his shoulders, his desire bloomed within him. He couldn't get enough of her, and he had no idea what to do about it.

Finally, voices from the corridor beyond brought him back to his senses, and he reluctantly let her go. She looked up at him, her eyes hazy, her cheeks flushed, and her lips thoroughly ravaged.

"I would apologize," he said, hearing the gruffness of his voice as he fought to regain control, "however that would mean that I regret my actions, and the truth is, Phoebe, I would do that all over again."

"I had always thought you to be a patient man," she replied with an arch of her brow, and he wondered how she could keep such control upon her emotions. "It seems I may have been altogether wrong about you."

He chuckled low at that and would have kissed her again just for her tart reply, but he sensed a presence in the doorway and turned to find the Earl and Countess of Torrington entering with a look of some incredulity on their faces.

"My apologies, Lord Torrington, Lady Torrington," he said with a nod of his head. "It has been some time since I have attended the theatre, and I seem to have found myself in the wrong box. I hope to speak with you later on this evening."

And with that, he led Phoebe out the door, fully aware that they would soon be the subject upon the lips of all in attendance.

Now he had to make it through five acts of a Shakespeare tragedy with this siren sitting beside him. If Phoebe wished to witness patience and control, well, she was about to do just that.

CHAPTER 17

*P*hoebe nervously twisted her hands in her lap as she attempted to concentrate on the play before her, the large stage filled with extensive scenery and a continual exhibition of actors. They were extremely talented, that she knew. Her fingers itched to remove her tablet from her reticle and take notes. *The Women's Weekly* should certainly have a column on theatre, she decided, and determined that she would write the very first review herself.

But first, she had to make sure she knew of what she was writing.

The Berkley box was on the second level, with an enormous chandelier hanging overtop of them. As Phoebe watched the actors, she found her gaze wandering to the elegant, lofty pilasters supporting the semi-elliptical arch, the royal arms looking down over all of them. She knew the construction of this building had been a triumphant success following the burning of the first theatre a few years prior. Certainly, it contained marvelous ingenuity, the way the slightest sound resounded around the theatre — such as the whispers of the man across from her as he unabashedly stared down into the bosom of the woman sitting next to him. Hopefully she was his wife, though Phoebe somewhat doubted it.

This was certainly a spectacle, and she was not speaking of the play before her, but rather the players that filled the theatre. What would it be like, she wondered, to be sitting down within the pit? How very different life would be. She noted these thoughts as well, determining that they would make an intriguing sidebar to her review of the play. Or perhaps the review should be the sidebar. She chewed her lip as she contemplated the idea.

"Stop it," Jeffrey whispered in her ear, and she turned sharply toward him, raising an eyebrow in question. "That thing with your lip," he explained in the slightest whisper directly in her ear. "It's driving me mad."

She stopped immediately but then thought only of him and the kiss in the Torringtons' private box for the rest of the act. Really, what had he been thinking? If she wasn't careful, Collette would be writing *her* into the next gossip column. Although perhaps that would sell more papers.

Phoebe was so distracted that she hardly knew to whom King Henry was currently married when intermission came about. They spilled out into the salon beyond the private boxes, which was suddenly filled with a symphony of voices as all of the attendees emerged with the same mission: to determine who was in attendance, and what they could take away as the gossip of the evening.

Phoebe swiveled her head from one side to the other to see if she recognized anyone, but then she felt a slight touch on her arm.

"Lady Phoebe, would you mind if we had a quick word?" Phoebe nodded in surprise at Lady Berkley's request, curious as to what Jeffrey's mother would wish to speak with her about in private. By mutual agreement, they wandered over to a corner against the wall. Phoebe jumped when she felt something dig into her back, but turned only to find that she had backed up too far, into the foot of a statue standing atop a pillar.

"It's quite an intriguing play, is it not?" she asked Lady Berkley with a smile, to which the marchioness nodded.

"It is. I have seen it many times, but never with such vivid actors onstage, who make it far too real. One forgets that this actually occurred many years ago," she said, a dreamy look on her face, before she shook her head as though clearing it. She took a deep breath and Phoebe's heart raced a little faster, though why she should be nervous about speaking with the amiable woman, she had no idea.

"I am being rather forward in speaking to you of this, Lady Phoebe," she said nervously. "And really, I should not at all. Please do not tell my son of this conversation, for he would be mortified. It is only ... Jeffrey has not portrayed much affection for any particular woman since he came of age. His father died fairly young, leaving Jeffrey with a great amount of responsibility, including four sisters who are, as I'm sure you have ascertained for yourself, a rather unruly bunch, for the most part.

"Jeffrey has always been so focused on his work, on caring for the rest of us, you see, that he has not taken much time to look after his own wellbeing, nor his own heart. As of late, he has seemed a bit more distracted than usual, to which I look upon as a good thing. As a mother, I want my children only to be happy, and with you, Lady Phoebe, he does seem so. Happy, I mean. He is taken with you, though he seems unsure of your own feelings toward him. All I ask, Lady Phoebe, is for you to take care of his heart. It takes quite a bit for him to share it and I only wish for it not to be broken."

Phoebe stared at her wide-eyed as Lady Berkley finished her speech, and unconsciously bit her teeth into her lower lip hard enough that she caused herself to jump slightly. Guilt began to roll through her. She had knowingly played Jeffrey, never dreaming that he would ever come to feel something for her besides outrage. She had slapped him, for goodness sake!

Their fiery discord from the outset had certainly led to passionate moments in which they showed one another just how much they physically desired one another, but as for what she actually felt for him…. She searched the room now, finding him standing with his sisters and her aunt. His sandy hair atop his tall, wide frame stood out among the crowd. He must have sensed her stare, for he returned her gaze, a slight smile crossing his lips, changing his face from its hard, imposing countenance to one that was warm and inviting.

She sighed as her heart thumped a traitorous beat in her chest. She yearned for him — she could not deny that as much as she wished to. She was also fully aware that her urge for him was running much deeper than a surface attraction. She had to put an end to it.

Or did she?

Of course she did, she thought, reminding herself that the man was out to destroy her publication and all she believed in. He himself believed all sorts of lies about women. It would never do. Besides all that, the moment he found out her secrets, he would lose any sort of attraction he had ever had toward her. For that was all it was. His mother was being hopeful — fanciful even.

She turned back toward Lady Berkley and the soft smile on her face, as she had clearly been aware of Phoebe's perusal of her son, likely believing it to be an amorous one.

"I—" Phoebe began, but halted, not knowing what else to say. She didn't want to lie to the woman, but she also could not very well tell her of the duplicity that began all of this. "I believe that all will work out as it should," she managed. "You have a wonderful family, Lady Berkley, and the marquess has proven to be quite a gentleman."

Lady Berkley beamed and placed a hand on Phoebe's arm.

"Thank you, my dear," she said, then leaned in and said warmly, "I believe you are just what he needs."

Just what he needs? She would have thought that she was the last woman on earth a man like Jeffrey would need. What was the marchioness on about?

As they returned to the rest of their party, Phoebe had to blink back tears as Lady Berkley's words left her heart and her mind at war with one another. She could very well tell herself all the lies she wished.

But the truth of the matter was, she was falling for Jeffrey Worthington, Marquess of Berkley, and there was nothing rational thought could do to stop it.

* * *

JEFFREY LONGED to know what his mother and Phoebe had been speaking of in the corner of the salon. Most men would look upon such a conversation as something to be fearful of, but Jeffrey had a unique advantage over most other men, which was the fact that his mother was actually a sensible woman who cared for more than only her children's marriage prospects and securing the highest social standing possible.

And Phoebe did not look particularly upset about the conversation. If anything, she looked… contemplative. When she and his mother rejoined them, he searched Phoebe's face, and she responded with a small curve of her lips. Well, that was encouraging, he supposed.

When it was time to return to the theatre, he took her arm and drew her close, dipping his head down toward hers. "Is everything all right?" he questioned.

"Yes, of course," she responded before turning to look at him with a quirkily raised eyebrow. "And you?"

"I have a beautiful woman on my arm, and the love of my family surrounding me," he said in all seriousness. "What more could a man ask for?"

His own words resonated around his mind as they re-took their seats. For there *was* more that a man could ask for. He could ask for a life with this woman. He imagined it, waking up every day with her lying next to him, her midnight tresses spread upon his pillow as the sun peeked through the gap in the curtains, bathing her beautiful curves with its light.

His heart beat quickly as his mind wandered, watching her open her green eyes to smile up at him as she lifted herself from his bed and reached for him. His daydreaming had him leaning over her, kissing those delicious red lips as he could whenever he chose, for she was his wife, and would be with him for the rest of their days.

In his mind, Jeffrey made love to her, her gasps in his ear more real in this moment than the play which had resumed on the stage below them. As he imagined her writhing beneath him, he reached over in their reality and took her hand in his, tightening his grip as in the dream Jeffrey and Phoebe entered into the throes of ecstasy.

Afterward, they would go down to breakfast, where they would share intimate conversation — this was his dream, so he needn't be concerned with the fact that they would likely have to share the breakfast table with his five siblings and his mother — and he would laugh at her wit before they both spent the morning together reading the papers of the day.

No, the papers were not something he should think of, as that only led him to consider the fact that there was still much upon which they disagreed. Not the papers, then. They would retire to the library, where they would share their secret affection for the latest Waverly novel.

There was Maxwell now, stretched out upon the rug that had cost a fortune and should not be collecting dog hair and muddy tracks, but of course Jeffrey could not bring himself to force Maxwell away.

Phoebe, sitting next to him on the settee, leaned in, and he was more than ready to bring those lips under his again, though he was content in simply staring at her, in hearing her laugh at something he had said.

The only thing that finally brought him out of his musings and back to the theatre was Phoebe's hand on his arm, shaking him.

"Are you all right?" she whispered softly, her eyes wide and concerned.

He must have looked as though he were in pain, which he was in a sense, but not the type of pain she was imagining. It was pain of another sort — desperation and frustration over the fact that the vivid images in his mind only left him desperately desiring more.

Jeffrey gazed down at her now. His dream may have been just that — a dream, but the face that looked up at him, the woman who sat next to him with her warm hand on his arm, was as real as the woman in his mind. He could hardly believe it himself, but he thought maybe — just maybe — he was falling in love with her.

He leaned down toward her, his lips coming close enough to tickle to the top of her ear. The words were out of his mouth before he even had time to think of what he was saying.

"Marry me."

CHAPTER 18

*P*hoebe stilled. She must not have heard him correctly. For if she had, Jeffrey Worthington, Marquess of Berkley, had just asked her to marry him. Which was preposterous. For not only would he never marry a woman like her, but he certainly wouldn't ask her in the middle of the theatre, surrounded by his mother, sisters, and her aunt. And definitely not while Henry VIII was onstage divorcing his wife and denouncing Cardinal Wolsey of all of his titles and possessions.

But Jeffrey's insistent gaze didn't leave her, and she was overcome by the musky, spicy scent of his cologne, the warm hand upon her, the hard planes of his face, and the set line of his lips. When she finally looked up to meet his eyes, they beseechingly searched hers.

"Will you?" he whispered.

"I… I…" she had no idea what to say. For her heart — her traitorous, mutinous heart — was telling her to say yes. To nod enthusiastically and tilt her head back just enough so that he could lean down and kiss her here, in front of an entire theatre of patrons. They would celebrate with their families and announce their betrothal, before having a beautiful wedding at St. George's, and she would live out the rest of her days as a marchioness.

But would they be happy days? Her mind intervened now. How could she be with a man with such vastly different beliefs than she held? The two of them had simply avoided returning to the conversation they had first clashed upon for some time now. Anytime she raised the subject, he quickly changed it, or they averted the argument altogether.

They couldn't, however, escape the inevitable for a lifetime. And what would Jeffrey do when he realized that she had, if not been lying to him, been evading the truth — that she was the woman he sought, the publisher of *The Women's Weekly*, which he so hated?

She couldn't, however, say no. The words wouldn't come.

"Later?" she pleaded instead, asking him for some time in which she could consider it, to determine what she should do. Slight disappointment clouded his eyes, but he nodded in understanding and leaned back in his seat, though he didn't relinquish her hand, for which she was grateful.

Of course, paying attention to the play now was certainly out of the question. Instead, thoughts swirled round her mind, as two vastly distinct futures stretched out in front of her. One as his wife, hosting events and welcoming children, waking up to his face every day. The other as a woman creating change, following her passions, and making a difference.

She managed to finish the evening without having to provide any type of response. With their families present, as well as the stream of acquaintances who came to greet them following the play, there was not a moment for the two of them to be alone.

When Phoebe and Aurelia took their leave, Jeffrey lifted her gloved hand to his lips, pressing a soft kiss against it, and she could feel the promise that he left along with it, as well as his hope for something more.

She would sleep on it, Phoebe decided. By the morning, she would know what to do.

* * *

BUT OF COURSE, in that, she was completely mistaken. She woke after a fitful night no closer to knowing what it was she should do regarding the request of the marquess.

Instead of preparing to go into the offices of *The Women's Weekly*, she prepared for a meeting of a different sort. She sent out notes of invitation to her three friends. She desperately needed advice, and there were no other people to whom she would prefer to turn.

And so she found herself, a couple of hours later, surrounded by the ladies in what she thought of as her mother's drawing room. Her father's parlor was far too distracting. At first, she had thought to meet in a tea shop somewhere, but the possibility of prying ears surrounding them was too great a risk. As it was, she hoped Aurelia was otherwise occupied.

Julia sat next to her, while Elizabeth and Sarah were side-by-side on the facing coral-and-white striped sofa. A tea tray sat between them, and Sarah was already helping herself to one of the pastries that lined the tray.

"Well, Phoebe, I must say, my curiosity is certainly piqued. Never before have you summoned us so urgently," said Elizabeth, her auburn hair pulled back in a neat chignon, not a hair out of place.

"I wouldn't say *summoned*," Phoebe said delicately. "Requested."

"Very well," Elizabeth replied. "Now, on with it. I can

hardly wait a moment more to know what it is that vexes you so."

"Lord Berkley has asked me to marry him."

She could have stood screaming as though she were stark mad and she didn't think she would elicit such surprise as she did from that one statement.

Phoebe looked around at her friends, who all stared at her with mouths and eyes opened wide. Sarah had paused with the pastry halfway to her lips, while Elizabeth sat frozen and Julia leaned in just slightly closer.

"Say that again?" Julia finally queried in a hushed voice.

"The Marquess of Berkley has asked me to marry him," Phoebe repeated, her voice just as matter-of-fact as it had been before.

"But what— when— how— what did you *say?*" Sarah finally managed.

"Last night. I said, 'Later.'"

"Pardon me?" Elizabeth asked now. "The Marquess of Berkley asked you to marry him and you told him, 'Later'?"

"Yes," Phoebe said, refusing to duck her head in any sort of shame as she defended herself. "He caught me off guard. We were in the middle of the Theatre Royal at Covent Garden, our voices likely echoing around the theatre. *Henry VIII* was onstage, for goodness sake! I wasn't going to accept a marriage proposal in front of a king who lopped off the heads of his wives."

"It was a *play*, Phoebe," said Julia with a sigh, as she tilted her head. "Oh, how utterly romantic. He asked you on a *whim*. His heart was so overcome with emotion for you that he couldn't wait a moment longer. Oh, you must agree."

"But the paper!" Sarah protested. "Does he know about the paper?"

"No," Phoebe said, biting her lip. "And therein lies the problem. He told me once that what he appreciates the most about me is my honesty. Well, I certainly have lied to him. He asked me if I knew the publisher of *The Women's Weekly*, and I outright told him that no, I did not. But I knew that if I told him it was *me*, he would likely never again speak to me again."

"And you did not want to push him away because you required information on his movements in regard to the publication, is that it?" Elizabeth asked cryptically.

"I suppose at first that was why," Phoebe said slowly. "Though I have to admit that from the very start, there has been something about him that draws me to him, something I cannot even put into words. At first it drove me mad that I should want to be around a man so vexing, however, I must admit that I have grown to enjoy our time together. He is not who I originally thought he was. He can be kind, and caring. The way he is with his sisters, his mother, his dog even. It is hard to reconcile the man I first met with the man I have come to know."

"But he is still there," Elizabeth persisted. "The man you slapped for his disparaging remarks toward you."

"Toward women," Phoebe amended. "But yes, I suppose, he is. So you see my difficulty now?"

"Phoebe," Elizabeth said carefully. "You know I love you, I do. And I hate to say that I told you this would happen but..."

"But you told me this would happen," Phoebe said with a sigh. "I know."

They were all silent for a moment as they contemplated her dilemma. It seemed none of them possessed any quick answers.

"Do you love him?" Julia asked softly.

"Pardon?" Phoebe said, her head snapping up toward her.

"Do you love him?" Julia repeated. "Can you imagine a life with him?"

Phoebe looked down at her fingers.

"I can picture that life, yes," she responded quietly. "But the image of contentment, of love, slowly slides into one in which the two of us argue, when I am bored by simply being the mistress of a house. The purpose I feel now with what I am doing — it is what I have always longed for, and I have never felt so complete. And yet … there is something missing."

"Him," Sarah said simply.

"Yes," Phoebe said, her breath coming out in a swift exhale. "Is it too much to want to have both?"

"It is more than most men would allow," Elizabeth said practically.

"Though, Phoebe, you have to know," Sarah said, leaning forward and placing a hand on her knee, "*The Women's Weekly* is something of which to be very proud. In a mere couple of months, you have created change. Not only do women now have a resource which matters to them, in terms of fashion and advice — and even horse racing," she bestowed a small smile upon Julia, "but women are speaking now of our role in this world. Conversations within salons and drawing rooms are expanding beyond gossip and theatre and sewing patterns to matters of Parliament, to the plight of those less fortunate, to the role of women in our entire society. *You* have done that. Do not forget that. I am not suggesting you give up on love. I am only suggesting that you do not give up on what you have created."

Phoebe blinked back tears at Sarah's words. She *was* proud of her work, it was true, but to hear such praise from someone she loved and respected meant more than the words of a stranger, and helped erase some of the words of hate that were often spewed toward her and the paper, most often through letters addressed to the publication.

"I believe you have two options, Phoebe," Elizabeth said, her head tilted in contemplation.

Phoebe looked up hopefully, grateful for a potential answer to her plight.

"The first is that you choose between your passion and the marquess."

Phoebe did not altogether like that suggestion.

"The second is that you tell him the truth, explain what you long for. He will either agree or force you to choose anyway."

"Or, perhaps, he would want nothing more to do with me anyway."

"That is another possibility," Elizabeth said with a nod, her mouth firm.

Phoebe squared her shoulders and took a deep breath.

"Well," she said. "I suppose I am the one to blame for being in this mess to start with. Now I must extricate myself from it. But you are right, Elizabeth. I can no longer hide within my fear. I'll tell him," she said with a decisive nod. "And then ... come what may."

"Come what may," Elizabeth agreed, raising her teacup to her lips.

CHAPTER 19

"*H*ead in the clouds, Berkley?"

Jeffrey came back to the present, looking across the green felt table of White's at his friend, the Duke of Clarence. As always, the Duke's hair was perfectly coiffed, his clothing immaculate. The duke prided himself on his appearance, be it the outward physical traits or his own behavior.

"It's not like you to be so distracted," Clarence continued as he took a sip of his brandy. "But it seems to have become a habit of yours as of late."

Jeffrey snorted. He was far too aware of the truth of his friend's words, unfortunately. And it was all because of a certain Lady Phoebe Winters.

Today, he would have his answer. When he appeared on the steps of her foyer, she would tell him, one way or another, if she desired a life with him as his marchioness.

He could hardly believe that he was pursuing a woman who might potentially say no to him, to turn him down. He was a man to whom all should say yes. He could have any number of young women of the *ton* and had been pursued by them and their mothers for years now. Unfortunately none of them, however, held any appeal to him. Now, the fact that he was even entertaining this idea of marriage to *Phoebe,* who was far from a sure thing … he shook his head. But he couldn't help it. He was infatuated with her.

"While I am not one to subscribe to the gossip columns or to listen in on women's chatter, one would have to be deaf not to hear the rumors surrounding the Marquess of Berkley and a certain Lady Phoebe Winters. Dances, visits to the theatre, a dinner with your family at your home, a walk in Hyde Park. You have not exactly been discreet."

"I did not know that I was required to be," Jeffrey said moodily.

"Of course not," Clarence said with a laugh. "I only meant that it is not difficult to sense the reason for your distress. You have a woman on your mind. Should that not, however, be cause for celebration? I cannot recall the last time you showed any more interest in an eligible woman than a dutiful dance or polite words at a party."

Jeffrey paused for a moment before lifting his own drink to his mouth, draining the contents of the glass before setting it back down firmly on the table.

"I've asked her to marry me."

Clarence choked on his brandy, nearly — but not quite — spewing the contents over his pristine white cravat. Jeffrey merely sat back and enjoyed the spectacle until Clarence finally collected himself.

"Well," he said, clearing his throat. "You certainly took some time to share your news. Congratulations, man."

He held out his hand, but Jeffrey made no move to shake it.

"Hold onto that thought," he said, "for the woman has yet to agree."

"What?" Clarence frowned. "Whatever do you mean?"

"I mean that I have not yet received an answer to my question," he said slowly. "When I asked her, it was not entirely a fit moment to discuss the matter. She said she would provide me with a response later, and today I will determine exactly what that answer is."

"She would be mad to refuse you," Clarence remarked, to which Jeffrey nodded.

"That may be, but she can be an unpredictable woman," he muttered. "Why I want her, the Lord only knows."

Though that was not altogether true. He wanted her because she was bright, intelligent, honest, and remarkably alive.

"Well," Clarence said, a wide smile on his face. "I wish you luck. And I sure as hell am glad that it is not me in your place."

A few weeks ago, Jeffrey would have thought the exact same thing.

He bid Clarence farewell and rose to leave when the Earl of Totnes approached, a paper in hand and two lords Jeffrey recognized trailing behind him.

"Berkley! A moment?" he asked, and Jeffrey resumed his seat with both annoyance and trepidation. He knew all too well what this was about, and he would prefer not to have to discuss this, for he was just as disappointed as anyone that he had been far too remiss in finding answers.

"Yes?"

"Have you seen the latest rubbish to destroy these fine pieces of newsprint?" the earl asked, throwing the paper down upon the table between Jeffrey and Clarence as though it were covered in manure.

"As of this morning, I have not," he admitted.

"Read it," the earl commanded, and Jeffrey looked up at him, raising an eyebrow at the fact the man would dare to command him to do anything.

"If you would," the earl amended, and Jeffrey opened the publication before him, perusing its contents.

"Is there anything in particular to which you would like to direct my attention?" he asked impatiently, wanting to leave White's and find his way to Phoebe's home now that it was an acceptable hour to call.

"Here," Totnes said, stabbing a meaty finger into the pages, and Jeffrey's eyes fell to the bottom of the page.

To all the women of London and beyond, consider this a personal letter, written to you directly from a lady.

Whether you are of the nobility, the landed gentry, or the daughter of an untitled man of sufficient means, you are likely expected to do but one thing with your life — marry, and have children. I understand that. It is what has been expected of women for generations.

While it is true that some women do work in order to make a living for themselves, there are few occupations that are acceptable and available for young ladies. Many women are required to work in order to support their families and typically find themselves performing laborious work. While it sounds like a difficult life to be sure, at times, I envy these women. It must be gratifying to have the ability to support oneself without reliance upon a man in order to provide the funds necessary for survival, which then provides him with the ability to determine what a woman will do with every waking moment of her life.

Not all gentleman are of such a mind, to be sure, but many do feel this way. Is this the way our world must continue? Why do women not have the ability to speak their opinions, to take whatever actions they wish, to marry whomever they choose and if they choose? When they do, should they not be able to retain whatever it is they bring into the marriage, without having to relinquish all to their husbands?

I am not suggesting that gentlemen are not capable of respecting women or their opinions, for there are certainly some that are understanding. What I am saying, ladies, is that we must take the next steps to fight for our rights to speak of what we believe in. To affect change. To work if we would so choose. To have a voice to create the changes that must occur in our country, in Parliament, to create a better life for all, not only for those who hold all of the power.

Together, anything is possible.

Jeffrey raked a hand through his hair. This was not good — not good at all. He was in a mess of trouble, that was certain. Why did it have to be him who was tasked with this unenviable position? Perhaps another could look further into it? He not only had enough to hold his focus at the moment, but he also had a household full of females, as well as a potential fiancée, who would not be altogether pleased if he took this route of persecution.

But someone had to. For this had all the workings of upheaval that he had been so cognizant of preventing. What would Phoebe say about this piece? It wasn't much of a question. She would agree with it, he was sure. Though he was positive that Viola would as well. How had he managed to surround himself with women of such strong, at-times ignorant, opinions?

"Well?" Totnes challenged him, his hands on his hips, his chin quivering as he looked down at Jeffrey — who was not particularly pleased that the man would choose to question him so, in front of many others.

"Well," Jeffrey said, standing to face him, as he knew he would tower over the Earl. "I said I would look into the matter. I have been and I will continue to do so. But really, Totnes, is such a piece truly so disturbing for you? Is it threatening your manhood?"

"I thought you agreed with me!" Totnes said, his eyes narrowing into slits.

"I do," Jeffrey said coolly, balancing out the heat Totnes

was throwing. "However, I am following up with this because I think it is the right thing to do, not because I am afraid of how a few women attempting to stir up trouble might affect me."

"You always have thought that you were better than the rest of us," Totnes sneered at him.

"Not the majority of you," Jeffrey corrected with a pointed look at the man. "Just certain men in particular."

And with Clarence's bark of laughter trailing after him, Jeffrey exited the building.

* * *

As he drove his phaeton to Phoebe's townhome, Jeffrey composed a list within his head of the actions he could take in order to put an end to this publication. He could compose a letter to the office, identifying himself as an advertiser and asking to meet with the publisher. He simply needed a way to make contact. That would be his in, and then he would reason with the woman, help her understand that her words were dangerous. He was sure that the threat of a marquess, as well as other men within the nobility, would be enough to worry her.

First, he needed to find the address of the blasted publication. Must it really be that difficult? The street urchins who delivered the paper had not been much help. He had actually been shocked by their loyalty. Their publisher must pay them well, for typically it did not take many coins in order to convince them for information, even regarding their employers.

Finding himself now in front of Phoebe's home, he halted his phaeton across the street, next to the square, and looked down at the paper resting beside him on the bench. He picked it up, rifling through the pages, perusing it for some clue as to who he may be dealing with. *Published by a Lady*, was all it said, and he wondered if he would end up knowing the woman. He had always assumed she would be of middle class, but perhaps he was mistaken.

He rifled through the pages, finding nothing and nearly throwing down the paper in disgust. But just then he paused — there, at the bottom of the back page, was a small mark. He looked at it more closely, seeing it was a lion and a seal poised overtop a ball. What in the— a printer's mark. Jeffrey smiled triumphantly as he realized what he had found, though he berated himself slightly for not considering this earlier. It was his distracted state — but no longer. After this visit with Phoebe, he knew exactly where he was going.

CHAPTER 20

*J*effrey admired Phoebe's home. She had clearly been meticulous about its upkeep following the passing of her parents, and somehow it suited her with its tidy walk, traditional brick, and untamed ivy strewn over the side wall.

He smiled as he strode up to the front door, wondering what they would do with the house after they were married. Would Aurelia remain, or would she prefer to join his household? He cringed slightly at the thought of adding not only Phoebe, but *two* more women to his home, but at the very least, he enjoyed the company of Phoebe's aunt.

The butler allowed him in, and Jeffrey was shown into a different room this time — not the parlor full of her father's curiosities, but a drawing room that was much softer, more feminine. He assumed it had been used by her mother, and he wondered which room Phoebe preferred.

He asked her as much when she walked into the room, finding her dressed in a plain blue morning dress that somehow favored her exotic looks with its simplicity.

"I couldn't say," she responded, her eyes widening in

surprise at his question. "I enjoy using both of them, for they are each so unique and remind me of my parents and who they were."

"And what of a room that suits you?"

"I have my private chambers for that," she said, pausing for a moment before smiling somewhat shyly and he swallowed hard but recovered quickly.

"Ah yes, the chambers you are currently redecorating?"

"Redecor—" she looked confused for a moment, but then her eyes cleared. "Oh yes! Just a few simple changes, really. It is nothing particularly disruptive."

Her expression shifted for a moment as she looked down at his hand.

"What have you got there?"

He looked down himself, shocked when he found that the newspaper was still clutched within his fingers.

"I had it with me in the phaeton," he explained. "It was sitting next to me on the seat and I must have picked it up without thinking once I arrived. Just a newspaper."

"That doesn't look like just any newspaper," she said, her eyes narrowing in on it. "That looks to me like *The Women's Weekly*. Are you interested in fashion advice, Jeffrey?"

"Oh, *The Women's Weekly*, is it?" he asked with a weak laugh. "Ah, I must have picked it up accidentally. Viola's been reading it, as much as I discourage her not to, of course."

"Of course?" she said, an eyebrow raised as she crossed her arms over her chest. "And why not? Viola's her own woman, well of age. She can do as she pleases, or, at the very least, read what she likes, can she not?"

"Oh, come," he said, his exasperation emerging after they had avoided this subject for so long. "The women in this paper may have ideals, but none of this is going to come to anything. All that will happen is that they will get hurt, and create unsubstantiated ideas in the minds of other women that will not go anywhere."

"Have you actually read any of it?" she asked, striding toward him, and he was momentarily distracted by the emerald of her eyes. But then they flashed at him with such anger that he was brought back to the present.

"Some of it, yes."

Well, perhaps three articles of all that had been published, but he was not going to admit as much.

"And what do you disagree with? That women should have minds of their own?"

"No," he said somewhat uncomfortably. A short time ago, he would have argued with much more vehemence, but he had learned that it brought him much more pleasure to enjoy the side of this woman that was amiable and bright, and he was reluctant to enter into a battle of wills — particularly because now he knew there was a very good chance she would win. "But what would happen if, as this paper suggests, women kept their property in a marriage? Do you know of all the estates that would go to ruin without the promised dowry of a potential wife?"

"And why do such estates fall into ruin?" she challenged. "Because of the lords who far prefer to spend their time gambling and whoring instead of taking proper care of what they are so fortunate to own!"

She was potentially right, but he wasn't about to admit that.

"Most women enjoy the status they are provided, and the opportunity to spend their lives raising their children and worrying only about what style of gown to wear to the next ball," he said, pacing the room now. "Why do you not feel the same?"

"You knew from the moment we met that I would never be a woman who felt such a way," she said, clearly angry and yet retaining an even tone. "Do I seem the type of woman who would ever be satisfied with a life in which my most important decision is choosing whether to wear blue or red?"

She certainly did not.

"If women and men were equal to one another," he continued, "what would come next? Women in fist-to-cuffs or brawling whenever they disagreed?"

"Of course not," she said with a sniff. "You are being ridiculous. First of all, men do not do so every time they argue. Secondly, women are much more civilized than that."

"So you admit that there is a difference between men and women," he said, stopping and turning to her with a smug grin of satisfaction.

"If you are generalizing, then often, yes there is," she agreed. "But that does not mean they should not be equal and respected in the same right."

"A true gentleman does nothing *but* respect women, do you not understand that? And what of this notion that women only marry men of their choosing?" he asked, raising an eyebrow. "As it is, women are not *forced* into marriage. Most of them choose to do as their parents ask of them. If all women chose for themselves, you would find all manner of classes marrying one another, and all of our society would be in disorder!"

"If status is such a concern of yours, then why are you wishing to marry *me*?" she asked, fire blazing from her as her body all but shook. "I am a lady, true, but the daughter of an eccentric viscount. Surely a powerful lord such as yourself could do much better. But do you know, Lord Berkley, that your mother does not suffer from the same afflictions and ego that you do? It is a pity that you did not inherit her grace."

He brought a hand to his head, rubbing at his temple where it had started to ache. He sighed and sat down in one of the pink floral settees. "I do not want to argue with you, Phoebe," he said, defeat filling him. "And I suppose at the end of it all, we do not think as differently as you may believe. I just worry about the repercussions of all women feeling this way."

He looked up to find her simply staring down at him, her face impassive, and he lifted his hand, palm up, to her in supplication. After hesitating for a moment, she took it and allowed him to pull her down to sit on his lap. He could still feel the tension radiating from her body, but she didn't push him away, and that, he considered, was a win.

"Oh, Phoebe," he said, bringing a finger to her chin, tilting her face to look at him. Her green eyes swam with passion in front of his own. "Whatever are we going to do?"

* * *

IF ONLY HE knew the extent of his question. For to him, it was simply a matter of disagreement in their views of the world. As important as that may be, it was not the end of it all. But for her, so much more was involved. It was on the tip of her tongue to tell him, to blurt out the fact that those words he so despaired of were her very own, but he had been angry enough over the fact that a lady in general had written them, and that she believed in them.

She closed her eyes to block the intensity of his gaze, his chiseled cheekbones and jaw so set and tense, and took a couple of deep breaths to control her temper and determine her next words.

"I believe, Jeffrey," she began, "that you, along with so many other men, are scared. You are scared of the power women can hold and wield. Life may change, yes, but it can only change for the better when all people are equal. I am not saying that women are going to displace you in Parliament or as the owners of your estates, certainly not. But perhaps our opinions should matter a little more, if nothing else."

She raised her bare hands to cup his face, his skin warming her palms and the rough stubble of his jaw scratching her hands.

"Do not be like the rest of them, Jeffrey," she said, her voice coming out as an urgent whisper. "Be better. Be brave. You know the power of women better than any. Show others what can happen when a man such as yourself takes that step of which all others are so afraid."

His eyes were filled with confusion and indecision, but he didn't refute her words. Instead he brought his large, wide hand to palm the back of her head, placed his forehead against hers, and after a moment of simply holding her with their heads together, he kissed her. She placed her hands on his chest in order to push him away — they were arguing moments ago about everything she believed in, for heaven's sake — but then his tongue touched hers, and instead of pushing, her fingers clutched the lapels of his jacket and drew him in closer.

He sighed into her mouth and she relaxed into him — oh, why was it so easy to allow all to melt away when this man touched her? — but then a quick knock on the door had her jumping backward.

Phoebe had just sat back in her own space on the settee when her Aunt Aurelia opened the door, a wide smile wreathing her face.

"Oh, Lord Berkley, so wonderful to see you!" she said, entering the room, either oblivious to what had been occurring before she walked in, or choosing to ignore the tension in the room. Phoebe assumed the latter. Aurelia was certainly not the strictest of chaperones, though she likely timed her visit accordingly, as, she always told Phoebe, she *had* made a promise to her father to look after her. "We must thank you for the wonderful night at the theatre. Why, I haven't enjoyed a performance like that in some time."

Jeffrey nodded at her, and Phoebe was amazed at how quickly he had recovered his wits. Perhaps he was used to doing so with a few unruly sisters, not to mention a dog that often made a literal mess of things.

They made careful conversation, polite of course, but Aurelia brought a sense of lightness out of everyone, Phoebe always found. Whatever tension remained in the room from both their argument and the kiss that had been prematurely halted soon dissipated, though Phoebe's nerves remained somewhat on edge. She had intended to tell Jeffrey of her role as publisher of *The Women's Weekly*, and it certainly wasn't a conversation she wanted to have with Aunt Aurelia in the room. Perhaps it might be a good idea, for then Jeffrey would be far less likely to become upset, but Phoebe would rather have the opportunity to have an honest, forthright discussion about it — whatever the result of that might be.

"Well," Jeffrey finally said, rising. "I should be going. I have some business to which I must attend."

"I'll walk you out," Phoebe said, placing a hand on his arm, feeling the warmth that radiated from him.

They were silent until they reached the front foyer.

"I suppose," Jeffrey said, finally turning and looking at her with a small grin. "If all of our arguments will end in such a kiss, I should not be altogether displeased with the thought of them."

She laughed. If nothing else, she enjoyed the fact that he could, when he so chose, bring levity to such a situation.

"Jeffrey…" she began, not knowing exactly how to broach the subject, or if this was even the right time and place, but he interrupted her by reaching out and placing his finger on her lips.

"I know," he said. "I will think on your words, and will take them into consideration."

She swallowed and nodded. "Do what you need to do, Jeffrey. At the end of it, it is your decision on such matters, despite my feelings regarding them."

For if he decided to persecute her and *The Women's Weekly*, well then, her role and their potential marriage wouldn't much matter anyway, would it?

"I know," he nodded, and he opened his mouth as though he were going to ask her something else, and her heart pounded. For if it was about marriage, she had no idea whatsoever how she should answer. He seemed to think better of it, however, as he turned to leave, though he paused in the front foyer, one foot between her entryway and the landing. He turned to her, looking back and forth behind her, though for what, she wasn't sure — the presence of anyone else, perhaps?

"Phoebe," he said softly, his eyes down at her feet before flying up to meet hers. "I just want you to know that I care about you very much."

And with that declaration, he was out the door and striding toward his phaeton without a backward glance. Phoebe could only stand there staring after him, her mouth open and her mind and heart in turmoil.

CHAPTER 21

*I*t took all he had not to turn around, to see her reaction, but instead, Jeffrey flicked the reins and drove away, attempting to refocus his thoughts on his next course of action. Fleet Street. It was where all the printers seemed to have set up shop, and where most of the newspapers did business. There, he would hopefully find answers and would determine his own next steps.

He had been about to ask her once more about his marriage proposal, to tell her so much more eloquently all that was flowing through his mind, but her words to him had told him something else entirely — that, perhaps, his decision on this blasted paper would affect her own thoughts.

And so, instead of asking what he had really wanted to know, he simply told her how he felt, leaving quickly so there was no pressure on her to return his words one way or another.

Jeffrey had the printer's mark now, but he wasn't entirely sure where to begin. He threw coin to a lad with promise of more to look after his phaeton, and then began walking down the street at a quick clip, looking in one shop window and then the next before he finally found what he was looking for. This must be a printer's shop, judging by the advertisements displayed on the window. He pushed open the door, waiting a moment until a man finally came out to greet him.

"Good day. May I help you, my lord?" the man asked, his thick mustache bobbing along with his words.

"I hope so," Jeffrey replied, holding out the paper. "I am seeking the publisher of this paper. I am unsure where to find the building's location, but I was hoping you may help me. This is the printer's mark — would this be yours?"

"No, my lord, I'm sorry, but I cannot help you," the man said with a shake of his head. "If you look at our sign, we have an entirely different mark." He paused for a moment. "If you find your way down the street a few doors, I believe you'll find the printer you're looking for. Though if you are needing printing of your own completed, be sure to come back here to Flynn's!"

Jeffrey nodded at him gratefully before he continued on his quest, soon seeing the sign the previous printer had pointed out. When he entered this establishment, it seemed not quite as clean, not quite as efficient, but then it was likely less expensive, which would be important for a fledgling publication.

"My lord?"

Jeffrey was shocked when a woman came out of the back to greet him. Well, he thought, recovering himself, this made much more sense. Of course, *The Women's Weekly* would choose a printer in which a woman was, if not the owner, firmly established within the business. Though this may prove trickier for him to determine how to receive the information he sought.

"Hello," he said with as much charm as he could muster,

though he was aware that it did not exactly come naturally. "I was hoping you could help me."

"I hope I can as well, my lord."

"I am an admirer of one of the publications you print, and I am hoping to get in touch with the publisher in order to offer my support."

She eyed him warily. Apparently this was not a usual request.

"Which publication are you interested in, my lord?"

"*The Women's Weekly.*"

Her eyes widened, and then she shocked him by letting out a snort of laughter. "I'm sure you are, my lord. Unfortunately I cannot help you."

"No?" he asked. "That is too bad. I have a substantial financial donation to provide them."

Her laughter died as she considered him. "And just what would a man like yourself be after with support of such a paper?"

"I am blessed with four sisters who greatly enjoy the publication," he said. "I would like to make the donation on their behalf."

"How about this?" she asked. "If you leave me your information, I will send it on to the publisher and have her contact you."

"Very well," Jeffrey said, realizing he wouldn't get any further with this woman, who was as loyal as everyone else seemed to be to this elusive publisher. He passed her his card. "As quickly as possible would be greatly appreciated."

She nodded and wished him good day, watching him carefully as he left the building. He did not, however, continue home. No, instead he waited around the corner. It took some time — longer than he would have liked. But he was rewarded for his patience, as soon enough, he saw a young lad — a messenger no doubt — scamper out the front door. Jeffrey had to set a quick pace to follow, but luckily it wasn't long until the lad opened the door of a building just down the street — 53 Fleet Street. It was fairly nondescript, not showcasing any of its true identity from the exterior. At the slab gray front punctuated only by a smoky window, he wondered at the prosperity of the publisher. While this clearly wouldn't have been the most expensive real estate available for offices, he questioned where a woman would find such funds. Perhaps the "lady" moniker was simply a ruse, and there was a man behind the scheme, making a significant sum off the publication that women were apparently flocking to in droves.

Did one knock at the entrance of such an establishment? No, he decided, pushing open the door, which creaked slightly as he did so. A small, scarred wooden desk sat near the door, a chair behind it, but no one was sitting awaiting him or any other arrival. He walked down the short corridor, looking in to find one small, dim, empty room, then another, before finally an open door revealed a rather large space, filled with rows of desks, a bank of long, narrow windows lining the side wall, showing nothing beyond but another building beside.

Here, a couple of women sat at the tables, one scratching away on the paper in front of her, the other lining up rows of sheets of paper, and he wondered if she was determining the layout for the next issue. The boy he had followed was just about to pass the note to one of the women, but paused when Jeffrey entered.

"Pardon me," Jeffrey said into the quiet of the room, and both women gasped, the one standing turning to him as she clutched at her breast.

"My apologies, my lord," she said a bit breathlessly. "I did not hear you come in."

"There was no one at the door when I entered," he explained, and she nodded.

"Quite right," she said. "Quite right. There will be in due time."

Whether she meant later that day, or later on in the future, he had no idea, but he didn't question it any further — it didn't make much difference to him.

"I am here to speak with your publisher," he said, and the woman's eyes narrowed slightly as she looked him over. She was a bit plump, around his mother's age, he thought, her hair dark with a touch of gray. But she looked quite... competent, he decided, and he wondered if he had found the woman he sought. "Would you be the woman I am looking for?" he asked when she said nothing.

"No," she said, shaking her head, not so much in denial of his words, but as though bringing herself out of a trance of some sort. "Forgive me. I am Mrs. Ellis. Rhoda Ellis, and I am the editor of this paper."

"'Tis a pleasure," he said with all of the politeness he had been bred with.

"Might I ask what business you have with our publisher?" she asked bluntly, not sharing any information in regards to whether or not she was available.

"It is a personal matter," he said, "One that requires a conversation with the publisher directly. You see, I am a supporter of the newspaper, and I wish to speak with her of what I could possibly do to help see to this publication's success."

Mrs. Ellis crossed her arms over her chest and leaned back against one of the tables. The other woman present — a girl, with blonde, swept-back hair, watched their exchange with interest.

"Our publisher... she is not in at the moment," replied Mrs. Ellis, and Jeffrey stored that piece of information — so the publisher was a woman, as he had initially suspected. But how did a woman manage an operation such as this? "In fact, it is the day when many of our writers are out gathering material for their columns and stories. Perhaps you might come back tomorrow?"

"Very good," he said. "Perhaps I shall do that. Mrs. Ellis, I do not suppose you might show me around the offices? If I am to offer my support, I should like to see where it is needed."

She was somewhat apprehensive about his request, he could tell, but finally she nodded her head and waved a hand for him to follow her.

"There's not much, really, not at this point," she said as they walked back into the corridor. "We were just in the room where the writers congregate when they are in the building, though many choose to write their columns in their own homes and send them into us. We do meet in there as well from time to time. Only two other offices are currently in use. This is mine, to your left, and then beside me, one door over, is our publisher's."

He stepped into the publisher's office, finding hardly anything of note with the exception of scattered papers across the desk, a quill pen on the surface of it, and smudges of ink upon the wood peeking out beneath it all.

Jeffrey leaned over the desk in an attempt to see what might be on the top of the pile, at the very least, but Mrs. Ellis was clearly aware of his intention as she stepped firmly in front of him, a strained smile covering her face as she held an arm out to usher him out of the door.

"That's all there is to see," she said politely, yet with some tension.

"I did not hear your publisher's name," he said as nonchalantly as he could as they continued back to the front entrance.

"That is because I did not tell you, my lord," she replied. "And what of yours?"

"Forgive me," he said, finding a card in his pocket and passing it to her. "Jeffrey Worthington, Marquess of Berkley. It was a pleasure to meet you, Mrs. Ellis. I shall see you again tomorrow."

CHAPTER 22

*B*y the time Phoebe herself arrived at 53 Fleet Street, she was no closer to retaining a handle on her emotions. She had a tendency to let her thoughts and opinions get away from her, to cause her to say things she shouldn't, or show too *much* thought or emotion. What was new to her, however, was this indecision that was plaguing her. Typically it did not take long for her to make up her mind and follow through with the next steps ahead.

She pushed open the door to the offices, rounding the corner to find a few of her writers were in the building, with Rhoda jumping to her feet the moment Phoebe walked into the room.

"Miss Winters!" she said, coming around and Phoebe's consternation rose.

"What's happened?" she asked, reading the concern on Rhoda's face.

"The man — the one that was asking around about you before, who Ned told us about? Well, he was here."

"The marquess." It was a statement, not a question, and Phoebe pulled out a chair and took a seat, suddenly noticing that Ned was in the room, sitting by the window, his feet dangling over the floor.

"Ned," she said, holding a hand out. "How are you?"

"Just fine, Miss Phoebe," he said. "Thanks very much to you. My mam said to thank you as well."

"Of course," Phoebe said, knowing Ned's circumstances: that it was only his mother at home, with no one else to provide. She was a seamstress, but with another couple of young ones, it was hard for her to keep up. Phoebe knew it wasn't exactly the best business practice to pay Ned — or the other boys — as much as she did for distributing the paper once a week, but at least it was helping to make a difference in families who needed a hand.

"When Ned stopped in for his pay, I asked him to stay for a moment so that you could determine if it was the same man, but it sounds as though you are already well aware of his identity," said Rhoda, and Phoebe nodded, leaning back in the chair.

"He asked to speak with you," Rhonda continued. "Well, not you specifically, but the publisher. He said he was here to meet with you about providing financial support to the newspaper, and he was quite believable, but I wasn't entirely sure. Told him you'd be back tomorrow if he wanted to speak with you directly. I wasn't sure if that was the right thing to do. I'm sorry if it wasn't."

"There is nothing at all to apologize for, Rhoda," Phoebe said, rising from her chair. "This shouldn't be your issue to deal with. In fact, he is right to ask for me, for as the publisher, this is my role — to handle these situations, while you look after the editorial. I know the man and I shall speak with him."

"Will he shut us down?" Collette asked from behind Rhoda, her eyes wide. "I need this job, Miss Winters. I have to work for a living, and if I'm not writing, well, my options are rather limited, I'm afraid. I have no training in anything but becoming a wife one day, being part of the gentry and all, but now supporting myself…"

Though she trailed off, Phoebe could practically read her thoughts. Collette had refused to marry her parents' choice of a husband for her, and so they told her the only other option was to leave. They would no longer support her, not when they had found a husband to do so instead. Collette had left her home in the countryside and made her way to London. She told Phoebe she hadn't the patience nor the skill to become a governess, she would likely be fired the first day as a servant, her sewing skills were dismal, and becoming a mistress was too frightful to bear.

When Collette had seen the ad for a writer, she had felt as though all her prayers had been answered.

And now Phoebe certainly didn't want to disappoint her, nor any of the women or young lads who worked here — and especially not the people who read and supported *The Women's Weekly*.

"We will not allow him or anyone else to threaten our existence," she said firmly, though truthfully she wasn't nearly as confident as she seemed outwardly. Men like Lord Berkley and his peers had power the likes of which she could never imagine. "Leave it to me."

And, entrusting the preparation of articles for this week's edition to Rhoda's capable hands, she left to her office, finding a sheet of paper and pen. She scribbled a note, sealed it, and then penned on the outside of one of the most respected addresses in all of Mayfair. Tonight Jeffrey would know not only of her role, but of her determination not to lose it.

* * *

JEFFREY WEARILY SAT down in the wide leather chair behind the desk in his study with a sigh. Peace and quiet — finally.

After his visit with Phoebe and then onto the newspaper offices, Jeffrey was filled with indecision. Stepping through the foyer of his home, he hardly had a moment to even take a breath before his sisters descended upon him. As always, they were eager to question him about the latest engagements they had been invited to, their requirement to find a new gown that was both in the latest fashion and yet completely different from what any other woman would be wearing, and to question him about what he himself had done all day.

"It's not fair," they would sigh regarding the fact that Jeffrey could do whatever he pleased, while they had to seek permission and a chaperone to accompany them wherever they went.

"I am a marquess," he would remind them, though they were not nearly as impressed by the fact as most other people, for they would only roll their eyes at him and continue their incessant chatter. After managing to escape them, he made the necessary niceties with his mother and then secluded himself in his office. There, he found correspondence awaiting him — of course. It never ended. His heartbeat quickened, however, when he noticed a note on top with what had become rather familiar handwriting covering its exterior.

"Well, well, what have we here?" he wondered aloud, and Harper, who was bustling around the office to ensure all was in order for his master, though Jeffrey assured him he wouldn't be long, looked up with question in his eyes.

"My apologies, Harper, I was speaking aloud to myself."

The butler nodded, but then Jeffrey continued. "When did this last correspondence come?"

"Shortly before you arrived, my lord."

"Very good," he nodded, wondering what Phoebe would have to say that was not already stated in their conversation earlier today. He was sure she was waiting to find out what he had chosen to do with his quest in bringing down *The Women's Weekly*. He knew she enjoyed reading the blasted paper but did it really mean that much to her? More than a marriage to him? Though deep down, he was well aware that it was more than the paper. It was the difference in beliefs that were instilled within each of them.

They were at a stalemate, and were this to go any further, one of them had to break, or else.... He didn't want to think on it. He quit wondering what could be and read her quickly scrawled note. It was no love letter, that was for certain, but rather she was requesting for him to come to see her tonight — long past an acceptable social hour, particularly for a man to be calling on an unattached young woman. Would her aunt be in attendance, or was this a request for the conversation he hoped — that she would accept his marriage proposal despite whatever he chose to do regarding his responsibilities as a peer? For that's what this was, and nothing more.

* * *

AS REQUESTED, Jeffrey found himself on the doorstep of the house bordering Cavendish Square at precisely ten o'clock. Should he knock? He instantly felt like an idiot at even thinking thusly. Of course he should knock. He was not here for some secret assignation. He had been invited here for a polite discussion with the lady of the house. True, it was not exactly conventional, but it was Phoebe who had invited him, and as he had previously ascertained time and again, she was not a particularly conventional woman.

He was slightly surprised when she herself answered the door. He could only stand there for a moment as he took her in. Her green eyes seemed as though they were beckoning to him, the way she looked up at him through the dim light. She wore a gown of midnight blue, which, though modestly cut, without gloves and her dark hair swimming around her shoulders, drew him in like a siren calling sailors into the rocks — full of danger yet completely impossible to resist. At this moment she could ask him anything and he didn't know how he could possibly refuse.

She stared back at him in equal measure, a lone sconce on the wall behind her outlining her silhouette, until finally she seemed to realize she had yet to say anything.

"Oh, forgive me," she said, shaking her head as a slightly abashed smile teased her lips and she opened the door wider. "Come in, please."

He did so, turning to face her once they were within the small, interesting foyer.

"Thank you for coming," she said, though he was finding it difficult to focus on anything besides the red of her lips as they moved. Then she reached out and undid the ties of his cloak, holding out her hand for him to remove it and pass it to her along with his hat. He was unsure of exactly how to navigate this, having never previously given a woman his outerwear.

"Where is your butler?" he asked instead.

"He has retired," she said. "He is rather elderly, and becomes exhausted past nine."

"And you still keep him on?'

"Of course!" she replied, somewhat indignant. "Glover has been with us for ages, and he will remain with us until he determines it is time to depart from his duties. He has been loyal to my family for years, and I certainly will not turn on him."

"I never meant to suggest—"

"My apologies," she said, her face losing its edge as she

took his cloak from his hand before he could protest. "I am slightly on edge this evening and I am afraid it is getting the better of me."

"What exactly is it that you have to be nervous about?" he asked, hoping it was that she had an answer for him, but not wanting to become too expectant.

She said nothing, but, having stowed his garments, turned to the stairs and began climbing.

"Come," she said, beckoning with her hand, and of course he was powerless to resist. "We'll avoid my father's parlor for this evening, I think. The other is far more comfortable."

He actually rather liked her father's parlor, though it was as eccentric as the man himself. It was interesting — unlike any he had ever seen before in all of England. But he did as she said, following her down the corridor. Wherever she chose to take him, he seemed inclined to follow, was he being honest.

The room they entered was dimly lit, the roaring fire in the hearth casting a glow throughout the room, illuminating the fine furniture, the gold walls, and the face of the woman who sat on the settee before him. As much as he longed to sit next to her, to run his fingers down her face as he watched her changing expressions, he had a feeling that this was more of an occasion for serious conversation, and so instead he took a seat across from her, where he could hopefully better concentrate on whatever it was she had to say.

"Will Lady Aurelia be joining us?" he asked, though he knew the answer before she began to shake her head.

"No, Aunt Aurelia is out at an engagement this evening," she responded.

"And you chose not to attend with her?"

"No," she said with another shake. "It is a gathering amongst friends she has been well acquainted with for years.

I am afraid if I accompanied her, I would be the youngest by a couple of decades. They have no wish for me to attend!"

"I believe you would always make for a welcome guest at parties," he murmured, and he squinted in the dim light to better ascertain whether her cheeks had turned pink. Was Phoebe blushing at a simple compliment from him? She really was out of sorts tonight.

"I would not say that is always the case, Lord Berkley."

"Jeffrey."

"Yes, Jeffrey, my apologies," she said, coloring all the more. "But you see, sometimes I can be found arguing with and slapping very polite, well-respected marquesses in the drawing rooms of balls, which does not make me the ideal guest."

He laughed at that, and the tension in the room eased somewhat. He loved that she could bring this out of him — the carefree side that was so often hidden under the weight of his responsibilities.

She took a breath, stood, and then came to sit beside him on the settee. Oh, he wished she hadn't done that. Now she was far too close, and her scent of oranges and cinnamon filled his senses, emanating from her unbound hair. His well-ordered, calculated thoughts began to flee, replaced by only thoughts of her, with him, under him — he took a sharp inhale of breath.

"Phoebe," he murmured, taking her hands in his and pulling them into his lap. "Before you say anything, I feel there are some aspects of our... relationship that I should clarify. When I whispered those words to you at the theatre, they seemed impulsive, and perhaps presumptuous. So I would like to better explain to you my thoughts."

He looked deep into her eyes, which were as murky as the waters of a country pond. Hidden within them were her thoughts regarding him and his words, but he could no more make them out than he could determine a pattern of the stars in the cloudy sky.

"When we met, it was… passionate, I suppose you could say, though not in the way one might expect. Everything I heard you say went against all of my morals, all of the long-held beliefs with which my father raised me. And yet there was something about you that took hold over me and wouldn't let go. You refused to leave my mind, and every time I saw you, I actually found more that I liked about you, that attracted me to you all the more. You get along very well with my family, who can be rather difficult. You love my dog, who most find rather trying, and you are kind. You are generous, honest, and good. You stand up for what you believe in. And even if I do not share those same beliefs, well, a husband and wife are bound to disagree time and again, are they not? As long as they care for one another and their families, that is what truly matters. So please, be my wife, Phoebe Winters."

Her eyes became watery as he spoke, and he smiled gently at her, for he knew that, despite her tough exterior, Phoebe's heart was true.

"Oh, Jeffrey," she said with a bit of a moan, and he took that as acceptance, and leaned in, softly brushing his lips over hers. He simply tasted at first, slowly nibbling her bottom lip, softly licking the top. Her hands came to his chest, and for a moment he had a strange worry that she would push him away, but instead her fingers dug into his chest, and his breath hitched.

He wrapped his arms around her and pulled her close, heady with the thought that everything this woman was — trying, but true — would be his, forever.

CHAPTER 23

*S*he really should not be doing this. No, she should put a stop to this kiss, push him away and tell him the truth — her truth. As he had spoken to her, his words had brought the strangest combination of emotions swirling within her — guilt, yes, but also passion and a swirling within her chest that took her a moment to recognize. As he kissed her, his body flush against her, the masculine heat of him radiating toward her, she had nearly jerked in surprise at the sudden realization that flooded her mind. She loved him. She loved Jeffrey Worthington, the contrary, impossible man. Bloody hell. This was not good — not good at all. For when he rejected her, and she was certain he would, damn but it would hurt, more than anything she could imagine since the death of her parents.

Tell him, Phoebe. Push him away and tell him this instant.

But oh, he was delicious, his taste a mix of brandy and coffee that surprisingly appealed to her. Her hands moved from his chest to curl around his neck, and at that moment she despised the cravat that so carefully, tightly hid the skin underneath. She wanted to run her fingers down his neck, his chest, to feel upon them the strength of the muscles she could only imagine were hidden beneath his layers of clothing.

Goodness, what was he doing to her? He was turning her into an addle-brained ninny, it seemed, as thoughts flew out of her head, to be replaced only by the need to be closer to him, to have more of him. Clearly she wasn't alone in her feelings, for Jeffrey placed a hand behind her back as he slowly eased her back down upon the settee, the giltwood creaking under their weight.

The narrow piece of furniture was certainly not made for two people to stretch themselves across, and Jeffrey grunted with apparent frustration as he attempted to keep the two of them on top of the quaint piece of furniture. When he lifted a hand to bring it to her hair, she nearly rolled off the damn thing and gave a squeal of surprise.

"Bloody hell," he muttered, and then with astonishing strength, he picked her up before placing her down on the Aubusson rug at their feet. He hovered above her, a quick grin spreading over his lips. "Much better," he said, before descending once more.

Now that he had full use of his hands, they seemed to be everywhere at the same time — running down her bare arms, caressing the top of her shoulder, raking through her hair. Soon she felt her strands brush over her surprisingly bare shoulders, and his lips moved to caress her collarbone, before lowering to the top of her bodice. His breath tickled the rise of her bosom above her dress, and he shocked her by taking the top of her bodice between his teeth before inching it lower so that her breasts were exposed to him. With delight evident his face, he cupped one and then the other, stroking her reverently with his thumbs.

"You are exquisite," he whispered, his face full of rapture, and a thrill coursed through her at the thought that such a look at her would cause these feelings within him. She knew she ought to cover herself up, to hide from him, but she found that she wanted him to look at her, needed to see that desire evident in his eyes, which had become so dark they were nearly black.

He brought his lips to one breast, and she nearly came off the floor with the sensation that coursed through her as a result. What in the—

"Do you like that?" he murmured.

"Perhaps."

He moved to her other breast, this time slightly scraping her nipple with his teeth, and she let out a moan.

"I will take that as an affirmative answer," he said, tilting his face to look at her and smiling wickedly. She swallowed hard, wanting nothing more than for him to do it again, an unknown wave of heat filling her when he complied with her unspoken thought.

This was unlike anything she had ever felt before, and yet, somehow, she wanted more than even this. Her fingers came to that damn cravat, untying it and removing it with one great yank before tossing it to the side, exposing the skin she had so urgently wanted to explore.

Her hands came around his neck, sliding down over the stubble that stretched over his Adam's apple, before finding smooth skin that led to a slight whorl of hair at the top of his shirt. Gripping the lapels of his jacket once again, she pushed it down over his arms, before her fingers came to unbutton the waistcoat underneath. When only his shirt remained, she hesitated for a moment, suddenly shy, but when his fingers began to slide up her legs, which were bare underneath her muslin dress and chemise, she was emboldened once again and made quick work of his shirt buttons.

"You have done this before?" he asked with an arched eyebrow, and she shook her head fiercely.

"No, but I am an efficient, determined woman, Jeffrey," Phoebe said, winking at him, and he let out a noise that was part-chuckle, part-groan as he left her legs alone for a moment to lift his shirt overhead, and now it was her turn to push him back onto the floor, and she rose above him so she could have a better look.

She had been right. Those muscles that she had imagined as quite solid underneath his shirt were so defined from his chest to the bottom of his torso that her mouth went dry as her eyes ran over him. The pattern of hair on his chest was as blond as the hair on his head, and she reached to run her fingers over it, entranced by this, her first view of a half-dressed man up close. Well, he had certainly been correct about one thing. There were differences between men and women that could not be denied. And yet, even here, their two bodies fit together, complemented one another, as it should be in all aspects of life, should it not?

Her thoughts trailed off as she continued down his body, noticing that the hair tapered off over his abdomen, but for a slight trail that led from his navel down beneath the waistband of his pants. Phoebe's eyes widened as she took it in, her fingers becoming slightly less brave as they wandered in that direction.

Sensing her hesitation, he took advantage. He covered her fingers with his, rolling them both over so that they lay on the plush carpet side by side, their faces even with one another. Not breaking eye contact, he went back to his previous ministrations, his fingers reaching down to lift her leg up a bit higher for better access. He wrapped his hand around her ankle, caressing it with his thumb, and she was grateful that she was wearing only her simple day dress with a chemise underneath. His fingers slid slowly upward, seemingly leaving no section of her leg unexplored as he continued.

When he crested her knee, her nerves seemed so exposed, her body so jumpy, that she wanted to bolt upright and run out of the room, but the sure gaze of the warm chocolate of his eyes steadied her, holding her in place. She knew with absolute certainty that she could open her mouth and tell him to stop, that she no longer wanted this and he would do as she said, but that would be more of a lie than anything else she had previously said to him. Her breath came quicker the higher his hand rose, her heart pounding so hard and rapid that she was sure he could hear it, louder than even the ticking of the ormolu clock on the mantle of the fireplace.

But then she noticed that he was slightly panting himself, and she was curious at the fact that he would be so affected when he was the one who was doing this to *her*. She closed her eyes for a moment, both hiding from him and reveling in the sensations, but then he whispered her name, and her lids flew open to find him again.

She gasped when his fingers came between her thighs, and he lifted his knee to rest it between hers to open her up to him. Was she a harlot for wanting him to continue, for not driving him away? But no, she realized as she kept her gaze focused, her eyes wide open on his face, which had now taken on a strained expression. This was what it meant to be with someone you cared for greatly or even loved. For she did. She loved him.

Her thoughts fled when his fingers reached between her folds and found the most sensitive place in her entire body. His thumb stroked her, and she finally broke their locked gaze, throwing back her head with a cry as he mercilessly continued to fondle her, his thumb increasing its pressure as it moved in circles, driving her to madness. If this was how it could feel with just his fingers…

Restless, she brought her hand to the fall of his breeches, and he shook his head.

"Phoebe," he murmured, "Let me please you. You do not have to—"

"I want to," she whispered, urgently looking at him as if to ensure him of her desire. "And I do nothing that I do not wish to do," she added.

He nodded, his eyes intent upon her.

"If at any time, you want to stop, just say the word," he said in a low, gruff voice, and she nodded, completely understanding and trusting in what he told her. His hands fell away as he allowed her to clumsily undo the fall of his breeches, and he rolled up above her, until he was between her knees, and his body, in the flickering light of the sconce on the wall and the candle atop the table beside them crossing over it, was astonishingly beautiful.

She reached up to draw him down toward her, and he complied. She braced herself for him to enter her, but instead, after first lifting her skirts to settle around her middle, his hands found her once more, this time were much more insistently, much more urgently, and she found herself falling away from the present to lose herself in sensations as she never had before. It was only when her entire body began to pulse, waves of the finest flames she could ever imagine coursing through her, that he sheathed himself inside her, and she let out a gasp as pain and pleasure intermingled.

He brought his forehead to hers, kissing her lips softly before raining kisses over her cheeks, nose, and chin, then dipping his head to find her breasts once more, suckling and making the desire begin to build all over again. The pain began to recede, and she tentatively moved against him ever so slowly to experiment how it might feel. And it was... good. It felt very, very good.

Jeffrey looked down at her with question, and when she nodded, he began to move, a slow back and forth, and it was nearly torturous. His pace began to increase, until finally, just when she didn't think she could take anymore, she arched into him at nearly the same time he gave a shout, and they tumbled into the waves together this time.

CHAPTER 24

*P*hoebe laughed with gleeful abandon, and the sight of her brilliant smile warmed Jeffrey thoroughly inside. He was surprised at just how much the happiness of another could bring happiness to himself. A slight sense of guilt began to fill him — not remorse, for he would love nothing more than to do that all again, but still, perhaps he should have ended it before it even began. Though once she had given him her assent — no, more than that — her own desire, he didn't think there was anything that could have kept him back from following through with what she wanted of him.

"Phoebe…" he began, wanting to apologize, but not knowing how. She apparently understood his thoughts, however, for she brought a finger to his lips, silencing him as she shook her head.

"Don't you dare express any regret for that, Jeffrey," she practically commanded him, and at his apparent persevering look of uncertainty, she continued. "We just made love, and it was magical, better than anything I could have ever imagined. I desired it, I asked you for it, and if you apologize, then I will take that as a sign of disrespect. Understood?"

He nodded weakly at her words, understanding that Phoebe Winters would never do a thing she didn't completely choose herself.

She lifted her bodice to cover those glorious breasts, before reaching for his clothing, which was scattered across the carpet, his shirt sprawled over the brandy decanter and glasses on the table.

When she looked back at him, however, her face had softened, and she bestowed the most beautiful smile upon him.

"Thank you, Jeffrey," she said, with another quick kiss on his lips. She lifted the shirt back over his head, seeming to enjoy helping him dress nearly as much as she had to undress him. The smile she wore seemed somewhat sad, though why he had no idea.

"How are you feeling?" he asked.

"Like a different woman than I was an hour ago," she said on near a whisper, and they shared a quick kiss, wordlessly speaking to one another of the secret that would remain between the two of them.

Finally he was dressed, though not as immaculately as he would have been with a valet, despite Phoebe's skill with a cravat. Phoebe stood before him, her fingers tangled together, and she stepped toward him.

"Jeffrey…" she began, but then there was a knock at the door and Aunt Aurelia sailed in.

"Phoebe, darling I— oh."

They all stood there staring at one another, until Jeffrey, having been bred and raised with only impeccable manners, broke the silence.

"Lady Aurelia," he said, striding to the door, picking up her hand and kissing it. "It is lovely to see you."

"And you, Lord Berkley, although I am not exactly sure

this is proper, for the two of you to be alone together at eleven o'clock at night in a home without any chaperone."

"That would be my doing," Phoebe said, stepping up to the pair of them where they were standing by the door, and Jeffrey shook his head at her. He appreciated the fact that she was willing to be honest about the original circumstances of their meeting, but he had an overwhelming need to protect her name, even if it was only in front of her aunt, who he was sure knew her better than nearly any other.

"Actually, Lady Aurelia, I'm afraid it was my fault. I called upon Lady Phoebe, unsure of whether or not you would be in residence," he said, which was in fact, entirely the truth. "I should have left upon finding that you were not home, but I could not keep myself from a moment with your lovely niece." He was proud of himself for not telling one word of a lie to Phoebe's aunt, though his "moment" was greatly underplayed.

"Now then, I suppose I should be going," he said, striding out the door, turning to take a few steps backward through the threshold. "It was wonderful seeing both of you. Phoebe — Lady Phoebe — we must speak again soon. *Very* soon."

He sent her what he hoped was a meaningful gaze, and he assumed she understood him as she slightly nodded at him.

"Goodnight," he said, holding her eyes.

"Goodnight," she whispered softly, and with that he was down the stairs, found his hat and cloak, and was out the door and into his carriage. He thought of stopping at White's but decided that what he had just experienced with Phoebe was so pure, so wonderful, that he didn't want to spoil it by going to the club and having to make pleasantries without being able to share what was truly in his heart. For now he knew. He loved her, and could not wait until she was truly his wife. He ordered his carriage home, whistling a cheerful tune all the way.

* * *

"Good morning, lovely ladies!" Jeffrey greeted his sisters and his mother as he sat down to breakfast the next morning. "And of course, good morning to you as well, Ambrose. It's wonderful to see you awake at this hour. Jolly good to see you're alive!"

He chuckled as he poured his coffee, but then looked up when he heard nothing but silence. Six faces wearing various expressions of disbelief stared at him. Penny had her fork halfway to her mouth, and now the morsel of egg she had been about to eat slowly slid off and back onto her plate.

Viola's eyes were wide behind her spectacles, Rebecca's mouth was open in a wide 'O,' and Ambrose had actually looked up from his plate. Jeffrey's mother wore a slight smile that was filled with confusion, and even Maxwell, who lay at his feet, had raised his head, while he typically kept it low to the floor in search of a dropped — purposefully or not — crumb of food. Annie was the first to finally break the silence.

"Are you all right, Jeffrey?"

"Of course!" he said with a bit of bluster. "What could possibly be the matter? It's the lot of you that is worrying me, sitting there staring as though you have lost all the words that are normally chattering about the table at this hour."

"It's just…" Rebecca began, looking around at her sisters for support. "You're almost *jovial* this morning. Has something happened?"

"I'm always jovial!" he defended himself, and Penny snorted at that, holding a hand in front of her mouth when her mother shot her a look of consternation. "Am I not, Viola?"

Jeffrey looked to his usual champion for support, but at

her hesitation, he realized he was going to lack defense even from her, and he was slightly put out for the moment.

"You are certainly pleasant, Jeffrey," she said with her usual diplomacy. "As for jovial, well, I wouldn't necessarily use the word to describe you, especially at the breakfast table. You much prefer to grumble about and read your papers. Which is fine. We cannot all be jolly in the morning."

He did grumble a bit, then, but even his family's astonishment couldn't break his spirits. The woman he desired more than anyone or anything he ever had before returned his affections and was going to be his wife. His affairs, his family, his home was in order. What more could a man ask for? Well, there was the business of that blasted publication, but he would worry about that afterward.

"It's the woman, isn't it?"

Jeffrey looked over at Ambrose, who now leaned back his chair, a sly smile crossing his face. Some of Jeffrey's joyful spirit slightly diminished. He knew that smile, and it wasn't one of which he was particularly fond. For when Ambrose smiled like that, it spoke of trouble.

"I believe you mean Lady Phoebe, Ambrose," Lady Berkley slightly admonished her son, and Jeffrey smiled at his mother, always the peacemaker, as she had to be with six — well, make that five — slightly unruly children, and then himself.

"Very well, then," Ambrose corrected, though the glint in his eye remained. "The lovely Lady Phoebe. Has something happened?"

They all looked at Jeffrey, their shock turning into expectant expressions. Jeffrey shifted slightly in his chair. He and Phoebe had not had the opportunity to actually *discuss* much of their betrothal, and he felt somewhat uncomfortable in sharing the news with his family until he had the opportunity to speak with her again. And yet, he had never lied to them, and he wasn't about to start this morning.

"Something has happened, yes," he said, and one of his sisters — Annie or Penny, he wasn't entirely sure which — squealed from the other end of the table, while his mother gasped and Viola and Rebecca both grinned. Ambrose simply regarded him with a calculating look on his face.

"And?" Rebecca prodded, but he shook his head.

"At the moment I am not able to say anything further," he responded but accompanied his words with a slight smile. "But rest assured that you will be the first to know should there be any further developments."

"Ooh, Jeffrey, you can be positively vexing!" Penny exclaimed, and he winked at her, to which she did not entirely know how to respond, as Jeffrey was not the type to wink at anyone, least of all his sisters.

He felt a cool, soft hand on his arm.

"As long as you are happy, Jeffrey, that is all that matters," his mother said gently, and he smiled at her. He knew how lucky he was to have been raised by a woman like her. He had loved his father as well, of course, but in a different way. He had been impressed by him, respected him, but the marquess had expected so much that Jeffrey always felt he had fallen short of what the previous Lord Berkley had required in an heir. Then again, most young gentlemen did not take on their title at the age of eighteen, so he supposed if he had more time before doing so, his father might have appreciated his efforts a little more.

But that was neither here nor there at the moment.

"Thank you, Mother," was all he said.

"Oh, Jeffrey," Rebecca called from down the table. "You haven't forgotten about the Dennington's party this evening, have you?"

"Of course not," he said, he hoped somewhat indignantly,

though, in fact, he *had* forgotten all about it. He wondered if Phoebe would be in attendance, and hoped very much that she would.

"Good," his sisters said, approving of him for once, he thought, and he shook his head ruefully as he let the idle chatter and speculations as to his current state of relationship status continue around him.

CHAPTER 25

*P*hoebe paced the floor of *The Women's Weekly* writing pit, as they had come to call it — the place where the lot of them congregated. She noticed Rhoda and the other writers glancing up at her from their pages time and again, but there wasn't anything she could say to them. For how could she explain that she had fallen in love with the man who was trying to put an end to their dream? He could destroy not only the publication, but also their very livelihoods and what they held dear – the moral beliefs that she had pushed them all to share, that they risked their very reputations to defend.

The door creaked open — Phoebe made a note to have it fixed so it didn't make such a noise — and footsteps echoed down the corridor, Julia walked in with a smile on her face. Phoebe had never been so pleased to see her friend. She needed counsel more than anything right now.

"Julia!" she exclaimed, walking toward her and taking her hands in hers. "It is *wonderful* to see you."

Julia beamed. "Such a welcome certainly makes one feel

appreciated, Phoebe," she said, then spoke in a near whisper so no one else would hear her. "Is anything amiss?"

"Everything," Phoebe said forlornly, and Julia's eyebrows jumped in surprise.

"That is not exactly what I expect from you, Phoebe," she said, her voice continuing in its low tone, but Phoebe had enough of her writers' questioning looks, and she pulled Julia back down the hall and into her office.

"I came to deliver my column in person — I love the idea of being a part of this, with the other writers, but if I am not mistaken, it seems that I am required for something other than my love of racing and my surprising writing skills," Julia said, gingerly taking a seat in the second office chair, the rickety wooden thing that seemed as though it would break even under Julia's tiny frame.

"Sit here," Phoebe said, ushering her instead into her own chair, which, while faded and ugly, did not look as though it were going to fall apart. "I cannot sit anymore myself."

She continued her pacing, though it was significantly more difficult in her office, which was so much smaller than the larger room down the hall.

"Phoebe, you must tell me what is the matter before you fall over from your exertions, or wear a hole in the floorboards," Julia demanded, her voice surprisingly strong and fierce, and Phoebe obeyed, stopping to face her.

"I love Jeffrey. And I made love to him."

Julia sat there, stunned into silence as she stared at Phoebe, who could feel tears beginning to prick the back of her eyes.

"Oh, say something, damnit!"

Julia stood and crossed over to Phoebe. While Julia said nothing, she wrapped her slim arms around her, squeezing so hard that Phoebe could hardly breathe. With her friend providing her the support she so needed, Phoebe finally let the tears begin to fall down her face, and Julia simply held her, letting her feel all she needed to emote.

Finally Phoebe nodded into her shoulder, telling her she was all right, and Julia stepped back, holding up a dainty handkerchief. Phoebe took the offering and wiped her eyes and nose before finally sitting, defeated, in the rickety old chair that, despite its questionable look, faithfully held her up.

Julia sat on the edge of the desk in front of her, a sympathetic look on her face. She placed her hands under Phoebe's chin and lifted her face.

"I know you are in turmoil right now, Phoebe, but for a moment, celebrate the fact that you are in love! How wonderful does that feel?"

Phoebe smiled ruefully. "That part of it, I suppose, is rather lovely."

"And," Julia continued, a wicked look coming into her eye. "You *must* tell me what it was like to make love to a man. I can hardly wait!"

Phoebe laughed at that, though she found that she couldn't say much about it. What had happened was something to be kept between her and Jeffrey, and it was too difficult to murmur a word of it even to her very closest of friends.

"Honestly, Julia," she said instead, "There are no words that can accurately describe what it is like to make love to a man for whom you hold such feelings. Not that I would know what it is like to be with a man whom I do *not* love, but still… it is nothing like what I could have ever expected, and no one could ever have properly prepared me for such a thing."

Julia smiled dreamily then, before she was brought back to Phoebe's plight when Phoebe sniffed into the handkerchief.

"As for your conundrum with Lord Berkley," Julia said, attending to the matter that she knew was ruining Phoebe's hopes for happiness, "I can see how you might be in some distress."

"Oh Julia," Phoebe began, running her hand over her hair, which was tied back today in a messy chignon, for she had not had the patience this morning to allow her maid much time with it. "My time with him was glorious, and yet my heart was breaking with the realization that it was likely the first and last occasion I would be with him. Was it worth it? Yes. For while I have not been able to use words to express what I feel for him, I was able to show him with our physical love. He proposed to me once more, said all sorts of lovely things to me, but never once did he say that he loved me, so I could hardly say the words first, now could I?"

"Of course you could have!" Julia exclaimed from her perch on the desk. "You are too proud, Phoebe."

"Perhaps," Phoebe said with a sigh. "But he keeps speaking about my damn honesty, and here I have been lying to him for weeks now. When it all comes out, he will not believe anything I have said. I meant to tell him all last night, Julia, truly I did, but then things got out of hand, and Aunt Aurelia came in—"

"Aurelia came in? During…." Julia's shocked expression made Phoebe burst into laughter, and she shook her head vehemently.

"No, thank goodness. Afterward, when I was about to tell him once more of the paper and my role as publisher. Then he left, and now I must make an effort once more. I never exactly responded to his request for marriage, but I suppose he now believes following my actions that I am in agreement."

"Well, of course," Julia said, nodding. "A man such as the marquess would not take such liberties with just any woman, nor expect them returned by a young lady. But one who was his betrothed… well, it is more likely."

"He attempted to apologize afterward, but I quickly told him that was rubbish and if he respected me, he must dismiss those feelings of guilt at once," Phoebe said with a nod. "Anyway, I must choose now. For even if, after I tell him the truth, he decides he still wants to marry me, then his quest to bring down *The Women's Weekly* is complete. For you know as well as I that if he were my husband, all of this—" she held her hands in the air to signify her surroundings "—becomes his. The building, the staff, the paper, all of my funds that are tied into this, and even those that are not. He can do whatever he likes with it all, and we know that he will not keep it in operation. Is my heart worth this? Is it of equal value to the change that we are making, the jobs of the women who write for me, the very fabric of all I feel is so important to make a difference among society? Is it selfish for me to choose love?"

She was breathing heavily now, so impassioned she felt about what she was saying, and Julia nodded in agreement.

"I understand, Phoebe, truly I do," she said. "And I am afraid I do not have the answers you are looking for. All I can suggest is that you follow your heart, that you do what feels right. And perhaps, once you speak with him, all will not be as lost as you currently feel it is."

"I don't know, Julia," Phoebe said, shaking her head sadly. "I just do not know."

But even so, despite her melancholy, regardless of the knowledge of what the future could bring, she penned a note in deliberately neat handwriting — altogether different from her usual scrawl — requesting a meeting with the Marquess of Berkley tomorrow at 2 o'clock in the afternoon, at the offices of *The Women's Weekly*. Signed, A Lady, the Publisher.

* * *

JEFFREY WAS ABOUT to leave Parliament to begin his trek to 53 Fleet Street when he was intercepted by a secretary and a piece of correspondence for him. He was delighted by what he found inside — an invitation to meet with the publisher of *The Women's Weekly*, tomorrow. Splendid. It was exactly what he was after — a chance to reason with the woman, to make her come around to his way of thinking. It was far preferable to have an invitation than to push his way in the door uninvited.

He whistled as he wandered down the corridor. All was going very well in the life of Jeffrey Worthington, he realized, though his spirits somewhat dimmed when he found his brother awaiting him outside the doors of the Palace of Westminster.

"Ambrose," he greeted him with a nod, though he didn't stop. "What can I do for you today?"

"I was hoping for a word with the great Marquess of Berkley," Ambrose said, pushing away from the wall and falling in step with him as he turned down Abingdon Street.

"You have my ear anytime you wish, as we live in the same home, though I should say it is high time you found your own quarters," Jeffrey said, looking ahead at the bustle of people on the walkway in front of him. "Surely you must have good reason for finding me here, in the middle of London, after I had to conduct business?"

"I do not understand how you do it every day," Ambrose said with a sigh, shaking his head. "I would find it altogether far too boring."

"Which is why it is fortunate for all of us that you are the second son and nothing untoward has yet happened to me," Jeffrey said with a stiff grin, and Ambrose smiled ruefully.

"I suppose this is true," he nodded. "And despite your noble demeanor, I am well aware that you do not always attend when sittings are held."

"I have a less than perfect attendance, I will admit," Jeffrey said. "But I do my very best, as do most lords similar to myself. Now, what can I do for you today, Ambrose?"

Ambrose's mouth was set in a grim line, and when he didn't answer immediately, Jeffrey only sighed, wondering what it was Ambrose had gotten himself into now.

"What is it, Ambrose?"

"You remember Hector, do you not?"

"Hector?" Jeffrey struggled to place the name, searching his memory for the man to whom his brother might be referring.

"The man who could make us money, who you so rudely ignored?"

"Ah, yes," Jeffrey said, grimacing. "I was hoping to not have to revisit that unfortunate circumstance."

He heard Ambrose sniff beside him, angry at his words, but Jeffrey didn't altogether care. Ambrose had been foolish to even entertain the idea that Jeffrey would consider parting with any funds to such a disreputable source.

"Well," Ambrose continued, "I thought it was a fine idea, despite your reluctance, and so I invested some with him anyway."

Jeffrey stopped walking then and turned to his brother. His tone was measured and even, but he couldn't mask the anger from his voice. "You did what?"

"I invested with the man," Ambrose said, holding his chin high. "And Hector says the investment is doing well. He just needs a bit more—"

"Oh, bloody hell, Ambrose," Jeffrey said, throwing his hands up in the air and continuing his forward progress to where his phaeton awaited, leaving Ambrose behind. As his brother continued to follow him, waxing on of all the benefits of investing in this unfortunate scheme, Jeffrey finally turned to him once more, a finger leveled at his chest.

"I told you what your options were, Ambrose — the Peterborough estate, a commission with the military, or to continue your education. I have given you enough time to ponder all of this, so tell me now — what do you choose?"

Ambrose glowered at him, the two brothers locked in a battle of wills.

"I choose to make my own way."

"Fine," Jeffrey said, his words coming from between clenched teeth. "Then do as you wish. But you will not do so with any help from me. You may live in Berkley House, but your allowance is cut off. You will have what you need to survive, but you will not be wiling away any more of our family funds, do you understand?"

"You were always so high and mighty, Jeffrey," Ambrose spit back at him. "But fine, if that is what you wish, then so be it."

Ambrose turned and walked off in the other direction, and as Jeffrey watched him, his anger faded, to be replaced only by sadness and some regret.

CHAPTER 26

*J*effrey escorted five ladies to the Dennington's party that evening. While they were each perfectly delightful and he loved them with his entire heart, he wished that he had another woman on his arm — one that he sought out the moment he arrived at the house that was but two streets away.

It was not an official event and therefore all of his sisters were in attendance. Rebecca was determined that she would spend the entire night on the dance floor, that all of the men would be so eager to fill up the list on her dance cards. Jeffrey hoped it was true. His sisters were all beautiful women, but they were also known for causing a bit of trouble — with the exception of Viola, of course. It would be up to him to help them find men who were worthy of them and yet could handle them as well. It wasn't a task he was looking forward to, but he wouldn't entrust it to any other person, either.

Jeffrey scanned the crowd now, looking for the dark, midnight curls of Phoebe's hair, but while there were many beauties with dark hair, he couldn't find the stunning woman who so held his attention. He sighed, hopeful she was simply late, as he made his way through the crowds to find a drink. Once his brandy was in hand, the Duke of Clarence found him leaning against one of the four pillars that held up the ceiling, which was painted in a scene of what he supposed was to be heaven.

"Berkley."

"Clarence."

They tipped their drinks at one another before each took a sip. They made a bit of conversation about nothing and everything before Jeffrey left to find Viola, hoping she had perhaps seen Phoebe as she traipsed around the room with her friends.

"Vi," he said, snagging her arm as she walked past, and he was both intrigued and pleased to see a few scrawls on her dance card.

She must not have heard him, however, for she continued on, and Jeffrey was waylaid for a moment by acquaintances who wanted a word of hello. By the time he caught up with his sister, she was engaged in conversation with a circle of her closest friends.

"What do you think of it?" he heard one of the women ask, and a tangle of voices responded, but Jeffrey heard the voice of his sister above the rest.

"I think it is an intriguing prospect," Viola said. "To have the *Marriage Act* changed? Why, the lives of women would never be the same. Women would have responsibility, would have the ability to actually make choices for themselves, without fear of what marriage could possibly mean for them."

He heard a rustle beside him, and Ambrose appeared. Jeffrey rolled his eyes but held up a finger to silence him, wanting to hear more of this conversation. For once, Ambrose blessedly did Jeffrey's bidding.

"And what did the article suggest to change?" One of the young women asked, to which another responded, "Simply that when a woman marries, all of her possessions must not necessarily be given directly to the man. That she might have her own finances, her own possessions that she keeps for herself. There would still be a dowry, to be sure, but she would no longer have to sacrifice all."

"Do you believe that would be wise?"

"I do," Viola affirmed. "For then, a woman need not be so fearful of entering into marriage. She would not only know then that a man truly loves her, but she would also be able to build a life for herself and keep it. Think of women who work, who have earned for themselves. They must be so fearful that marriage would take all away from them. They could enter a union willingly, without that fear. I know it is not likely to happen soon, but it is an intriguing prospect."

Ambrose snorted beside him, and Viola turned quickly, catching both of them in her gaze. Jeffrey felt his face warm slightly at being caught eavesdropping, but nonetheless, he smiled at his sister.

"Good evening, ladies," he said to the other women, all who stared at him with doting faces. The title of a marquess did bring that about. "Vi," he said, leaning toward his sister, "I do not suppose you have seen Lady Phoebe this evening?"

"No," she said, shaking her head. "Nor have I heard that she is to be in attendance. Now," her look darkened as she glared at her brothers. "Will you kindly stop listening to my private conversations? You, Jeffrey, have developed a very un-*noble* habit of eavesdropping as of late."

She was absolutely right, and he felt like a chastised schoolboy for having been caught. He continued on his way with Ambrose trailing behind him, and he wondered what it was his brother wanted. Ambrose had clearly not been pleased with him the other day, though Jeffrey doubted he was here to beg his forgiveness.

"I hope you are making progress in bringing down that awful newspaper," Ambrose said, once they were a fair bit away, and Jeffrey turned to him with surprise.

"I was not aware that you had an opinion on the subject either way," he said, and Ambrose shrugged.

"Can you imagine a woman keeping funds to herself? Whatever would she do with them? Purchase more hats and ballgowns? It is laughable, really."

Jeffrey was silent for a moment. The words coming from the mouths of his siblings tonight — first Viola's sensible thoughts and now Ambrose's bluster — had him thinking. The opinion Viola brought forth on *The Marriage Act* was actually somewhat valid, as much as he didn't want to admit it. It would cause uproar were anything to ever change, that was true, but it would not altogether upset the order of society. Another point of discussion to be had with this publisher, he thought ruefully, and Ambrose narrowed his eyes at him.

"You *are* following through, are you not?"

"Absolutely," he said, which was not a lie. He was following up on the situation. He just didn't know to what extent. "In fact, I have a meeting with the publisher tomorrow."

"Oh, good," Ambrose said. "Give him — or her — hell, Jeffrey." He placed a hand on Jeffrey's shoulder, looking at him with eyes that were like a reflection of his own. "It's what father would have wanted. He'd be proud of you."

And with a wink, he was gone, leaving Jeffrey to wonder what his brother was up to.

Ambrose had been right. His father would be proud to know he was taking down such a paper. But his mother —

would she feel the same? Or his sisters? And most of all, Phoebe?

He sighed and downed his drink, lamenting the late hour and the fact that Phoebe hadn't yet arrived, meaning she likely wouldn't at all. It was going to be a long night.

* * *

JEFFREY KNOCKED on the door of 53 Fleet Street the next day at precisely two o'clock, and the grey-haired woman — Mrs. Ellis, if he remembered correctly from the day before — ushered him in. Her face was pleasant, but it certainly didn't seem as though she were smiling at him, but rather was, perhaps, a bit anxious. Clearly, she didn't believe his story from the other day of becoming a supporter of the paper, and nor did he blame her. He knew he wasn't overly convincing.

She didn't say much as she led him down the short corridor, stopping in front of the small room he had entered during his previous visit, the office being that of the publisher. Mrs. Ellis extended her arm, gesturing for him to enter the small office. There wasn't much to look at, its owner clearly not having occupied it for long. A square window let some light in through the glass, which had obviously been scrubbed, though streaks remained, apparently resisting the effort. This time he noticed the ugliest chair he had ever seen in his life sitting behind the scarred oak desk, while a chair so rickety he didn't dare chance it sat in front of the desk. An old, lopsided bookshelf in the corner held stacks of papers and a few odds and ends.

Mrs. Ellis caught his gaze and smiled slightly. "We haven't been here long and this furniture remains from the previous tenants," she said, slightly apologetically. "We are awaiting the new furnishings to arrive."

He nodded in understanding.

"The publisher will be with you in just a few moments, my lord," she said, then turned and continued down the hallway, her footsteps echoing behind her, and as Jeffrey waited, he contemplated what he was going to say. Initially, when he had begun this quest, he had been determined to shut down this damn paper. He still felt that it was somewhat of a nuisance, but between Phoebe and his sisters, he had become swayed toward the idea that perhaps it wasn't entirely fair for him — or any man really — to take away the opportunity for women to have something of their own. As his sisters had pointed out, there were articles within the paper regarding fashion, advice, and other endeavors that gentlemen would hardly be interested in.

It was the articles that incited change, that suggested women should challenge the very fabric of society that had held them together for years, that bothered him somewhat. If he could reason with the publisher, convince her to be slightly less controversial, then all could co-exist peacefully, could they not?

Jeffrey stood waiting, his hands behind his back, as he heard footsteps advancing down the hall ever so slowly, and he waited impatiently. What was taking the woman so long? For he assumed the publisher was a woman.

The oak door, which Mrs. Ellis had left slightly ajar, was pushed open wide. And Jeffrey could only stare in surprise.

CHAPTER 27

"*P*hoebe? What the devil are you doing here?" Jeffrey asked, looking around her to determine if the publisher was approaching. Had Phoebe followed him here? He hadn't seen her since they made love, and he had desperately wanted to speak with her, but prior engagements — such as this very one — had prevented him. "Would you mind terribly if we spoke afterward? I am awaiting a woman with whom I have long been trying to arrange a meeting. Once I am finished, I will meet you out front."

She looked stunning, of course, as she always did. Today she wore a fine crimson dress, and her hair was piled high on her head, with a few curls cascading around her chin. However, as much as he could stand here all day and admire her, it would not do to show up with his betrothed in tow, and besides that, he wasn't altogether sure that the three of them would fit in this room at the same time.

Phoebe said nothing, but advanced into the office, shutting the door firmly behind her. She astonished him by rounding the desk and taking a seat in the ugly green chair.

"Jeffrey," she said slowly, clasping her hands in front of

her on the desk, and he could only stare as the obvious truth of the situation began to seep through and into his mind, as much as he wanted to deny it.

"No…" he began, but didn't know what else to say as he looked around the office, his eyes lighting upon the shelves once more. There were no books, true, but now he looked again and saw a few things upon the wood — a small magnifying glass, a carved statue in mahogany — items of curiosity very similar to those found in the parlor of her home.

She nodded, and he could have sworn a sheen of tears covered her eyes, or perhaps it was just a trick of the dim light filtering in through the window.

"You wanted to meet with the publisher of *The Women's Weekly*," she said, and some part of his conscious noted just how tightly she gripped her fingers together. "Well, here I am."

She gave a little laugh, but it was so forced it sounded hollow. "I am sorry, Jeffrey, truly I am. I never set out to lie to you. I never thought we would form such an attachment to one another, and by the time I had realized my feelings for you, well, it was too late. With how you feel about this publication, I knew that if you were aware of my involvement, you would no longer want anything to do with me, and it was a difficult thought to bear."

She took a deep breath. "But once you proposed marriage, you needed to know the truth. I couldn't say yes until you did, as much as I wanted to accept. I tried to tell you, so many times, but it seemed something would always happen or we would be interrupted, and I never found the opportunity. So here we are."

She stopped speaking then, simply sitting and looking up at him, where he still remained standing.

"You've got to be jesting with me," he finally managed, choking out the words, and she shook her head.

"I would never jest about something so important," she said, standing now, though he was still a head above her. "You have to understand. I always thought that things should be different, that someone ought to do something to push for change. Then one day, I thought, why shouldn't *I* do it? Hardly anyone knows about me, no one cares about my movements, and I have the ability to do so. We all cannot sit around wondering whether someone else will be the one to take action. So, here I am, the publisher of *The Women's Weekly*. Will you not say something, besides the fact that you still believe me to be deceiving you?"

He opened his mouth to speak, but nothing came out, so he cleared his throat and tried again. "Phoebe… this is insanity. You are a lady. You cannot publish a newspaper such as this one."

"Whyever not?"

He tried to think rationally through the fog that had come to surround his brain.

"Because… it will be difficult to finance such an operation."

"I was left a fairly significant inheritance when my parents passed and I am using it for a purpose with which I hope they would be pleased. In addition, the paper has been doing much better than I initially anticipated, and therefore we now operate on revenue and the initial investment will soon be recovered."

"Well," he said with a whoosh of breath. "How very… fortunate for you."

"I like to think of it as hard work and the courage to take the necessary action to do what is right."

"But how do you know that what you do is right? What if you up-end all order?"

"That, Jeffrey, would be the goal. Tell me, what did you want of this meeting, not with Lady Phoebe, the woman you have come to know, but Miss Phoebe Winters, publisher of *The Women's Weekly?*"

"Well," he began, contemplating exactly what he should say to her, proud that he was maintaining his calm demeanor while his was in turmoil within. "I did not come with the intention of halting the publication, though that is what some of my colleagues would prefer that I do. I simply hoped that you would, perhaps, be slightly less vocal in some of your more controversial ideas. Like the idea to change *The Marriage Act*, for example."

"You would prefer to have control over all of your wife's finances and property?" she asked with a raised eyebrow, and he noticed that she did not refer to herself as his wife, but rather a woman in general.

"Phoebe, there is one aspect of what you are doing that does not make sense," he said, not answering her question as she continued to stare at him with eyebrows raised. "If you want change within Parliament, giving this notion to ladies is not going to revolutionize anything, as they are unable to make any sort of difference."

"True," she countered. "But their fathers and brothers will, and some men listen to the women in their lives. In fact, I have heard on good authority that many men even seek out such advice."

She gave him a pointed look, and he thought for a moment of himself seeking out his mother's opinion, or Viola's, and he could understand her words. But, he realized, as an unrecognizable feeling of dread continued to accumulate in the pit of his stomach, all that they were talking about paled in comparison to a matter of far more importance — that of his heart. For Phoebe had taken his trust, his belief in her and who he had assumed her to be, and broken all of it by keeping such a secret from him, one that was such an essential part of who she was.

"Phoebe," he said, attempting with all that was within him to keep his voice impassive, as though nothing was bothering him in the least. "There are arguments to be made for and against the content of your paper, I understand that, but that is not what is most concerning to me."

"It isn't?"

"Not at all," he said, crossing his arms over his chest. "I have told you, time and again, how important honesty is to me, how much I have admired it in you. Now I find that you have been completely lying to me for weeks, pretending to be someone you are not."

"That is not true at all!" she said, her words much more heated than his own, though he felt the same emotion as she. "I am the same woman I always have been. In fact, the words you heard me uttering to my friends on the very night we met are the same as those you will read in my paper each and every week. I have simply taken this opportunity and made it into something much bigger than myself, something of which I am awfully proud. You made your opinion abundantly clear, and it was not as though it seemed you would change your thoughts just because you came to know me. What was I to do? For to tell you would have only meant you would have tried to bring about the paper's ruination that much sooner, would it not have?"

He ran his hand through his hair, not knowing what to say. For much of what she said was true, that was certain. And yet, she had still lied, and that rankled deep within him.

Jeffrey paced back and forth, his emotions fraught, every nerve seemingly on edge. She had taken him off guard, and he needed time to process all of this, to think through her revelation.

Now that he knew the truth, his own stupidity rankled. It all made sense. Phoebe's opinions, her proclivity to say whatever she felt, her determination to make a difference, to change the world. Her frequent daytime outings not entirely in keeping with a woman of her station. He knew the publisher was likely a woman, and she signed her very name as "a lady." Why had the thought never even occurred to him?

Because he wouldn't have wanted to accept the truth, even subconsciously, he admitted to himself. He wanted to *marry* her, and how could he be married to a woman who not only supported, but actually published, such a scandalous newspaper?

He groaned aloud as he sat in the rickety old chair that creaked dangerously under his weight, and placed his head in his hands as he leaned onto the old desk. Phoebe took a seat across from him, saying nothing for a moment, as she allowed her words to resonate with him.

"Do you see now?" she asked gently. "If I had told you from the moment we met, what would have happened? You would have wanted nothing to do with me, and we would never have had the opportunity to develop… feelings for one another. I am still the same woman you wanted to marry, Jeffrey, and I have so badly wanted to accept your proposal, but I couldn't. Not with this secret between us. I am well aware of how this may change your feelings toward me, but please know that I am still the same woman you asked to marry you, the same woman who would like to agree. My ideals have never changed — simply the fact that I have actually taken the step to do something about them."

"Would you cease this production if we were to marry?" he asked.

He wasn't sure that he would actually ask her to do so — in fact, he wasn't altogether certain of anything at the moment. But it would surely tell him just how much she actually cared for him — if it was more than this blasted publication.

"I— I would not want to," she said, dropping their locked

gaze for a moment, looking down at her hands. "I would hope that you would not ask it of me. However, if it was a condition of marriage to you... I would consider taking a step back, but not entirely leaving it behind, nor ever destroying it. I would ensure that it remained in good hands."

"I see," he said, leaning back in his chair now, crossing his arms once more and nodding his head. It was not the answer he had been looking for, but nor was it an outright rejection of him. "At least you are being honest with me now."

"I never *meant* to be dishonest!" she cried. "How could I have told you the truth? Once I learned that you were the one who was trying to find the publisher of *The Women's Weekly*, to *destroy* the newspaper that I worked so hard to build, I knew that if you became aware of what I was doing, you would do everything you could to bring me — this — down."

He looked intently at her then as her words stirred a thought within him.

"That's when you began to pursue me," he said, standing once more and leaning over the desk, looking deep into her eyes, studying her face to determine her reaction to his words. "After you knew that I was the lord who was interested in learning more of the publication. Before that, you hated me. You slapped me! And then this sudden interest. Your appearances at events I frequented, where I had never seen you before. Your coy looks, your slightest touches, your apparent interest in my life, my *family*." He paused for a moment as he read the guilt in her eyes. "By God, you used me."

"I— it wasn't—"

"You *intended* to be close to me. You wanted to know what my actions were, of what I was aware. Not only that, but — perhaps unknowingly, I'll grant you — you distracted me from my goal. And like a fool, I fell for your games, for your lies. You are not only a talented writer, Phoebe, but you are a clever actress as well."

Horrified, he stepped back from the desk, the realization of his complete and utter stupidity draping over him like a cloak he could not pull from his body.

"I thought your dishonesty was simply that you did not tell me of your role here, but now I realize it is far, far greater than that. Our entire relationship is a lie."

"Jeffrey," Phoebe finally cut in, desperation written all over her face and tears pooling in her eyes as she stood and rounded the desk. She raised her hands up toward him, but he pushed them away, not able to stand the thought of her touching him at the moment.

"Jeffrey, what you say... well, I cannot deny it. There is certainly truth to your words. Except you must know that I have been attracted to you from the moment we met, even during that awful conversation we had in the Earl of Torrington's drawing room. And yes, it is true that I did want to be aware of any progress you were making in your investigation as it were, but once I began to know you, the man you truly are — aside from your nonsensical beliefs regarding women — then I became far more than attracted to you. I began to fall for you, Jeffrey. I never thought you could want anything to do with a woman like me for more than a flirtation, so trust me, no one was more surprised than I over the fact that you not only courted me but then asked me to wed you. Every time we are together, I only..."

Tears began to fall down her face, and he steeled himself, determined not to give in to her dramatics. For that's what they were, were they not? More dishonesty as she attempted to make him feel sorry for her?

"You only what?"

"I only fall more in love with you."

He looked at her, at her tear-stained cheeks, her ink-stained hands, her stunning face that he had come to care so much for, and could only think of how it had all been a lie.

Jeffrey shook his head despondently, turned from her, and before she could say another word, slowly strode out the door.

CHAPTER 28

*P*hoebe was rolled in a ball in her bed the next morning, her knees wedged into her chest and the bedclothes clutched tightly around her. She heard a knock on the door, but she squeezed her eyes shut, not ready to face the day.

In fact, she had barely been able to sleep through the night. After Jeffrey had left her office, she had sunk to the floor and allowed the tears to flow freely as she realized just how much it hurt, knowing she had lost him. While he had never said the words, she had felt it, deep in her soul. She hadn't been aware of the depth of her emotions toward him until her dreams for a future with him began to seep away from her. It wasn't fair, she had thought, shaking her head against the truth of it all. Why could she not follow her passions and make a difference, while still finding the true love she had never thought would be there for her?

The worst of it all was that she could see the situation from Jeffrey's point of view. She *had* used him. She *had* lied to him. She had done everything of which he had accused her, and there was no use arguing with him, for all she could say was that he was right — and that everything had changed for her.

But why would he believe her now?

All of these details flowing through her mind, after Jeffrey left, Phoebe wasn't sure how long she had sat at her horrible desk. She had finally come to her senses when there had been a soft knock at the door. At Rhoda's quiet question regarding whether everything was all right, Phoebe rallied herself enough to call out that all was fine, and finally after enough time had passed, she composed herself, collected her belongings, and left, calling out to her staff that she was not well and would return tomorrow.

Since then, she had been desperately trying to determine how she could save it all. By the time she had fallen into bed, physically and mentally exhausted, no brilliant ideas had come to her, and she had despaired of waking up the next day to face it all again.

But she did. For that's how time worked, did it not?

And now... well, for the moment she would have to put aside her own heart, or what was left of it, and focus on other matters. For by telling Jeffrey of who she was, she had not only risked her heart but her entire paper as well. Now it was in his hands, and she had no idea what that would mean for her or her staff. What he would do with the information he had gleaned yesterday. She could wait and see. But she would have to be the one to speak to the people who worked for her, to prepare them for what may come.

Nancy came in quickly after Phoebe rang the bell, and Phoebe managed a small smile for the girl, who had likely been waiting outside the door, aware that her lady was not entirely in her best state of mind.

"Good morning, my lady," Nancy said quietly, and with her somehow unhurried efficiency, began to search through the wardrobe to choose Phoebe's clothing for the day. "You will be in at the office today?" she asked, to which Phoebe nodded. She didn't want to go. She didn't want to face it all. She would far prefer to sit here and cry over the love she had never sought but had found and lost all the same, all by her own doing. And yet, life went on. Other people depended upon her. And so she would put on a brave face along with her clothing for the day, attend to matters at the newspaper office, and then return home where she could allow herself to *feel* once more in private.

"The gray, I think, Nancy," Phoebe said, choosing a smart gown the same color as her mood. Nancy nodded, finding the dress as well as the accessories to accompany it, and Phoebe reluctantly pulled herself from the bed to begin dressing. After Nancy arranged her hair in a tight chignon that Phoebe found pulled at her head but allowed her to feel rather efficient, she went down to breakfast, sighing when she saw that for once in her life, Aurelia had decided to come down first thing in the morning. She loved Aurelia, truly she did, but why today, of all days, did she decide to join her, when Phoebe would far prefer to sit in her own miserable silence?

"Good morning, darling," she said, and Phoebe attempted to smile as she took a seat. She didn't miss Aurelia's shrewd perusal of her face.

"Good morning, Aunt Aurelia."

"And how are you today?"

"I am fine, thank you."

"Are you?"

Phoebe knew she wasn't exactly at her best, but she didn't think there was anything particularly amiss with how she looked. Perhaps Aurelia had been seeking her out last night when she had remained in her rooms.

"I am feeling better than yesterday. I must have had some sort of megrim or something."

"You never have megrims."

"It seems that yesterday, I did."

Why was Aurelia questioning her so today? Typically her aunt primarily left her to see to her own affairs, without any interference.

"Phoebe." Aurelia reached across the table and placed her hand over hers, and Phoebe looked up at her in surprise, her fork stilling in her other hand in its work of shuffling food from one side of her plate to the other.

"Yes?"

"Has something happened? I may be an old spinster, but I know what one's face looks like after her heart has been broken. Has something happened between you and the marquess?"

And with her aunt looking at her so pityingly, Phoebe put down her fork. She began to assemble a story that would tell the truth while leaving out a few details, but soon enough the tears were flowing once more, and it all came spilling out — every bit of it, from her original intentions and her dishonesty, to falling in love with Jeffrey and his visit to the office yesterday, to her fear for the paper and her desire to continue her quest. She only left out the intimate bits.

"Oh, Aurelia, what do I do now?"

"Well," Aurelia said matter-of-factly after consoling Phoebe, "the first thing you do, that you *must* do, is continue to live your life. For wallowing in self-pity will help no one, including yourself. Secondly, if you love him as truly as you say you do, you must tell him of this — again, after he has had time to recover from hearing all that you shared with him. And lastly, Phoebe, I cannot tell you how proud I am of you and all that you have done. You must save that publication. I can hardly believe that Jeffrey would do anything to ruin all that you have built, but others will come after you. It cannot be helped. You can protect it, and you can fight for it. Do not quit."

Phoebe looked up at her, her eyes watering with unshed tears once more, but she nodded. That was one thing she could do, that she had some control over. *The Women's Weekly* would not fall, not on her watch.

"You are right," she said, with some determination now. "I cannot fail. I refuse to. Wish me luck?"

"You, Phoebe Winters, do not need luck," Aurelia said with a loving smile as she squeezed her niece's hand tightly. "You simply needed a nudge in the right direction. With your intelligence and your determination, you can do anything you set out to do. Now go."

Phoebe rose, rounded the table to bestow a quick kiss on her aunt's cheek, and then set off to Fleet Street where she would put all to rights.

* * *

"WHAT DO YOU MEAN, we must pack it all up?"

Collette's voice, slightly shrill, rose over the din of chatter in the writer's pit. Phoebe had known she would be one of the few who would question her, and she was prepared for it.

"I have reason to believe that some of the nobility, who are not exactly enamored of us, may attempt to put a close to our publication," Phoebe explained calmly. "And we all know what that could mean for us, do we not? I do not want to lose this paper, and I am assuming that none of you do either."

Most in the room nodded, a few voicing their agreement with her, to which she was pleased. Rhoda stood next to her in support. The two of them had spoken privately before-hand, determining the best message to share with their small group of writers. They didn't want to lose any of them, and in fact, were doing all they could to protect them and their livelihoods.

"We have kept all of your identities concealed as best we can," Rhoda said, though she herself was perhaps most at risk as Jeffrey knew of her name. "So you should have nothing to fear as individuals. We do not believe that legally anything can be done to bring about our demise as a business; however, when powerful lords band together, well, it seems nothing is impossible."

Phoebe noted quite a few worried stares from around the room, and she attempted to smile reassuringly.

"We have not much to move, should the need come, as we are still a small operation, and of course we do not utilize our own printing press — that connection is actually what hailed to our discovery. At any rate, our address is now known, and we do have some supplies, and of course copies of the paper itself and material for upcoming editions. I suggest we pack much of it away so that if we must, we can easily move it from the building until we find new premises to where we can relocate."

"Is the building not rented in your name, Miss Phoebe?" one writer asked, and Phoebe nodded.

"So your name is known then."

"I have been discreet, but yes, it is likely."

"We appreciate how much you are risking," said Rhoda, who knew more of Phoebe's identity, and likely suspected more regarding her relationship — or previous relationship — with Jeffrey than any of the others would, with the exception of Julia, who had come in as well when Phoebe had written to her of the urgency of their meeting this morning. Julia now eyed Phoebe with a crestfallen expression covering her face, and Phoebe knew that the romantic Julia was likely just as, if not more so, upset about Phoebe's loss of love than the potential loss of the newspaper.

"It's worth it," said Phoebe with emphasis, and she looked around the room at each writer. "Sometimes something bigger than yourself comes along, and you have the unique opportunity to be a part of it. It can be difficult to see this through the day-to-day tasks, but what we are doing could create change and affect the lives of so many women. Women who are in marriages in which they are beaten, who have no rights for themselves or for their children. Women who feel alone, hopeless, in whatever situation they find themselves in. Or women who simply need something to help them pass the time, to show them that this world is made for more than men."

She saw heads nodding, and her spirits began to rise slightly, knowing that her words were taking effect.

"All we can do — besides a little packing — is continue in our work, with the knowledge that our words are being read, understood, and discussed. I wish to thank each and every one of you for the work you do in making this not only the best women's periodical in England, but the best periodical of all."

The room broke out into a round of applause, and Phoebe smiled at them all, hoping her words rang true. Finally, sensing the mood had somewhat lifted, Phoebe returned to her office, needing to decide her own next course of action.

CHAPTER 29

*J*effrey stared moodily at the drink in front of him as he sat in his library, alone, in the near-dark. It had been a day since he had spoken with Phoebe, and he had not done much of anything. Oh, he had seen to his paperwork, he had met with his secretary, he had breakfasted with his family — who were filled with remarks about how he was compensating for his cheeriness by becoming even more surly than his usual self — and he had even taken a walk with Maxwell through the nearby park. But now he sat, brooding. Maxwell snoozed at his feet, twitching now and then as he let out sleepy barks, likely dreaming of chasing after birds and rabbits, Jeffrey thought with a rueful grin. If only life were as simple as that of a dog.

But, of course, it wasn't. No, life was filled with women you shouldn't want but did anyway, who surprised you at every turn. It was filled with responsibility that you never asked for, but that others would do anything to take from you. And it was filled with indecision, at least for him. On what was the right action to take, on whether he should follow his heart or his head. On the greater questions of life, such as whether or not society was based upon the correct foundation.

Phoebe Winters had upended his entire world — well, every part of his world that wasn't already chaotic. The aspects of which he thought he had entirely under control. Now … he wasn't so sure about anything.

There was a knock at the door and Jeffrey said nothing, hoping that if he were silent enough, whoever was desiring entrance would go away and he could remain deep within the soft leather of his mahogany chair. He was not so lucky, however, as the door slowly eased open, and Maxwell woke up and gave a traitorous cheerful yip of welcome.

"Shush," he said as he took another sip of his drink. Whiskey tonight. He needed something more than brandy, of which he was typically quite fond.

"Jeffrey?" came the soft voice, and he sighed. If there was one woman he could never turn away, no matter the circumstances, it was his mother.

"Come in," he said, attempting to hide his reluctance to invite her into his sanctuary for the evening. The library was shared amongst the family, of course, but, besides his study and his bedchamber, it was one room where he could usually be alone, or if not alone, in silence. Viola was often seated upon the chesterfield in the corner, but she always had a book in hand and let him be. They had a rather extensive library for a London townhouse, with floor-to-ceiling shelves that lined the walls, much like his office but in greater volume, and more throughout the room within recesses, all filled with various books from multiple eras, in many different genres. They had accumulated over the years, and it seemed that no Marquess of Berkley had felt the need to be rid of any of them, nor to substantially change anything about this house itself. It seemed aversion to change was a Berkley trait that had been passed down, and now lay in residence within his very own soul.

Lady Berkley softly padded into the room, taking a seat across from Jeffrey in a matching leather chair.

His mother was still beautiful, of course, and possessed a gentle soul. Yet, she had been strong enough to raise six children, and to continue to counsel them upon the death of her husband, a man she had loved with all of her heart — though with whom she hadn't always agreed.

She looked at Jeffrey now, with the deep love in her eyes that she held for all of her children, a look that told him she knew some of the pain he now held.

"Jeffrey, tell me what's happened."

It was a soft, silent command, yet a command it was. Jeffrey took another sip of his drink.

"Nothing, Mother," he said but attempted a smile, though he was concerned that perhaps it came out as more of a grimace. "Please, do not concern yourself. It is nothing I cannot determine how best to handle."

"Truly, Jeffrey?" she asked, her eyebrows raised. "I have never known you to shutter yourself away, to be so surly to your sisters and me. They may have jested with you, true, about your attitude at breakfast this morning, but that is not how I raised you. If something is wrong, you share it, so that we may help you with it. You do not take your anger out on the rest of us, Jeffrey. You can be silent and read your papers, I understand that. But when Rebecca asked you to pass the sugar, you made it seem as though she had asked you to travel across the world to get it for her!"

Jeffrey looked down at the drink in his hand, remorse filling him as his mother chastised him like a child, and he knew very well he deserved it.

"You are correct," he said finally, rolling the glass between his hands. "Something has happened. I fell in love with Lady

Phoebe Winters, but then I found out she is not the woman I had thought her to be. She was dishonest with me, hid her true self from me, took actions that I could not condone were she to become my wife — as I asked her to be. Yes," he said at his mother's look of surprise. "I asked her to marry me, and what did she do? She revealed herself to be a woman who I could never accept."

Lady Berkley held his stare for a few moments as she took in his words.

"And this ... revelation — did it come before or after she accepted your hand?"

"She told me that she would accept my proposal, but only if I still wanted her after what she told me."

"Well, that, I suppose, Jeffrey, is considered honesty," she said.

He reluctantly nodded, but continued.

"This was after weeks, Mother. Weeks in which I thought we were developing a relationship that was leading to something. However, she was using me. For nothing more than her damn paper!"

"Ah, I see," said Clarissa, not looking the least bit surprised, and Jeffrey eyed her warily.

"Do not tell me that you knew of her role as publisher of that rubbish!"

Jeffrey's mother stared at him calmly in response, not rising to his anger.

"I had my suspicions," she said with a lift of one shoulder. "I knew her opinions on matters such as those written, was aware that she would have the means to create such a publication, and I also knew her parents. They would have raised her to be a woman who would speak her mind, to not hide behind the trappings of what is expected of a young lady, and to believe life held more for her than what is typically expected of a woman. You may not want to hear this, Jeffrey, but I admire her. She is brave and doing what she feels is right. You do not necessarily have to agree with her, but you must understand where she is coming from."

His mother leaned forward now, and Jeffrey was taken aback at her passion for the subject, for his mother was most often fairly reserved in her opinions, allowing her children to express their own instead.

"Think of it from the other way, Jeffrey. Imagine if the roles were reversed, if men were relegated to the household, to marrying well and bearing and raising children."

He snorted at the idea, but she ignored him and continued.

"How would you feel about it? Would you feel stifled? Would you not want your voice to be heard?"

"You can hardly compare, Mother, for then I would not have been raised with the expectations that I currently hold."

"That is true," she conceded. "However, you did not know Phoebe's parents as I did. They raised her to be aware of her true potential, and now she is sharing that knowledge with other women, who are awakening to the possibilities that may be available to them. It is a powerful thing, Jeffrey, to learn the world may not necessarily be as stifling as one thought, to find a sense of freedom in knowledge. For that is what Phoebe is providing — knowledge."

She paused for a moment, then leaned forward and rested cool hands on his cheeks as she looked into his eyes.

"All I am asking, Jeffrey, is for you to consider my words, and then consider hers."

She stood and walked over to a corner cupboard. She opened the bottom doors, rummaged around a bit, and then, finding what she was looking for, she returned to him with a pile of newsprint in her hands and held the sheets out to him.

"Read these, Jeffrey," she said. "Not just the headlines, but truly read the articles. Do not think about how they might affect you, but of how you would react were you a woman. What would you think? How would you respond? And not only that, imagine if every other newspaper you read was only for those of the opposite gender, and finally, there is now something you feel comfortable reading. How would you feel?"

He reluctantly took the papers from her, and she lit another candle, bringing it over to him so that he would be better able to read, as his current near-burned candle was far too dim.

She began to walk to the door, but stopped and turned her head to look at him over her shoulder. "Oh, and Jeffrey?"

"Yes, Mother?"

"I simply want you to be happy. And from what I can tell, Lady Phoebe Winters certainly makes you so. It does not matter whether or not she would make the perfect marchioness. What matters is that she would be the perfect wife for you."

With a pointed look telling him that she expected no argument, she left as quietly as she came, leaving him alone with his newspapers, his drink, and his swirling emotions — or so he thought.

"Well, you certainly have a conundrum, do you not?"

"Ambrose!" Jeffrey shot up in his chair at his brother's voice, which came from the depths of the library. He stood, looking between the shelves, until he found him, leaning nonchalantly against one bookshelf up against the wall. Jeffrey squinted to make him out in the dim light, glaring at him and his smug expression. "How long have you been here, eavesdropping on my private conversation, observing me for whatever sick purposes you may have?"

"Long enough," said Ambrose, uncrossing his arms and advancing toward Jeffrey. "So, dear brother, you have a choice to make. Do you maintain your reputation as the perfect marquess, filled with honor and responsibility, or do you bend your wills for a woman, one who would be oh, so unsuitable, despite what Mother may think? And what would happen then, with Phoebe's little publication? Would you tell your friends, the Earl of Totnes, the Duke of Clarence, and all the others, of the true identity of the publisher — your betrothed? Oh, what a scandal it would make!"

"Yes," Jeffrey said, tight-lipped. "It certainly is, as you say, a conundrum. But," he made the decision that instant, one he had known deep inside but had not spoken aloud. "Whatever happens, I will not tell anything of Phoebe and her role with *The Women's Weekly*. It would be too great a betrayal, and whatever should happen between the two of us, I do not want to see her persecuted or hurt by any other."

"No? How very gallant of you," said Ambrose. "But what if someone else were to find out?"

"To whom would you be referring?" Jeffrey asked darkly, knowing full well what Ambrose was insinuating.

"Well, Jeffrey, I see you are taking far longer to make this decision than you have with any decision *I* have ever brought to you. So I suggest that you think much harder about what I have asked you. Just a pittance, really, for your own brother. And no, I have no plans to vacate to the country, nor to take up a commission. Me, in the military? Ha, it is laughable! Yes, Jeffrey, think hard on your next actions, I *implore* you."

He chuckled as he walked around Jeffrey and out the door, his laughter echoing along the corridor. Jeffrey stood with fists clenched tightly as he watched his brother's shadow depart.

CHAPTER 30

The expressions her friends wore were mostly filled with pity as they listened to Phoebe's tale. Julia already knew most of it, but Sarah and Elizabeth were just learning many of the details. Phoebe had finally joined them on what had once been their usual walk together, and she felt a pang in her chest when she noted just how surprised they were to see her.

It was difficult juggling so many priorities, but her friends were not one that should have been neglected.

The day was warm as spring was progressing, though Phoebe couldn't help the chill that had invaded and wouldn't seem to leave her, ever since Jeffrey's visit to *The Women's Weekly*. The grass was beginning to green, the trees were starting to leaf, but despite the beauty emerging all around her, Phoebe was having a difficult time seeing any positivity in the day. Today she had awoken just as she had the day before, wishing everything had simply been one of those terrible, utterly realistic dreams that plagued her when she was stressed by any type of situation.

"Oh, Phoebe, I'm ever so sorry," said Sarah in a sympathetic tone. "But maybe, just maybe, you can right it all, do you not think?"

"I am not sure," Elizabeth responded before Phoebe could say anything. She paused for a moment to smile at another group of ladies strolling past before continuing. "We knew from the beginning that a happy ending likely would not be the result of such a complex relationship, particularly with the unconventional role that you have played. I am sorry, Phoebe, that you lost your heart, truly I am, though, as harsh as it is for me to say it, I cannot say I am overly surprised."

Julia and Sarah turned to look at her incredulously, that she should speak so callously to their friend who was hurting, but Phoebe held up a hand to halt their defense of her, grateful though she was.

"Unfortunately, Elizabeth is right," she said, finally looking up from the ground to turn to Julia on her left, Elizabeth and Sarah on her right. They flanked her as though they were her guards, here to protect her from anything that may deem to harm her, and she hated that they would see her as such a fragile being at this moment. "When I began to attempt to charm Jeffrey, I never dreamed that it would become anything — why, I hardly believed he would even notice me, let alone lose his heart to me and mine to him. I was as shocked as any. However, as much as my heart aches at having lost him, I also feel a burden relieved from my shoulders at the fact the truth is now known to him."

They all nodded at that. The truth was always best, was it not?

"Will you speak to him again, do you think?" Julia asked. "What will you do if you see him at an event?"

Phoebe paused for a moment in contemplation, and they all slowed their steps along with her.

"Actually," she began, "I have decided that I must speak with him anyway."

"You will? Whatever will you say?" Sarah asked, her eyes wide.

"I must apologize," said Phoebe decisively. "No matter what feelings may have developed, no matter that I still believe he was misguided in believing that the paper should be discontinued, it *was* also wrong and dishonest of me to attempt to become close with him in order to determine his progress. I played with feelings — his own as well as mine, in the end — and I learned my lesson from it, I suppose. Only it was a most difficult lesson that I rather wish I had avoided."

"So you would prefer you not loved him at all?" Julia asked softly.

"I have no idea!" Phoebe cried. "I suppose it is too much to ask for love as well as the opportunity to have purpose, to do what I want with my life?"

"For a woman?" Elizabeth asked, an eyebrow raised. "Perhaps, yes it is. And for that reason, Phoebe, you are right for doing the work that you do, for attempting to change the world we live in. For if you were a man, the answer to that question would be entirely different."

They were all silent as they contemplated Elizabeth's words, and they continued walking along the Serpentine within the park, nodding at acquaintances they passed along the way.

"When are you going to speak to him?" Sarah asked.

"Tomorrow," Phoebe said morosely as she thought of the conversation to come. It would likely be their last and would be the slamming of the door upon what could have been, what would never be.

"And the paper?" Sarah asked.

Phoebe shrugged. "Nothing has happened as of yet. Perhaps Jeffrey has not said anything. Or mayhap he is biding his time. I am not entirely sure. We are prepared, however. If we must vacate our property quickly, we will. We do not believe there is any legal recourse that can be taken, but with the power of a noble name, anything is possible. We will, however, persist. I will not allow *The Women's Weekly* to cease operation simply because cowardly men feel that it might harm the way of their world."

"That's the spirit," Elizabeth said, attempting to smile at Phoebe, but it was a rather pained expression as they all knew the likely outcome of Phoebe's situation and the fact that, while she could fight, it would be a difficult battle.

Phoebe swallowed hard to avoid the tears that threatened, and her steps were heavy as she continued on in silence.

* * *

THE DAY after his mother provided him with her wisdom, as well as the stack of papers Viola had stashed away, Jeffrey slept through most of the morning, which was so unlike him that Lady Berkley sent his valet upstairs to determine if he was well.

He had, however, been awake until the early hours of the morning reading through *The Women's Weekly*. Only a few issues had been printed at this point in time, but he read each article carefully, then re-read it, then sat there, contemplating the words, his thoughts on the subject, and how the article may affect the women who read it, as his mother had suggested.

He could hear Phoebe's voice in many of the articles. Oh, not the ones on fashion or gossip, which of course would not interest her, but the editorials, the ones advocating for change, or describing society life — the words came as though she herself were speaking. Her intelligence shone through, her wit brought a smile to his face, and her propensity for determining the exact truth in every situation or opinion astonished him.

Now, he sat in his study, the papers lined up on the desk in front of him once more, as he tried to ascertain his own feelings toward them. Maxwell slept on the dog bed near his feet, completely oblivious to Jeffrey's melancholy, snoring as he lay on his back with all four legs up in the air.

"Jeffrey?"

A head poked in the doorway, and at his nod, Viola entered the room, sitting in front of his expansive mahogany desk. Maxwell merely snorted.

"I see you've been reading," she began, and he crooked a smile at her.

"How much did Mother tell you?"

"Not much," she said, then at his raised eyebrow, she reddened slightly. Viola could never tell a lie. "All right, she told me a bit of it when I couldn't find my recent paper. That you were reading them to determine if there is any truth to them besides what you read on the surface. And that you were now aware that Phoebe is the publisher of *The Women's Weekly*."

"You knew as well?" he asked, running a hand through his hair.

"Stop that, your hair is now standing straight up," she said with an admonishing frown, and he couldn't help but smile as she sounded like a nursemaid. Or a mother. "But yes, I had my suspicions. How could you not?"

"It seems I did not want to believe such a thing," he said wearily. "Though apparently everyone else who knew her was aware."

"We were not entirely sure," said Viola reassuringly. "However it seemed somewhat likely." She tilted her head and studied him. "It looks as though you have been reading."

"I have," he nodded, though said nothing more.

"And?" she asked.

"And what?"

"And what do you think now, Jeffrey?" she finished, rolling her eyes at him.

He smiled at how easy it was to rankle her, as it was with all his sisters. They were rather predictable that way. Unlike his brother, who was completely the opposite.

He leaned back in his chair now, contemplating his answer, for he knew how much importance it held — not only for Viola but for his own understanding, as it could determine the course of his very future.

"I believe," he began slowly, "That I possibly made some assumptions about *The Women's Weekly* and about Phoebe's own opinions that were, perhaps, not altogether true."

Viola's eyes brightened behind her spectacles, but all she said was, "How so?"

"I had thought that Phoebe wanted to create great change, to upend our current society, to cause chaos," he continued reflectively. "But her articles seem to state that, in fact, what she believes is that women should have a voice, should be able to express themselves and have a forum where they can feel comfortable, in both finding items to read that intrigue them, while also opening their minds to other possibilities. That does make sense to me. There was also something Mother said — about imagining what it might be like to have both your opinions and your potential stifled. It is a difficult thing to conjecture, having been raised with every door open to you, but I suppose I would feel completely closed in."

"She does propose changes to some of the acts, to providing women more freedoms, more choice," Viola pointed out, and Jeffrey was aware that his sister was ensuring he was completely aware of the full implications of the potential choice he might make.

"Yes, I realize that," he nodded. "I cannot lie and say I agree with every one of her articles or opinions, 'tis true. And yet, there are some which I do understand. If women had

231

more power to look over their own marriage contracts, for example, that could make quite a difference, would it not? And I agree with her that there should be a law in place to protect a woman from a man who would put her in harm's way, though how one would ever determine the guilty party in such a matter, I have no idea."

Viola tilted her head, a slow smile beginning to spread on her face. "So tell me, Jeffrey, what will you do? Will you go to her? Make amends?"

He frowned.

"Despite the fact that I better understand many of her principles, that does not change the fact that she was completely dishonest with me, that she used me for her own purposes, made me into a fool."

He drummed his fingertips absently on the top of the desk, and Viola leaned forward and placed her own hand atop them to still his movements.

"Do you not understand why she had to do such a thing when you were of a completely different opinion but hours ago?"

He stared down at the desk, at Viola's gentle hand, and closed his eyes and sighed. He did not want to give in, did not want to admit any errors in his own ways, but perhaps Viola did have a point.

"What is pride worth?" she persisted. "More than losing the love of your life?"

He passed his hand over his eyes as he couldn't help but chuckle ruefully at Viola's words, that she displayed such maturity and grace, and she smiled back at him with pleasure as she patted his hand.

"That's the spirit. Now, what are you going to do about reporting on this wicked publisher you so determinedly tracked down? For you have some men who will be waiting to hear what you have to say, and you must be prepared."

"I suppose I shall just say that I could not find her."

Viola snorted. "That is a terrible lie and they will never believe it. No, you must say that you tracked her down, but she evaded your grasp. That you found their place of work, but she got away."

"That is certainly not believable either — that I let a woman and an entire building escape me?"

"It will if you are convincing, and if you concoct a story that is believable — and you must help ensure that no one will ever find her. How did you determine the address of the publication?"

"I visited the print shop, asked the proprietor to deliver a message to the publisher, and then followed the messenger."

"You see?" Viola said with a pointed look. "You must work backward to help Phoebe hide her tracks from any other."

He nodded absently and was about to reach for pen and paper in order to contact Phoebe, but the door flew open and Rebecca burst in, her long blonde hair billowing behind her in her rush to find him. She slammed the door dramatically, ensuring it was closed before continuing her breakneck pace, then came to a halt at Jeffrey's desk, splaying her hands over its top. Her eyes were wide as she looked at first Jeffrey and then Viola. She hardly noticed Maxwell as he attempted to jump up into her arms.

"Jeffrey," she said, her breaths coming in quick gasps, as though she had run through the entire house to find him — and it was very well likely she had. "I've just overheard something completely wicked."

"Oh?"

"Ambrose was speaking with his valet, and, oh Jeffrey, he is going to bring down Phoebe's entire publication! Not only will it be destroyed, but she will be completely ruined as he is going to expose her secret to the world!"

"Calm down," he said, rising and bringing his hands to his sister's shoulders, as he looked her in the eyes with as measured a gaze as he could manage. "Start at the beginning and tell me what you heard, when and where you heard it, and then we will determine our next steps from there."

She nodded, beginning to catch her breath, and Viola tugged at her hands to encourage her to take a seat next to her.

"Very well," Rebecca said, her words still coming quickly as she finally sat, though her hands continued to wring together worriedly.

"I was passing by Ambrose's chambers, for as you know, his rooms are next to mine. I heard voices, and a few words caught my ear."

Viola gave her a look out of the corner of her eye, and Rebecca rolled her eyes. "Fine, I eavesdropped on purpose. Are you happy now, Vi? Ambrose is always up to some adventure or another, and I wanted to hear the latest. So anyway, my ear was to the keyhole of the door, and I heard Ambrose saying he was going to do something that would prove to you, Jeffrey, the fallacy of attempting to control him, of not supporting him in his own endeavors. He told his valet that Phoebe was the publisher of *The Women's Weekly* — as we all guessed, Vi — but that you, Jeffrey, were not going to do a thing about it as ... well, perhaps I shouldn't repeat exactly what he said, but something to do with you being fairly besotted with Phoebe. Anyway, he said he had a plan to take her down himself. That he was going to gather Totnes and all the rest of them who wish to see the paper destroyed, and go down to the office and take everything they had, destroy the building, and then report the names of every woman they found working there."

"He would do all of that — ruin the lives of all of these women — in order to make *me* angry?" was the question

Jeffrey first asked, ire simmering within his belly. He knew his brother was completely self-centered, but why take this action against the woman he loved, to women who would have no effect upon him?

And that was the very 'why,' he realized. Ambrose had no care for others — just look at the scheme he became a part of, which preyed upon those with little to their name. He had determined, rightly so, that it would hurt Jeffrey far more to see someone he cared for ruined than to take revenge on him directly. Rebecca affirmed his suspicions.

"He said that this is what you deserve, for supporting a woman more than you would one of your own family members. He said that now you will see what happens when you cross him."

Jeffrey lowered his forehead into his hand, rubbing at his temples.

"My God," he muttered. "Did he say when he proposed to take action?"

"He will put everything in motion the next time you speak to the gentlemen, when you compose a lie. He said he would then out you, providing his proof. He said it will cause you to look a fool to all — as you always make him out to be. His words, not mine."

"So we at the very least have the ability to set the time ourselves," he mused.

Jeffrey rose from the desk, paced back and forth behind it, and then finally rounded its corner, and picked his sister up in a huge hug, one she seemed completely unaccustomed to as she let out a yelp of surprise. Maxwell jumped up from his slumber and began barking excitedly as he seemed to think they were beginning to play some kind of fun game.

"Thank you, Rebecca," he said, placing her feet back on the floor and then lifting Viola and doing the same to her. "And you as well, Viola. Not only for your words today, but for your presence in my life to keep me from the stuffy, boring marquess that I could have been, who would never have known how to see past his own prejudices and learn that, perhaps, there are other opinions out there worth listening to. Now," he left the two of them where they were standing, gaping at him, as he grabbed his cloak and began walking out of the study, "I have much to do within a few hours. And please, ladies, do not allow Ambrose to know you've spoken to me of this. Thank you again."

And, without another word, he left.

CHAPTER 31

Phoebe stared at the note in her hand. She had dressed so carefully that morning, prepared to go speak with Jeffrey, perhaps for the last time. And then the note had arrived. The paper was crinkled, as she had read it multiple times already, far too many to be acceptable. It was rather sad, was she being honest. What he could want with her now, she had no idea, but she had a feeling it couldn't be anything good, now could it? She allowed no hope to enter her heart, for she could no longer take the disappointment that would crash down on her when she would, no doubt, be utterly wrong.

She placed the note on the desktop before her, smoothing down the crinkled edges. She looked up and around at the office that she thought of as partly still her father's, partly now her own, and sighed deeply. She was an independent woman, true, and she prided herself on that fact, but there were times, such as in this very moment, she longed to speak with her parents, to know what they would advise her to do.

She looked back down in front of her.

. . .

PHOEBE,

I would ask you to meet with me in two days' time. I will collect you at two o'clock in the afternoon.

Jeffrey

THAT WAS IT. Short, to the point, yet written in his hand, so it was not as though he had dictated it. There were no words of undying love. Not even a "Yours, Jeffrey."

What could he possibly want? Was he taking her into the authorities, to turn her in as the publisher? But of course not. For she had done nothing illegal, nothing wrong, despite how many would likely feel otherwise. Phoebe took a breath to calm her trembling hands. Should she go ahead and do his bidding?

Well, she supposed she had wanted to see him anyway, to apologize. But she had been looking forward to doing it today, to be done with it so she could move on with her life, if she could. She would try her utmost, anyway.

She reached for a piece of paper and her pen, to return his note before she could talk herself out of it. She was a strong woman, she told herself, and she was not going to allow heartbreak to change that, to make her weak or indecisive. And, despite the fact that they both knew she was capable of writing much more eloquently, she allowed herself a slight moment of pettiness as she responded to him in much the same vein as his original note. She thought about addressing it to The Marquess of Berkley, but perhaps that was going a bit too far.

JEFFREY,

I will see you at two o'clock on Wednesday.

Phoebe

* * *

THE NEXT TWO days were both the longest and the shortest of Jeffrey's life. He spent them concerned about whether or not he could succeed in both winning Phoebe's hand as well as keeping her from the persecution of his brother, the Earl of Totnes, and the many others in the nobility wishing for her downfall — a group that he himself had been a part of not long ago. If only he could convince them of some of what he had come to realize himself — that just as two parties coexisted among Parliament, so too, perhaps, could the differing ideas of those who agreed with Phoebe's beliefs and those who opposed them.

He had become accustomed to seeing her regularly, and the time without her presence stretched interminably. He considered what his life would be like should she choose a path without him, and it seemed infinitely bleak and desolate without her in it. Even now when he considered his life before she had entered it, it seemed devoid of the vitality he had come to know, created by her smile and her wit, which had invaded his soul and captured his heart.

It had, however, been a busy few days. He had much to accomplish in order to ensure that all was in order, but, with a little help from his faithful and efficient secretary, he had completed all by his self-imposed deadline.

Now his carriage drew up to Phoebe's home, and he twisted his hands together in his lap, determined not to show any bit of nerves once he was in her company. He disembarked and was halfway up the walk toward the door when she stepped outside, her maid following. Ah, so she had decided this would be a formal visit, with a proper chaperone today.

He wasn't sure how to greet her, but she solved the problem for him.

"Jeffrey," she said with a nod as she drew close, and his heart ached with the need to reach out and take her in his arms. For her face was drawn, her cheeks pinched, and that full bottom lip that constantly beckoned to him was currently being nibbled on by her own teeth.

But instead, he simply returned her nod and extended his arm.

"You look lovely," he said as they walked to the carriage, and it was true that her gown, peeking out beneath her billowing navy cloak, was a scarlet red that perfectly suited her complexion, and nothing could hide the sultry green of her eyes, nor how striking her face was. He would bring vibrancy back into it very soon, he promised himself, and as much as he wished to tell her what awaited her, to do so would ruin everything.

"Thank you," she said, and as she stepped into the carriage, she finally showed some emotion when she noticed Maxwell was waiting for her, his tail wagging excitedly. She took his face in her hands and gave him a quick kiss on the nose as she took a seat in the carriage, her maid settling in up top with the driver. When they were finally alone — save the dog — she looked at Jeffrey pointedly, slightly unnerving him. Jeffrey sat across from her, his legs outstretched, though she quite clearly moved as far from him as possible so that there was no risk of them accidentally touching. Phoebe sat with her hands fisted together in her lap, her posture so straight that even the strictest mother of the *ton* would approve. Her face was stoic, no emotion playing over it, and he desperately wished to know of what she was thinking.

"Where are we going?" she asked bluntly.

He smiled. She always did get to her point as quickly as possible.

"You will find out soon," he promised, and she narrowed her eyes.

"I would like to know if I should be concerned about our destination."

But of course. She was worried that he had collected her in order to bring about the demise of *The Women's Weekly*. It rankled at him that she would suspect such actions of him, that she did not understand that his feelings for her were strong enough to overcome whatever else may have once been a concern.

"Do you truly think so little of me?" he asked, looking up at her from across the carriage, leaning forward toward her with his elbows on his thighs.

"Why would I think otherwise?" she asked, one fine eyebrow arched high. "It was your intention from when we first met, was it not? And all else aside, *you* have been nothing but honest with me."

She paused for a moment, her gaze on the floor as though she were deep in contemplation. "Jeffrey—"

But he held out a hand. He didn't want her to say anymore to him, not until they reached their destination and he unveiled what was within.

"Bear with me for another moment," he said. "Then we can have a candid discussion. All right?"

She nodded and then lapsed into silence, and for the next few minutes, the only sound to be heard was the clopping of the horses' hooves and the rattle of the carriage wheels on the cobblestones beneath them.

* * *

SHE WAS BEHAVING LIKE A LACKWIT. Why could she not demand that he tell her where he was taking her, and why could she not force out the words of apology? It should be an easy conversation. Then he could simply turn around and take her home, and all would be forgotten. Or so she hoped.

It was torture sitting here across from him. She only had to move ever so slightly and their legs would rest against one another. Or if she leaned forward toward him, she could reach out a hand and touch him. She closed her eyes for a moment as even the thought of twining her fingers within his sent warmth running through her. Oh, how she missed him. She hadn't wanted to admit it, not even to herself. But if she couldn't go two days without him, how was she to survive the rest of her life?

Perhaps she shouldn't have come to this meeting after all. For then she wouldn't have to go through this pain again of being so close and yet so far. She tried to calm herself by petting the dog, who was content to lie on the seat next to her, his head upon her lap. Thank goodness he was here to somewhat quiet her nerves.

She was jolted out of her reveries as the carriage began to cross a bridge, and she peered out the window at the Thames below, surprised to find that they were in Lambeth — what were they doing in this neighborhood of London? It wasn't far from her own offices, true, but what purpose would Jeffrey have to bring her here? When she looked at him, her eyes wide in question, he simply smiled and motioned her out of the carriage.

She stepped out, finding nothing in front of her but a nondescript building. It looked as though it would be fairly large inside, and Jeffrey held out an arm to her, a gleam in his eye and a smile on his lips as she reluctantly took it, still silent. It was on the tip of her tongue to ask where they were and what they were doing here, but she knew he wouldn't answer her question and she would find out soon enough. At the very least, she doubted he would be looking at her with such satisfaction if he were going to do something nefarious, would he?

Phoebe looked back and told Nancy she could remain

with the carriage if she'd like — the day was warm, and Nancy looked as though she was enjoying herself with Jeffrey's driver, as they were currently in the midst of an animated conversation. It was not as though Jeffrey was going to seduce her in the middle of what looked to be an abandoned warehouse, and besides, it was certainly too late for him to ruin her, was it not? Nancy smiled and nodded, and Phoebe turned to follow Jeffrey with some trepidation.

Jeffrey called to Maxwell to stay, but the dog had other ideas and was soon happily trotting along behind them.

The buildings to the right and left were warehouses of various sorts. One looked to be a furniture manufacturer, and her suspicions were solidified by the sounds of men constructing within. The other side looked to be some kind of clothing manufacturer, and the building they were walking into was completely devoid of any clues as to what it might hold within. It was built of red brick, with a simple arched window in the front, offering a glimpse of nothing but darkness beyond.

Jeffrey procured a key from his pocket to open the door, and Phoebe looked up at him questioningly.

"Do you own this building?" she asked, to which he simply smiled but said nothing in confirmation. "Oh, you are maddening," she muttered, and he chuckled slightly under his breath as he pulled open the door and ushered her in.

The front foyer was open but sparse, with exposed brick walls and a plain hearth in one corner, with nothing else of which to speak occupying the room. There was a small corridor at the end, and Jeffrey ushered her down toward it and through, then bypassed the doors to the left and right and opened the door at the end of the hallway.

"You are not meaning to kidnap me and keep me in this building as your captive, are you?" she asked, becoming more curious by the minute.

"That was not my plan, but now you have given me an idea," he said with a wicked grin, and she couldn't help the reluctant smile that played on her lips at that. He pushed open the door, and she stepped in, squinting in the dim light, trying to determine what lay before her. Her eyes were beginning to adjust to the darkness when she heard the scratching of Maxwell's nails and the echo of Jeffrey's boots on the floorboards behind her, and soon he was pulling back curtains to allow light into the room. She gasped when the sun flooded in, dust particles swirling in the air in front of her, but not distracting her from what lay before her.

"A press," she whispered almost reverently, and she turned to Jeffrey, who was grinning broadly now, his hands behind his back as he watched her reaction.

"Your Mrs. Ellis told me upon my first visit to *The Women's Weekly* that you had everything you needed for your paper but a printing press," he said. "Well, now you have one."

She could only gape at him in astonishment as she walked forward, running her hand along the machine. It was by no means new and had obviously done some work in its time, but it would do an admirable job, and was, apparently, hers — if she chose to accept it.

It was the most thoughtful gift he could have ever chosen for her. While most women would enjoy jewels or ballgowns in the latest style, for Phoebe, this meant more than any finery ever could.

"But …" she turned to him, confusion coursing through her, "Why?"

"That's something of a long story," he said, taking a hesitant step toward. "But first I must know — would you accept it? And in doing so, would you accept me?"

CHAPTER 32

*P*hoebe stared at him in shock, overwhelmed by not only his gift but his words. Accept him? After all that had occurred?

"But Jeffrey," she started, lifting a hand but then dropping it, unsure of what she meant to do, or even say. "After everything that happened, all I did — you still want me?"

"Phoebe," he crossed the room to her, knelt in front of her, clearly oblivious to the dust and debris that had settled on the floor beneath his knees, his fine black breeches now covered in their dirt. "I was taken aback at your confession, I must admit. And were I the same man that I was the night we first met in the drawing room at the Earl of Torrington's home … well, I would certainly have had a different reaction. But since I met you, since I spent time with you, I have come to know who you truly are, and in doing so, I understand much more of the way you see life, of the roles we all play. You may have lied, 'tis true, but I now understand why you did so, and never did you stray from the woman you purport yourself to be."

He paused for a moment.

"I will also admit that I had some help in seeing the error of my ways. I am blessed to have women in my life who are never fearful of sharing their infinite wisdom with me. I was upset with your dishonesty, truly I was, although I am beginning to understand why you chose to keep such truths from me. But more than anything, Phoebe, I have come to realize that I cannot spend my life without you. You are everything I need in a woman, though I never knew it until recently. You are strong, independent, determined, brave, and will have no qualms in ever telling me exactly what I need to hear. I do not know how I lived without you, and I would ask that you not force me to attempt to do so ever again."

Phoebe didn't realize there were tears falling down her face until she saw one drop onto Jeffrey's hand where he clasped hers, and she tore off her gloves as, at that moment, she needed to feel his warm hands upon hers. She intertwined their fingers then, and sank down to the floor with him, forgetting completely about the dust below.

"Jeffrey," she said leaning in toward him, looking him in his dark brown eyes that were no longer hard, but warm and caring, just like the man himself. "I didn't think I could spend another moment with you, knowing how torturous it would be to leave you again. But I had to meet with you in order to apologize, and before we go any further, you must allow me to do so. For you were right. I did use you, at least at first. But then I found myself falling completely in love with you, and I had no idea what course of action to take. I tried to tell you the truth, again and again, but it seemed my every attempt was thwarted, either by the presence of another or … distraction." She colored slightly at that, and he grinned as he seemed to understand exactly of what she meant.

"I can do nothing to fix that wrong but apologize. And yes, of *course*, I will have you. I will have you and your amazing family and your wonderful dog," who was currently sniffing around at her feet, wondering what the two of them could possibly be doing, she was sure. "You have already proven that you know me better than likely anyone else, though there was no need for you to go to such extremes to prove what you feel for me."

"Actually," his face darkened slightly, "There is more need than you know. But come, we will speak of that in the carriage. Your beautiful dress is likely ruined by now."

"Nothing that a good washing will not fix," she said, though she allowed him to help her to her feet.

She leaned into him now, wrapping her arms around his neck.

"I love you, Jeffrey, and I will spend the rest of my life showing you just how much," she said softly.

"I will hold you to that," he said with a laugh, and then caught her mouth with his. He pressed a warm, firm kiss on her lips before drawing back slightly. "And I love you, Phoebe, more than you could ever imagine."

He kissed her once more, this time harder, more insistent, and she all but melted into him, her pulse racing at the thought that she would have this, have him, for the rest of her life. She had never thought it would be possible, but now that it was, that he accepted her for all she was, her heart seemed as though it might burst with joy.

And as for the paper ... well, there was still one more obstacle between them, she supposed. She pulled back slightly as the thought dipped into her mind, reminding her of what had caused the distance between them to start.

"What of the publication?" she asked, and he wrapped an arm around her waist, leading her out the door.

"Come," he responded, and Maxwell seemed to believe the command was to him, as he quit sniffing around the corners and loped toward them, following them out the door. "I will tell you all."

* * *

JEFFREY WISHED he could take this moment to bask in celebration of the fact that the woman he loved was going to be his wife, had accepted him after all they had been through, over what had seemed completely impossible. But this was life, and life had a way of interrupting even the happiest of moments. And so, first, they had to determine how to best face the adversity that remained. He outlined all that had occurred as succinctly as possible.

"So your brother now wishes to put an end to *The Women's Weekly*," she murmured in response from her place in the carriage — on the seat beside him this time, where she belonged, though Maxwell looked at them slightly forlornly from the seat across from them.

Jeffrey nodded. "Yes, although Ambrose is only choosing to do so in order to take revenge on me. It has nothing to do with you."

"It does now," she said, grasping his hand tighter. "For many reasons. It is my paper, and if he is coming after you, then I take that as an affront to both of us."

His chest swelled at her words, at the fact that she now saw the two of them as one.

"I myself would have faced the dilemma anyway of what to say to all those who would continue to question me as to the progress of my task of determining how to cease your publication," he said gravely, "Though it would have become much simpler without Ambrose involved, who has far more knowledge than we would like. I have a plan, however, one that should hopefully protect you."

"What changed your mind?" she said suddenly, breaking through his thoughts as she turned toward him. "I realize that your mother and sisters played a part, but why did you eventually decide that the paper should continue — as I am hoping, from your words, you no longer have the urge to strike it down?"

Jeffrey nodded slowly, understanding her question.

"I must tell you, Phoebe, that I will never exactly become a subscriber to *The Women's Weekly*," he said with a bit of a laugh. "However, I had the opportunity to read the thing — actually read it, from cover to cover. And after a few conversations of my own, I began to attempt to place myself in the role of a woman reading it, and I can certainly see its appeal."

She snorted somewhat at the thought of him as a woman, but he simply raised an eyebrow and continued.

"I also cannot say that I completely agree with every argument presented within its pages — particularly the editorials by 'a Lady.' Though I have found that she makes a great deal of sense, is eloquent, witty, and presents issues in a method that is extremely difficult to argue against them. At any rate, I no longer believe that its publication will bring complete discord to our society. But that brings me to the reason for the press. And the location we found ourselves in."

She nodded, and he leaned forward.

"Oh, Jeffrey," she said, breaking into his soliloquy, and running her soft, cool hands over what he knew were sure to be the lines on his face. His sisters were forever telling him that he needed to smile more, or he would continue to age at a far more rapid pace than would be desirable.

And he knew then, at that moment, that he now had what — or, rather, who — he needed in order to keep him young, to keep him much more happier, carefree, and understanding, than he would ever be alone, or should he have chosen a wife for anything other than love.

"You place far too much of a burden on yourself," she continued, and he smiled, knowing her words to be true, and that she was beginning to know him better than most others.

"Such is the way of a man with four sisters, the responsibility of multiple estates, and a conniving brother who knows nothing of responsibility himself," he responded. "Which is why it has proven fortunate that I find a woman who can look after herself, though I am unsure why such a thought never previously occurred to me."

"Oh, is that the only reason you wanted me?" she asked with a laugh, and he shook his head slowly.

"I must confess, there was far more than that," he said, no longer laughing himself as he gave in to the thoughts and desires consuming him and wrapped an arm around her. He tugged her toward him so that she was flush against him, and he leaned down to kiss her. Just a taste, he told himself, and then it was on with business.

But his body, it seemed, had something else in mind, and Phoebe certainly did not seem to have any issue with it. He kissed her hard and fast, drinking in the woman he had feared he had lost forever. She tasted so sweet, like tea and pastries, he thought, though there was an edge to her that he had never before experienced with any other women. It was desire, he realized. She wanted him as much as he did her, and that drove him crazy with his longing for her.

The carriage came to an abrupt halt, and he pulled back dazedly from Phoebe to see that they had returned to her house.

"Is your aunt home?" he asked, his mind in a fog.

"No, I believe she was going out visiting this afternoon," Phoebe responded, and Jeffrey let out a breath in an attempt to slow his racing heart, to quench the fire raging through him.

"Perhaps we should disembark and walk," he said, his fingers tapping mercilessly on the seat beside him, knowing the only way he would be able to resist making love to her this very moment was to be somewhere public, somewhere he would not have a choice in the matter.

For his stubborn will was slowly seeping away from him. This woman had the power that no one else seemed to possess — the power to make him forget all, to throw away caution, and to allow himself to live.

She looked at him now with some incredulity and simply held out her hand.

"Come."

He took it.

CHAPTER 33

$\mathcal{P}$hoebe led him into her house, asking Nancy to bring tea to the drawing room.

Nancy was quick, and the moment she had delivered it, Phoebe dismissed her, telling her that she and the marquess had some pressing matters to discuss, and they were not to be disturbed until Phoebe called for her. Whether Nancy understood the undertones of the conversation or not, Phoebe wasn't sure, and Nancy didn't seem to care.

"I suppose she will likely be outside flirting with your driver anyway," Phoebe murmured, but then her thoughts of Nancy and the driver fled as Jeffrey stepped up behind her. His body came flush against her back, and he bent his face to her neck as his fingers began to trail up her arms. She shivered, though she was far from cold, and his lips kissed the sensitive skin above her shoulder. She arched back against him, reveling in the fact that this man was hers, that he accepted her for all she was and all she did. There were no secrets now, nothing between them — except, perhaps, a few too many layers of clothes.

"Come," she said again, this time in near a whisper. She

opened the door of the drawing room, taking his hand and leading him down the corridor to her own chamber. She pushed the door open, the crimson and cream room greeting them, and she saw Jeffrey pause momentarily to take in the cascading curtains, the writing table, and the bed, where his focus remained.

"And just where has the redecorating occurred?"

Phoebe flushed and turned to face him as she bit her lip at his question.

"We may have used the redecorating excuse as a ruse to explain my busyness," she said, looking up at him quickly, hoping he wouldn't be upset at what had been another lie, although it was connected to the first and had actually been Elizabeth's quick thinking and not her own.

He shook his head at her as he hid the grin that seemed to be teasing his lips, and Phoebe realized that he had never believed the fib.

She now took both of his hands in hers, looking up at him with a smile, but he intercepted her.

"Should we wait to make love again until after we are married?" he asked, but his voice was gruff, husky, his throat filled with uncontained lust — for her. It made her quiver with anticipation to feel him against her, inside her, once more.

"Perhaps we should," she responded, keeping her face a mask, and he nodded, though his was in turmoil.

She gave him but one more moment of suffering before she began to laugh at his agony and he looked at her, perplexed.

"I'm sorry, that was evil of me. Perhaps..." she said, her smile fading as she leaned into him once more, "We should live in the moment and succumb to what both of us are currently longing for very, very much."

She wrapped her arms around his neck then, and he

groaned before leaning over her, taking her mouth with his. It was a kiss of desperation, true, but there was more to it. It was also a kiss of promise, one that solidified the love they had spoken to one another, as the pent-up desire and emotion flowed between them.

In one fluid motion, Jeffrey swooped down, a strong arm coming underneath her knees as he lifted her up and carried her to the bed. He laid her down upon it gently, and for a moment she wondered where his passion had gone as he stilled. But then she looked up at him and saw it pooled in his eyes, which were sharper than ever before.

"This time," he murmured, "I am going to do this right."

"Was it so wrong the last time?" she asked, arching an eyebrow.

"I wouldn't exactly say there was anything wrong with it — in fact, it was *very* right, for that particular moment," he confessed, and a lock of his blond hair fell over his brow. "However, today, you will feel *loved*, Phoebe Winters, soon-to-be Worthington."

He began by raining tender kisses over her face, before repeating the featherlight kisses she loved so much over her neck. He began to inch down the bodice of her dress, his touch driving her mad as he reached behind her and began to unfasten the buttons down the back of her gown. Fortunately it was a simple day dress, not anything complex that would cause him any sort of vexation. He had the dress down around her waist in moments, and with the ease of a magician, he had soon banished it to the floor. He began to work on her undergarments next, and her body tingled with anticipation. When he finally had her lying naked before him, however, Phoebe — who never in her life could recall being shy — had the sudden urge to cover herself. What would he think of her? Before, she had not fully undressed, but today—

"You," he said, his voice even deeper than it had been before, "are incredibly beautiful."

She felt a flush covering her body, then, beginning in her cheeks and racing down to her toes, from more than just the fact she was lying here exposed to him.

"Your turn," she said cheekily, and he grinned and acquiesced. She sat up then, undoing the buttons of his jacket, his waistcoat, and eventually practically ripping off his cravat.

"And they say women wear far too many layers," she grumbled, and he chuckled.

"This is no laughing matter," she muttered as she dispensed with her attempts to unbutton his shirt, leaving it to him as she went to work at the fall of his breeches, satisfaction filling her once she finally freed him.

"Well done, love," he said, before descending upon her once more, scarcely giving her time to take her own fill of him. What she saw, however, made her nearly pant breathlessly. For he was divine. He was all hard muscle, his well-defined chest covered with the slightest sprinkling of blond hair, his torso sculpted all the way down to where the muscles descended into a vee. If she hadn't known better, she would have wondered how it would be possible for the two of them to fit together.

But her mind cleared of everything except the sensations coursing through her when his hard, hot body came flush against hers, and she moved restlessly against him. He found her lips with his, while his hands held her head, divesting her hair of the pins that had kept the chignon on top. Soon she could feel her hair flowing loosely around her shoulders, as she had come to learn was exactly how he liked it.

His hands seemed to be everywhere at once — in her hair, then skimming down her arms, the gooseflesh rising behind where he touched her. He was slow and gentle, as much as she yearned for him to simply take her, to have her right then and there. This was torture, she thought with a gasp as he circled her nipples with his thumbs, and by the look on his face, it seemed that he felt as she did. So why, oh why, was he not releasing her from this madness, allowing them both to find fulfillment? He bent his head then, his tongue coming so lightly to her breast, circling it, and she cried out his name.

"Jeffrey, will you just ... oh, my—"

She had no words as he continued to do delicious, torturous things with his tongue, to first one breast and then the other. His hands began to find their way lower, until they were on her hips, which jerked up toward him in response. He slid his fingers down her legs to her knees, and then ever so slowly they began to find their way back up to the silk of her.

Having had quite enough of this, Phoebe decided she would show him just exactly what he was doing to her. She placed her hands on his own chest, feeling coarse hair underneath her skin, before running them down over the fine, supple muscle of his torso. She kneaded insistently as she went lower still, and just when she had found the vee below his waist that she was so admiring earlier, she wrapped her arms around him, bringing them to his backside and digging in as she pulled him toward her.

"Phoebe," he gasped. "Do not ... you are—"

"What? Torturing you?" She asked wickedly, and he closed his eyes tightly and nodded. She laughed then, and before he even realized what she was doing, she flipped herself up, throwing a leg over him so that now she was on top and in control.

"Phoebe, what are you—"

"Hush," she said, bringing a finger to his lips. "We are doing this my way now."

"You do understand that my intention was to delicately

make love to you," he said dryly, and she laughed, shaking her head.

"Well, you will be sorely disappointed then," she said in a low voice, leaning down to nip at his bottom lip, and he let out another groan.

She wasn't altogether sure what she was doing but knew only what she needed at this moment, and that was him.

Phoebe lifted herself up, and, with his hands on her hips helping to guide her, she slid down on top of him, then experimentally began to move back and forth. Oh, this was beyond words, she thought as she threw her head back as the pleasure filled her. Jeffrey guided her back and forth, and when she looked down at him, she saw the mix of pain and pleasure on his face that equally filled her entire body.

She leaned forward over him, her body now finding the pace that was as natural as anything had ever come to her before, and soon she was near sobbing in anticipation of what was to come. His hands rose once more to her breasts, and the moment he began to tease her nipples, pleasure began to course through her in waves, an inexplicable exhilaration that she could not put into words.

Jeffrey gave a shout himself, and soon was pulsing into her, her release allowing him to find his own.

When they both finished, Phoebe collapsed down upon him, spent as well as filled with a joy she had never known possible. For unlike the last time, now she knew that this was not just a moment in time between the two of them, but rather the beginning of a life to come together. She could still hardly believe it, and wanted to check with him once more that this — she — was what he truly wanted, and yet she knew it was true, knew that he was the man for her, just as she was the women for him.

"Have I told you how much I love you?" he murmured into her hair.

"A couple of times," she said, "though I do not believe I should tire of hearing it."

"I love you, Phoebe," he said. "And while I could spend all day in this bed making love to you, I have been distracted for far too long. There are a few ... urgent matters that we must discuss. Your future — our future — could depend upon it."

"Well, that sounds awfully grave," she said, sitting up now, and when he nodded, she was shocked at the serious expression that had once more covered his face. All she wanted to do was lean over, take his perfectly clean-shaven face in her hands, and kiss those strong, grimacing lips. She would kiss away his frowns, smooth the lines that covered his face, soothe away his worries. All she vowed to do for the rest of their days together. But first, he clearly had something on his mind, and she knew better than to continue to distract him from his purpose. So instead of doing as she wished, she clumsily slid off him, off the bed, and began to pick up their garments.

Finding that her dress was even dirtier than she would have thought, she crossed over to her wardrobe, searching through to find something appropriate. She chose a violet dress that was fairly similar to the red and turned around to find Jeffrey pulling his shirt over his head.

"Do you fancy the role of lady's maid this afternoon?" she asked, and when his face was visible again, he nodded.

"I promise to do my very best, my lady," he said, "though I confess I can do nothing with your hair. I am much more adept at taking apart, so it seems."

"So you are," she said wryly, donning her chemise and then lifting her gown overhead, turning around toward him. "I'm ready."

Even the brush of his fingertips against her back set her nerves on edge once more, but apparently there were things to discuss. Once the two of them were each dressed — to an extent — she led him back out the door into the drawing room, where the tea had grown cold, though the pastries remained, beckoning to them.

"So," Phoebe said, taking a seat on one of the settees. "What was it that you had to tell me?"

CHAPTER 34

*J*effrey sighed, wishing he could forget all else and simply take this woman back to bed, where he would continue to ravish her, showing her how much he loved her. Or even take her home and share the news with his family that the two of them were to be wed. How happy his mother would be, and he could already imagine his sisters' glee at the thought of a wedding. But first, there were more serious matters to which they must attend.

"You are aware that I set out to learn more about *The Women's Weekly* not completely on my own terms, but due to the urging of other noblemen," he began, leaning back against the settee. He had to sit across from her, or else he would be tempted to forget all that he wanted to speak to her about once more.

She nodded, and he continued.

"I am, obviously, not going to tell them of your identity, nor have I had any thoughts to do so in some time. It was going to be easy enough to tell them that you could not be found, though it would require you moving out of your current building."

"Hence the building you bought?" she asked, raising an eyebrow.

"Partially, yes," he said. "Though matters have become somewhat … complicated by the fact that my brother, Ambrose, is aware that you are the publisher of said publication. Ambrose holds a vendetta against me for not supporting him in his rather nefarious, questionable schemes, and now he feels he can find justice by not only making me out to be a liar but by discrediting the woman I love."

"I see," she said, looking off into the distance, and he could practically see her mind working as she chewed her bottom lip.

"He means to follow me to the club, and feels he has proof that can establish that I am not all that I seem," he said. "But I will demonstrate that this is not at all the case."

"And how do you plan to do that?" she asked.

"First," he said, leaning forward, "It will now require quite a bit of work on your part. It is partially why I purchased the printing press. For there can be no ties back to you. I found your printer, Phoebe, and unfortunately it did not take much to follow up on that lead. As it was, I was rather … preoccupied in courting you and therefore was no longer hunting you, or I would have found you even sooner. If someone else much more determined takes on the crusade, then you must be untraceable."

She held up a hand, and he stopped for a moment.

"Yes?"

"While I was aware that you were no longer persecuting us, as it were, are you telling me that you have no issue with me — as your wife — continuing on publishing such a paper?"

He reached across the table and took her hands in his.

"Phoebe, I have come to learn that part of what makes you the person you are, the woman I fell in love with, is the purpose and the passion that you hold. If I were to take that away from you, you would only grow to resent me, would you not?"

She looked down at the ground and then back up at him.

"While I would like to deny it, I suppose this is somewhat true. Of course I would still love you, but I would resent the fact that it was all taken away from me, yes. There is another issue, however. We are making money now, but much of the paper is still dependent upon my inheritance, the money that I bring into it. And I am the sole owner. If — when — we marry, that will all become yours."

He nodded slowly, warm at the thought she would trust him with all that was hers, and yet at the same time aware of what it would mean for her to give it all over to him.

"When we marry, Phoebe, what's mine is yours and yours is mine. If it would make you feel better, however, we can make a small adjustment to the marriage contract so that you may retain some of the funds in your own name — and the publication."

She smiled at him then, one of great thanks, and it warmed his heart.

"I suppose there will be much of these negotiations to come," she said, chewing that bottom lip again, and he nodded. "But if we do so with only the thought of one another, then I'm sure all will work out fine."

He leaned forward, kissing her ever so gently on the lips, before settling back on the settee.

"Now, for discrediting my brother," he continued. "I know just how to do so."

* * *

JEFFREY STRODE into White's the next day, confident in his plan, though a slight bit of nerves coursed through him. For if he should fail— but he would not. That was not an option, not now that he had finally accomplished nearly all for which he had been searching for so long.

"Berkley!"

A table full of gentlemen greeted him as he strode in. He could read the speculation in their gazes, with the exception of one — Clarence. Instead the Duke leaned back with a smirk on his face as he watched Jeffrey, as though he were eager to learn what Jeffrey would have to say to the lot of them.

Jeffrey nodded to them his greetings before ordering himself his usual brandy and settling into a chair at the corner of the table.

"Well?" Lord Totnes asked, his face already ruddy from too much drink, despite the fact that it was still early in the afternoon. "Have you finally anything to report, Berkley, or are you still finding other matters much more important?"

Ignoring Totnes for a moment, out of the corner of his eye, Jeffrey was not at all surprised to see Ambrose slip through the door, and it was concerning when his surprise at seeing Jeffrey was completely convincing.

"Ah, brother!" he said, taking a seat next to him. "I did not expect to see you here, for you so scarcely visit these days, now that you have found yourself a woman."

Jeffrey turned to him with eyebrows raised.

"I do not recall you being a frequent visitor to White's."

Their father, who had always had a soft spot for Ambrose while foisting all of the duty and responsibility on Jeffrey, had, before he passed, secured a membership for his younger son, though Ambrose far preferred less reputable establishments.

"Well, one cannot argue with the quality of their whiskey," Ambrose said with a wide grin.

"'Tis true," Jeffrey replied, though he wondered at how Ambrose could afford such spirits when he was constantly practically begging Jeffrey for money.

"Berkley!" Totnes barked again, determined not to be ignored, and Jeffrey finally turned to him with an exaggerated sigh so that the man was aware of exactly what he thought of his summons.

"Did you have a question for me, Totnes?" He asked sardonically as he took a sip of his drink.

"You know very well I do, Berkley," Totnes said, leaning forward across the table and pointing a finger at him.

"If you think you can simply point a finger at me like that, Totnes, and I will obey your commands, then I will tell you just what, exactly, you can do with that finger."

Totnes turned even redder, were it possible, but he sat back in his chair and crossed his arms over his chest, mumbling to himself as he did so.

"What Totnes was so rudely attempting to ask," Lord Torrington said, "is whether or not you have made any progress in determining the publisher of this women's magazine that you so disdain, so as to bring about its demise."

Jeffrey heard Ambrose snort slightly behind him, and he paused a moment to glare at his brother.

"As a matter of fact," he began slowly, knowing that he needed to play the role required of him if he was going to sell this properly. He took a sip of his drink nonchalantly, as though what he had to say was of not much consequence, "I did find the building where the publication was located."

"That would not be altogether difficult," said Totnes. "I imagine you just had to ask around. It can hardly be a secret."

"It was fairly simple," Jeffrey agreed. "I visited the building — on Fleet Street — and was met by the editor. She advised me that the publisher was not in the building, and I should come back in two days' time."

"Very well," Torrington said, "And then?"

"And then I returned, and they had all vanished."

"What?" came the chorus of voices from around the table, all shocked at his words.

"All had vanished," Totnes repeated. "You cannot be serious. Do you mean the people?"

"The writers, the editors, their files, hell, even their pencils — it was all gone. Cleared out."

"Just like that?" thundered Totnes. "Did you continue the search?"

"Of course I did," Jeffrey said, holding his nose high in the air with all of the noble status he could muster. "But they have completely disappeared."

"So you have failed," Totnes said with a sniff, looking as though he wanted say more but, at the last moment, he refrained from doing so. "Very well. If that is your response, we will assign someone else to the task."

"An excellent idea, Lord Totnes," Ambrose finally chimed in, and Jeffrey smiled. He had been waiting for his brother to speak. Ambrose continued. "I am afraid my dear brother here has become slightly … prejudiced."

"Prejudiced?" Torrington cut in. "In what way?"

"Well," Ambrose said, relishing this moment, and he sat up, breathed in, and puffed his chest out as far as he was able. He looked around the room to ensure he had the full attention of all. "The publisher of *The Women's Weekly* is none other than … the woman Jeffrey is courting."

There was a pause for a moment as the heads of each man at the table swiveled around to him, unsure of how to react. Jeffrey waited for a beat before he burst out into laughter. The moment his guffaw began to echo around the room, Clarence joined in, and soon the remainder of the men added in their chuckles, though none were quite as exuberant as Jeffrey, for Ambrose was still looking particularly determined for them to believe his words.

"It's true! Lady Phoebe Winters. She is the publisher, and she is running *The Women's Weekly*. Jeffrey has fallen in love with her, and she has softened him to the extent that he thinks nothing of allowing such a wretched publication to continue."

"Are you serious, Ambrose?" Jeffrey finally asked, his merriment now containing itself, as he noticed Totnes still looked somewhat skeptical. "You think that *Lady Phoebe* — a lady, interested in a fine marriage to a marquess — would risk her entire future by taking up such an endeavor? And besides that, do you believe that I would make such a woman my marchioness?"

"Now I do," said Ambrose accusingly, "For that is exactly the path you have chosen."

"Oh, Ambrose, I really wish we wouldn't do this here, in front of everyone."

"Do what?" Ambrose asked, his eyes narrowing.

"Allowing all to know of our family matters — of your wish to bring about my disgrace, in hopes that you would then no longer be off to see to your own estate. I am aware your greatest dream is to be rid of me so that you yourself could become marquess."

"Though I would have to kill you in order to do so," Ambrose answered wryly, giving Jeffrey pause for a moment, until he smiled.

"Well, if anything should happen to me, we now have a roomful of witnesses who can speak of your intentions."

He chuckled as though it were all a joke, though his body was tense. Is this truly how his brother felt about him? He knew they were not on the best of terms, but this was going rather far, was it not? This was the one part of his plan that truly bothered him — though he would have to deal with his relationship with his brother following this encounter.

Jeffrey noticed Ambrose had begun to perspire slightly as he gave a tight-lipped nod. "Perhaps we best speak in private," he finally agreed, and Jeffrey now waved him away.

"Ah, no, we've started this now, and the men are interested to learn of the ending, are you not?" he asked them all, and the men nodded. Of course they were interested. Even the nearby footman was looking on with rapt attention.

There was a pause for a moment and Jeffrey waited, as everything rested on what happened next.

"To add an opinion from outside of the Worthington family," Clarence finally said from the corner, as nonchalant as ever. "Lady Phoebe could hardly be running a newspaper with her frequent social engagements."

"I hardly ever see her at a party," retorted Totnes, clearly much more inclined to believe Ambrose's words.

The Duke shrugged. "She's not much for those events, I'm told. But she spends a great deal of time with her closest friends. They walk daily, take tea together. I have become rather acquainted with their social calendar as I have taken an interest in one of Lady Phoebe's closest companions, though I shouldn't like to name her until we have determined the seriousness of our relationship."

"Oh?"

Jeffrey wasn't sure who asked the question. This was new gossip, and not only did it have the desired effect of providing credence to Phoebe's innocence of what they accused her of, but it also distracted the men. Jeffrey would have laughed if had been in private — or with Phoebe. For clearly the men were as interested in the gossip of the day as the readers of *The Women's Weekly*.

"Yes," the Duke said as though his words were of no

consequence. "She would have known if such a lady was running something like a newspaper."

Jeffrey nodded and sighed as though his next piece of news irked him slightly. "And it seems that my mother and sisters have taken a great liking to the paper. At first, of course, this greatly vexed me. However, now I am finding that when the five of them are occupied in reading of the latest fashions and gossip as written about within this publication, they are far less likely to disturb me while I read my morning news at the breakfast table. And that is something which I am not perturbed about in the slightest."

The Earl of Totnes stood now, though his gait was slightly unsteady as he walked around the table. "So you believe that we should allow this publication to stand because you like to drink your coffee in peace?"

"It's not just coffee," said Jeffrey. "Has there not been a time when you wish the women in your life left you alone?"

Totnes stopped for a moment to consider that, and while it took a few moments for Jeffrey's words to seep into his alcohol-laden brain, after a time his angry countenance changed into one that showed promise of being agreeable.

"So there are a few editorials of women voicing their opinions," Clarence said, and Jeffrey could have leaned across the table and kissed his friend for not only complying with his wishes, but going far beyond. "What does it matter? It is not as though they can actually *do* anything about it. As long as men maintain their power within parliament — and they always will — the women have what they have always had, simply their words. Just this time it's on paper. I say, gentlemen, that we waste no more of our efforts on this fruitless pursuit and leave the women to do as they please. Do you agree?"

There were some murmurings around the table as the men both argued and conversed amongst themselves until finally a few "ayes" came forward, and Jeffrey had to work to maintain his composure.

Mutterings reached him, primarily from Totnes and Torrington, of course, but this was the power of a duke such as Clarence — his opinion mattered more than most, and when he spoke, people listened.

"This is ridiculous!" Ambrose burst out from his end of the table, and Clarence turned, ever so slowly, to look at him with all of his ducal authority etched into his face. He raised an eyebrow at Ambrose, as though challenging him to continue his line of thought. Ambrose, unfortunately, was not quite as perceptive as he should have been, for words continued to spew forth. "You are all taking the word of a man besotted! Come, should we not, at the very least, pay a visit to this establishment to determine just whether or not my brother is a liar?"

There was a pause, as they all waited for Jeffrey's response to his brother's challenge.

"Go ahead," he said with a flippant wave of his hand. "I'm done with this business. Go, Ambrose, do as you please."

Ambrose nodded and stood, looking around to determine if any would follow, and finally Totnes began to totter after him, beckoning Torrington to accompany him.

Once the three of them had departed, Jeffrey breathed deeply, knowing they would find nothing, that this was finally near to over. As the others began to move onto other matters, Jeffrey found a seat next to his friend.

"Thank you, Clarence," Jeffrey said in a low voice, and Clarence shrugged, as though it weren't that much issue.

"I never much liked Totnes," he said, throwing back his drink. "It was a good excuse to get under his skin, if nothing else."

He laughed then, and Jeffrey felt fortunate that he was a

friend of the Duke's, for he would not want to be on his bad side.

"And I must say," Clarence continued, in a much lower voice now as he looked around to ensure the rest of the men were no longer listening. "You have found yourself quite a woman. I always thought I preferred a woman I could control, but now I am wondering if perhaps it might be more fun to find a woman with something more to her than a giggle and a smile."

Jeffrey simply raised his glass to Clarence in a toast, as he sat back with some satisfaction and now contemplated what the future might now hold.

CHAPTER 35

*P*hoebe filled the printing press with ink and checked that the paper was feeding correctly before she pulled the handle and set it to work once again. As the machine began to press the letters into the paper, she marveled once more at its capabilities. It was one thing to provide your copy to a printer and pick up the papers once they were prepared. It was quite another to watch the magic happen in front of your own eyes.

The door — closed to prevent as much noise as possible from reaching the writers — creaked open behind her, and Phoebe turned to find Rhoda had entered the room.

"You shouldn't have to worry about this now," Rhoda admonished her, though she wore a smile as she did so. "You have much more pressing matters at hand."

"Is something amiss?" Phoebe asked, turning to Rhoda now, worried.

"No," Rhoda said with a laugh, "But I believe your mother-in-law and your aunt await you at Madame Boudreau's."

"Oh no, I'm late!" Phoebe exclaimed and raced to the

door, but not before turning back to Rhoda. "You will look after the printing today?"

"Of course!" Rhoda said, shooing her hands toward the door. "Now go!"

Phoebe found her bonnet and raced out the door, though she was but halfway down the street when she remembered that Nancy was within, and realized that she was much too far to walk. Nancy had accompanied her today for the visit to the modiste's and the carriage was awaiting them down the street, so as to not draw attention to their location.

"Damn," Phoebe said, returned, and then encouraged the driver to hurry to the shop.

Phoebe raced in the door, out of breath when she arrived, but Jeffrey's mother either didn't notice or didn't much care. Today was the final fitting of Phoebe's dress. The wedding would take place in just a few days, this very Saturday. Jeffrey had felt it best not to wait overly long, to which Phoebe certainly agreed. Of course, there had been much to work out, what with the marriage contract as well as the entire situation with Ambrose, but somehow, it had all gone according to plan.

Phoebe was both shocked and pleased to walk in the door and find not only Aunt Aurelia and Jeffrey's mother, but also his four sisters and her three closest friends. Madame Boudreau bustled around them all with a long-practiced efficiency, and Phoebe was not quite sure how to express her thankfulness to have such women in her life.

"I cannot believe you are all here!" she exclaimed.

"Oh, we wouldn't miss it," said Sarah with a smile.

"Besides, we have to make sure you do not find out Jeffrey's true personality and leave him before you are married!" Rebecca exclaimed, and Phoebe didn't miss the elbow Viola nudged into her side. Phoebe simply laughed.

"Fortunately I believe I have come to know all sides of

him and will marry him anyway," she quipped, and Lady Berkley wore a look of such happiness that Phoebe nearly started crying at that moment. Goodness, when had she become such an emotional mess? She hurriedly found Madame Boudreau in order to try on the dress before she showed too much emotion before the lot of them.

And when she came out and turned in front of them, the lengths of cream satin swirling around her, the jewels on the dress glittering in the light, she could only hope that Jeffrey would feel as impressed as these ladies did, judging by the looks on their faces. She grinned at them all, wondering how she had ever gotten so lucky.

* * *

One week later
   St. George's, Hanover Square

PHOEBE BREATHED DEEPLY as she waited in the vestibule at the back of St. George's. People filled the pews before her, most of them faces she had seen in passing but didn't actually know well at all. They had all come to see the Marquess of Berkley marry a woman they had hardly heard of at all until recently — Lady Phoebe Winters. She had no real connections, hardly any family to speak of, and, to most, was as much of a mystery as the identity of the publisher of *The Women's Weekly.*

Two lives, she mused, and yet they were one and the same as far as Jeffrey was concerned, and he was all that mattered.

He was right down the aisle, she knew, and yet he was too far for her to see him, and so instead she focused for a moment on the stained glass, under which she knew he would be standing. Despite all the people filling the pews ahead of her and the man who waited for her at the end of the aisle, Phoebe had never felt quite so alone. She looked up above her to the rafters of the church, to the windows emitting daylight at the very top, and closed her eyes as she felt her parents' presence beside her, imagined her father was with her, holding onto her arm. Suddenly her arm was lifted, interlocked with another, and Phoebe's eyes flew open to find Aurelia beside her.

"Aunt Aurelia!" she exclaimed. "I thought you would be at the front of the church, in the very best seat."

"Well, I could not allow you to walk all that way alone now, could I? Particularly in all those layers of fabric. What if you tripped?"

She smiled gently and squeezed Phoebe's arm softly.

"Your parents would be ever so proud of you," she said. "You are marrying a handsome marquess, true, but what they would really be thankful for is the fact that you are marrying for love, and that this man will make you happy for the rest of your days."

"Yes," Phoebe said softly. "Yes, he will. Thank you, Aunt Aurelia, for everything."

"That's not necessary. I love you as my own, and always will," Aurelia responded, tears forming in her eyes, though she hastily blinked them away. "Now, we best get moving or else they'll all think you've jilted him."

And with that, she urged Phoebe forward, and they began the long walk to the altar. There were quite a few murmurings, of course, that Phoebe was escorted by her aunt, but she cared not at all. This was her life, and her wedding, and what mattered was the man standing at the end of this journey. Jeffrey was as handsome as ever, tall, broad, and imposing, his blond hair swept back immaculately from his hard, chiseled face. But then his eyes found Phoebe's as she neared, and his entire countenance softened, his lips curling upward ever so slightly, his eyes becoming a lighter shade, less harsh as love filled them. And when a lock fell out of his perfectly coiffed hair and onto his forehead, any nerves which remained left her and she returned his grin. For she knew the man that so many didn't — the man who was willing to accept her for who she was, for what her passions were, who overlooked her own many faults and loved her anyway.

Phoebe kissed Aunt Aurelia on the cheek and stepped up to stand next to the man who was to become her husband. She looked up at him, leaned in close, and whispered for his ears alone, "I love you."

* * *

WHILE THE CHURCH had been filled, the wedding breakfast was, thank goodness, simply for their families and closest friends. Jeffrey's London home had been outrageously decorated, the doing of his mothers and sisters.

"Was all this really necessary?" he asked them as they arrived home, and a piece of long pink fabric nearly fell on him from where it was draped above them over the balcony.

"Of course it is, Jeffrey," Penny said indignantly from where she awaited them, practically bouncing on the toes of her pink kid slippers. Jeffrey's sisters certainly had a taste for pink, Phoebe thought as she looked around her at the floral arrangements covering the entryway and the staircase. She could hardly imagine what the interior rooms must look like.

Though secretly, she thought, as they rounded the corner of the stairwell and entered the drawing room, she would guess that they simply did it to irk Jeffrey. His sisters loved annoying him, and Phoebe found it particularly entertaining, though she would never tell him so.

Jeffrey's mother, who had entered but moments before them, sailed over to greet them. She took Phoebe's hands in hers and kissed her cheeks. "Welcome home," she said, a tear sliding down her face, and Phoebe squeezed her hands in response.

She leaned in and whispered in Lady Berkley's ear, "I will ensure he is happy — I promise."

Which only, of course, led to more tears, and Jeffrey looked at Phoebe with something akin to horror. "Perhaps we best get on with this breakfast," he said, attempting to steer her away from his mother and toward the table, but Clarissa stilled him by placing a hand on his arm.

"Oh, Jeffrey, you were never one for tears," she said, taking Jeffrey's offered handkerchief. "You would think you would be used to it by now."

The moment was broken, however, when loud barking flowed into the room from the corridor outside, and Jeffrey looked around at all of the perfectly placed decorations, at the flower arrangements in their crystal vases. "No, no, no," he called out. "Maxwell! Stay—"

But Maxwell's keeper — none other than Annie, who ran in behind the dog — had lost all control, and Maxwell happily bounded into the room, nearly knocking Jeffrey over with uninhibited exuberance.

"How long has it been since you have seen him?" Phoebe asked as Maxwell turned his attention toward her, covering her face with a lick of his huge, wet tongue.

"Since before I left for the wedding," he said, shaking his head as he handed her what must have been a second hand-kerchief. Apparently he had anticipated a need for them today.

She laughed then, following her husband — goodness, it felt odd to say such a thing — into the dining room, where the table was piled high with every type of confection that one could possibly dream of, and where her new family and closest friends awaited.

It was not, of course, the type of wedding breakfast one might expect at the home of the marquess. In fact, Jeffrey told her, it was reminiscent of most of the breakfasts held at this house.

"This will likely be a change for you," he mused, and she nodded.

"That would be an understatement," she agreed. "Typically my company every morning is a stack of papers."

"Mine as well," he said, turning to her with a bit of surprise. "Though my reading is continually interrupted by never-ending questions and comments meant to drive me mad."

"Ah, so you are aware they do it on purpose."

"Of course they do," he grunted. "But I keep up the pretense, for I do not want to spoil their fun."

When she laughed, Jeffrey ruefully smiled before turning his warm eyes to his family around the table, though his gaze slightly hardened when it alighted on Ambrose.

"Did we have to invite him?" he asked Phoebe, and she nodded. She had, in fact, told Jeffrey in no uncertain terms that he absolutely must invite his brother to his wedding or he would never forgive himself in the future.

"I know he has acted absolutely appallingly, and I understand your reluctance," she had said, "But he is your brother, and one day you would look back and be upset that this would have only increased the divide between you."

"Fine," he had finally relented. "But after this, he is off to his country estate. The man must learn some responsibility, some decency."

To that, Phoebe agreed. After the scene at White's a few short weeks ago, Jeffrey had continued on to Phoebe's townhouse, where he related the entire incident, including the fact that Ambrose didn't return to White's, nor did Totnes. Torrington, however, was enough of a man to report back to all of them, somewhat sheepishly, that it was, in fact, as Jeffrey had said. The building was empty, with hardly a thing left in it to prove that anyone had even occupied it in the past month.

"I know you are still concerned that some may come after you," Jeffrey had told her, to which she nodded. She supposed part of her always would be. "But maintain your anonymity, and all will be well. And Phoebe," he had continued. "I am not asking you to keep your name from others because I am ashamed of you. I want you to know that. I would simply like you to be able to maintain your way of life as well do what you are driven to do."

Phoebe had nodded, understanding. Part of her longed to be able to show her face, to be proud of what she was doing, to attach her name to the publication that was a part of her now. But she understood Jeffrey's reluctance, and he had done so much for her, made so many compromises, that the very least she could do was to keep the name of Berkley from any disrepute. So she would continue in her current capacity, doing what made her happy, with the full support of the man she loved beside her.

CHAPTER 36

The wedding breakfast passed quickly, cheerfully, and afterward, while she knew Jeffrey was itching to begin the wedding night, despite it being the middle of the afternoon, she found her friends, leading them into the drawing room for a moment alone.

"Oh, Phoebe, I can hardly believe this is your home now," Sarah said, sighing at the romanticism of it all as she flounced onto the settee, her skirts billowing out around her. Julia nodded in agreement, placing a hand on Phoebe's arm and squeezing it gently.

"You have always been determined, Phoebe Winters — or should I say Worthington. I am so very proud of you and all that you have accomplished."

Elizabeth sat down next to Sarah, shaking her head in wonderment.

"I never thought it was possible, Phoebe, and I am sorry for it. I suppose I underestimated both you and Lord Berkley," she said.

"I can understand your feelings, Elizabeth. And you are correct. I myself underestimated Jeffrey from the very

279

moment I met him, so I can hardly blame anyone else for doing the same," Phoebe said from her seat on the corner chair. "And I thank you for always being honest with me. If nothing else, you are a moral compass that we are all fortunate to have as part of our lives."

"That is a very kind way of telling me that I am a pessimistic busybody who should keep her nose out of others' business," said Elizabeth with a sigh, but the rest of them quickly assured her that she was being far too harsh on herself.

"And, oh, Phoebe, the wedding was ever so beautiful," Sarah continued, and as her friends continued their chatter, Phoebe was silent for a moment as she took in all that surrounded her. She was fortunate to have friends like these, and she was determined that despite now being married, she would always make them a priority.

"What of Aurelia?" Elizabeth asked. "Will she move with you?"

"No," Phoebe shook her head. "We asked her if she would like to, but she said she would prefer to be on her own, so she will maintain the house. I believe she rather enjoys her independence and her ability to come and go as she pleases. Which is why she made such a terrible chaperone, although the perfect one for me. She will likely accompany us when we return to Jeffrey's country home for the summer, but here in London she will retain her own residence."

"That is actually lovely," said Julia, "For then your parents' home will remain within your family."

"It will," Phoebe said softly. "I do not think I could ever let it go."

"Nor must you," Elizabeth agreed, and Phoebe smiled, so glad she had women in her life who completely understood her.

* * *

"Have they finally gone?"

"Who, all of my loved ones?"

"Yes," Jeffrey said, as he stood beside his wife at the entrance to their home, where they waved at the departing carriages. "Now if I could only get rid of my own loved ones so easily."

Maxwell clearly understood his words, for he was soon standing at attention at his master's side.

"Oh, Maxwell," said Phoebe, dropping down beside the dog, oblivious to the fact that her satin skirts were all over the floor and Maxwell had no qualms about stepping upon them. "I hope you do not mind that I will now be monopolizing much of your master's time. However, you should be pleased as now you have a mistress as well."

"You do not truly believe he can understand you, do you?"

"To an extent, I suppose he likely can," Phoebe retorted. "Where does he sleep?"

"Originally he was supposed to sleep in the stables behind the house," Jeffrey began, already inwardly sighing at his lack of control over the damn dog. Or his family. Or his wife. "But he spent all night crying at the door, so we allowed him inside, where he was supposed to remain on a dog bed in the drawing room. But then…"

"He sleeps in your bed, doesn't he."

"He does."

Phoebe began to laugh at his vexation, and Jeffrey couldn't help but smile along with her.

"Well, Maxwell, you are going to have to move over tonight," she said, patting his head as she stood.

"I believe, wife," Jeffrey said dryly, "Maxwell will have to remain on the floor."

"Oh?" Phoebe said as he drew her in closer. "And why would that be?"

"Because I have plans for you involving the bed."

He brought his head down, intending to kiss her, to show her a sample of what was to come, when footsteps began to descend the stairs, and he stepped back from her reluctantly.

"The next order of business is to marry off my sisters," he muttered, causing Phoebe to laugh.

But it was not any of Jeffrey's sisters, nor his mother, nor a servant. Phoebe's laughter subsided somewhat as Ambrose came down the stairs, his valet behind him, laden with trunks in each arm. Phoebe's smile faded slightly as Ambrose came to a halt in front of them, looking at each of them in turn with hostility in his gaze.

"Well," he said finally. "I will be away, then, which I'm sure you will be pleased about, Jeffrey."

"I never wanted it to come to this," Jeffrey responded, his face hard. "But I do wish you the best of luck. I know if you set your mind to it, you will be successful."

"Well, there will be nothing else with which to occupy my time, will there now, in the middle of Peterborough?" Ambrose asked with sarcasm, and Phoebe stepped forward, surprise crossing Ambrose's face as she took his hands in hers.

"Be happy, Ambrose," she said, and he apparently had no response for that as he simply nodded curtly at her.

"I have said my goodbyes to the others," he said in a clipped tone as he turned toward the door, his valet following. "Farewell to the two of you."

Phoebe leaned her head on Jeffrey's shoulder as they watched him walk away.

"I do hope he comes to learn that you only wanted what was best for him," she said.

"Perhaps," Jeffrey replied. "Perhaps not."

The butler was about to close the door behind Ambrose when a boy came running up the walk. "Miss Phoebe? Miss Phoebe, is that you?"

Phoebe waved the boy in the door, and the butler closed it firmly behind him, some consternation on his face as he looked down at the street urchin.

"Why, Ned," she said, surprised at his presence. "Whatever are you doing here? How did you find me?"

The boy caught his breath. "One of the servants at your old house told me where you lived now." Before Phoebe could ask how the resourceful boy knew of her previous address, he pulled two sheets of folded, crumpled, partially stained pieces of paper from inside his jacket. "Miss Collette has two versions of her column for the paper, and she was worried about including a couple of pieces. Mrs. Ellis, who just returned from your wedding, told her not to bother you, that she would see to it, but Miss Collette asked me to deliver them to you anyway, and so—"

Phoebe nodded curtly, taking the two pieces of paper from him, reading them over with a quick scan.

"This one," she said, handing one page back to him. "We keep the suggestive pieces out, including only what can be proven."

"Miss Collette said—"

"She wanted my opinion, now she has it. Thank you for coming to see me, Ned, and it was industrious of you to find me here."

"In-dust…"

"You were very quick-witted."

"Ah," his face brightened. "Thank you, Miss Phoebe. Good day, and good day, sir!"

Jeffrey lifted a hand in response as the boy flew out the door as fast as he'd come. The butler shut the door behind him, and at Jeffrey's nod, continued down the hallway, out of the room.

Jeffrey paused for a moment. "I do not believe street urchins at our door help much with anonymity. But I must say, Phoebe, it seems we are alone, if you can believe it. Allow me to escort you to the bedchamber, where I will—"

"Jeffrey!"

Phoebe felt him tense, and when she looked up at him, his eyes were closed tightly, as though by shutting them he would block any sights or sounds that attempted to interrupt them. But his efforts, of course, were wasted, as Penny and Annie rounded the corner, chasing one another, curls and satins flying as they came to a sudden stop in front of them. It was Annie who stopped first, and Penny ran into the back of her so hard that she fell down on her backside.

"Jeffrey, I know that today was your wedding, but tonight there is a ball at Georgia's parents' house, and I so want to go, and I do not see any reason why I cannot, as it is a simple house party, and while Penny says that I am too young, I do not see why I cannot—"

"Annie," Jeffrey said, holding up a hand to stop the flow of words. "You can go to any ball or party you like — after your come out."

"But—"

"Do not argue, not now," he said with exasperation, and Penny stood up with her nose high in the air and a huge smile of glee directed at her sister. They continued on their way out of the room, Annie pouting as she left, shooting a glare at Jeffrey before she walked through the door.

"Are you sure you are prepared for all of this?" Jeffrey asked Phoebe, who knew her eyes must be wide.

"It is too late to decide anything else, is it not?" Phoebe asked, laughing, and Jeffrey smiled with some chagrin.

"You are correct — I have trapped you now," he said, and

Phoebe squealed in surprise when he reached down and picked her up. "Now, I will have no more interruptions. Come, wife, up to the bedchamber we go."

Maxwell barked in glee.

"Not you, Maxwell!" Jeffrey exclaimed, but the dog followed them up the stairs.

"I am far too heavy to carry," Phoebe protested, but Jeffrey shook his head.

"That is utter nonsense," he scoffed. "And if you continue that line of thinking, I shall believe that you do not feel me strong enough, which would be a quite the affront to my manhood."

She snorted. "That is ridiculous. A man is not defined by—"

He silenced her with a look. "I have come around to your line of thinking in many ways, Phoebe, but in this, you will not argue with me."

She raised an eyebrow at him, but when she opened her mouth to do just that, he silenced her by pausing in the upstairs corridor and bringing his lips down on hers, and she entirely forgot what it was she was going to protest.

In the background, Phoebe heard a slight peep from who she assumed was a startled housemaid, as she was sure that Jeffrey's sisters would have a lot more to say about such a sight in their hallway.

Jeffrey, however, no longer seemed to care as to who might be nearby or what any might think, as he used his boot to push open the bedroom door. Despite the fact that Phoebe had spent a great deal in the house over the past few weeks as they planned this wedding, this was the first time she had ever been in his bedchamber. It was masculine, of course, the walls navy and forest green, the brick of an impressive fireplace covering one wall, the fire just embers as they were not, of course, expected to be in the bedchamber in the middle of the afternoon.

Phoebe, however, did not require any additional warmth, as Jeffrey was soon covering her body with his own, and he was becoming even more adept at releasing her hair from its pins, though she had left half of it flowing down her back for their wedding, as she knew he loved it so. For the first time, he slowly, gently, undressed her, and she relaxed into it, not hurrying anything. She yearned for him, for his body upon hers, as much as she ever had before, and yet perhaps because now they knew for certain that it was not the last time they would be together, but the first of a lifetime as one, that they took the time to explore, to revel, to enjoy.

And when they came together, it was as magical as it had ever been, and Phoebe had to close her eyes at the bliss that filled her.

"I love you, Phoebe," Jeffrey whispered in her ear as she lay her head upon his chest afterward, her hand splayed upon his glorious abdomen muscles. He brushed a hand over her hair, then twined his fingers into her loose curls.

"And I love you too, Jeff—"

But her words were cut short by a knock at the door, to which Maxwell, who had been snoozing on the carpet in front of the bed, began to bark ferociously.

"Jeffrey?" It was his mother this time. "Are you in there? We cannot locate you, nor Phoebe, and we were wondering—"

He groaned aloud and raised an arm over his eyes.

"Coming, Mother!" he called out, and then placed a kiss on Phoebe's forehead. "Shall we resume this later?" he asked.

"We shall," she said with a nod and a laugh, and reluctantly they disengaged, with one last, quick kiss — knowing there were many more to come.

EPILOGUE

THREE MONTHS LATER

"*J*effrey?" Phoebe ran into the house in search of her husband. She had written what she hoped was a brilliant piece, and she could hardly wait for him to read it. Unfortunately, she did not immediately find him, though she did happen upon each of Jeffrey's sisters, as well as his mother, and therefore it was a good hour before she reached the library, where, she knew, she should have begun her quest.

"There you are," she said, exhausted now from not only her work with *The Women's Weekly*, but her quick ride home, her dash through the house, and dutifully listening to and agreeing with the plights of three of Jeffrey's four sisters.

Maxwell now bounded about her gleefully, and she knelt beside him to acknowledge his affections.

"Thank you, Maxwell," she said as he left a large, sloppy kiss on her cheek. "You do know how to make a woman feel loved."

"And I do not?" Jeffrey asked, rising from his desk with a wink.

"You do fairly well," she said, cocking her head as she looked at him, "though you could learn some enthusiasm from your dog."

He shook his head as he laughed ruefully, then kissed her cheek and stepped back, holding onto her shoulders.

"You look … excited," he acknowledged and she nodded, waving him back toward his desk.

"I wrote something," she said, sitting down across from him, Maxwell laying his giant head in her lap.

"It must be quite something," he remarked, "for you write every day, and yet I don't believe you have ever seemed so interested in sharing."

"Oh, just listen," she said, and then she began to read the piece that would be featured in next week's edition.

A woman finds herself in an interesting position. She is expected to marry well, to bear children, and to care for her home. All my life I never understood this. I thought it was not enough, that it did not give a woman true purpose. And so I sought to make a difference. I determined my passion. And with means I was fortunate enough to have been provided, I created an outlet in which I could share my thoughts with the world.

I still believe that women are capable of more than raising families and looking after one another, more than doing their societal duties at balls and dances, or whatever it may be.

And yet, I have realized, that in some ways, I was wrong. Marriage, when that marriage is to the one you love, is more important than anything else in one's life. And the privilege to raise children — to form people as they grow and mature to adulthood — is both a great responsibility, as well as the ultimate form of love.

I do not believe that means a woman must forsake all else in order to have love and marriage. For if she finds a man who loves her, who truly loves her, for the woman she is, then he will under-stand what she needs to thrive.

I am one of the lucky ones — a woman in love with a man who loves her, all of her, in return. Not all are so lucky. Some are lucky enough to have love, or to have purpose, or to have both as one and the same. Whatever you are fortunate enough to achieve in life, enjoy it. Love it. Love with all of your heart, and with all of your soul, and never be afraid.

She finished and looked up at him.

"I have been wrong about many things," she said. "I used to think that one could not love and be herself in the same breath. But love does not hinder anything. It only enhances it."

He took her hands and leaned across the desk.

"And I am proud to be the man who will enhance your life for the rest of your days," he said, a smile on his lips. "Your piece is wonderful. And will be well-read, as *The Women's Weekly* is now on the lips of all in London."

"Hardly," she said with a laugh.

"It's true," he insisted. "In fact, it is all I hear of. I do not know what caused it, but somehow you have gone from being scandalous to sensational."

"I'll tell you a secret," she said, leaning in, her voice low. "It's the ladies. They can accept it — and in doing so have changed opinions. The gentlemen believe they are in control." She winked at him and added, "But of course, they are not."

"Is that so?"

"It is."

She squeezed his hands.

"Oh, and one more thing."

"Yes?"

"With all of this talk of love ... there will be more of it soon."

His eyebrows furrowed. "Whatever do you mean? I know Ambrose is, ever-so-slowly, beginning to come around, particularly as he has fallen head-over-heels with a country miss but—"

"Which is lovely, truly it is," Phoebe interrupted. "But that is not to what I was referring."

"No, then what—"

And then she smiled at him, and that smile told him everything he needed to know. It would no longer be just the two of them — not that it ever was, of course, at least not in this house — but the love of which she spoke would grow beyond them as another would soon be joining their family.

And he could hardly wait.

THE END

* * *

Dear reader,

I hope you enjoyed the first book of The Unconventional Ladies! As a writer myself, I had a lot of fun writing Phoebe's story. She sees the Regency world as many of us would, were we to ever go back in time. She is certainly not the norm of the period, but all it takes is one person to start to make a difference.

Julia's story is up next. She explores the past and the loves she never let go of in both horse racing as well the man she fell for as a child. You can read a sneak peek of her story in the pages after this one, or download Lady of Fortune here.

If you haven't yet signed up for my newsletter, I would love to have you join us! You will receive Unmasking a Duke for free, as well as links to giveaways, sales, new releases, and stories about my coffee addiction, my struggle to keep my plants alive, and how much trouble one loveable wolf-lookalike dog can get into.

www.elliestclair.com/ellies-newsletter

Or you can join my Facebook group, Ellie St. Clair's Ever Afters, and stay in touch daily.

Until next time, happy reading!

With love,
Ellie

* * *

Lady of Fortune
The Unconventional Ladies
Book 2

WITH ALL THAT **stands against them, are they willing to risk everything for their forbidden love?**

Lady Julia Stone has everything a woman could ask for — parents who love one another as much as they do her, the ability to live her dreams by managing her own racehorse, and now, a duke who is interested in capturing her affections. So why does she feel unsatisfied?

Why can she not let go of her past love for another man?

Growing up the son of a maid and a groom, Eddie Francis knows how fortunate he is to have achieved his ambitions of becoming a jockey renowned throughout England. But a past secret and a current accusation against his character have him loathing the very nobles he works for, and questioning all he knows to be true.

Everything changes during one fateful race on a

Newmarket racetrack, when Julia makes an impromptu decision to disguise herself as a jockey and takes the reins herself. When she is discovered by none other than Eddie Francis, the man she once loved, she must put her trust in him to keep her secret and help her find victory.

AN EXCERPT FROM LADY OF FORTUNE

PROLOGUE ~ 1807

"*C*atch me — I dare you!"

Julia laughed with the abandon of youth as she dug her heels into her mare, Princess — so named by her brother as he felt the horse reminded him of Julia — to urge her to run even faster.

The impromptu race was on as they galloped over the green pastures of her family's country estates. She had to win, if for no other reason than to prove to Eddie that she was more than the fourteen-year-old girl he saw her as, but nearly a woman now.

She dared a quick look over her shoulder, letting out a shriek when she saw that Eddie was gaining on her, a wide grin on his handsome face.

"One hundred yards, Julia, and I'm coming for you!"

Julia leaned further over Princess' neck, speaking words of encouragement in her ear. Princess responded with speed, and Julia let a shout of victory ring through the air when she reached the lone pine at the edge of the field first, signaling her win.

She continued her celebration as she twirled Princess around, stroking her withers in praise. She finally looked up to find Eddie slowing his own horse as he caught up to her, a smile teasing his lips, despite the fact he was clearly trying to hide it — which was never an easy feat for Eddie, who seemed to live in a perpetual state of happiness.

"Well done, little one," he said, leaning over his own mount, patting the horse's neck. "You ride well."

Julia beamed with pride at his words, knowing how much they meant from a man who knew horseflesh and the quality of a rider as well as he did. Eddie was four years her senior, and she longed for not only his respect for her as a rider, but as a woman as well.

"It's thanks to you," she said, her eyes on the ground so he couldn't see just how much she admired him. It was difficult to hide when not only was he the best rider she had ever known, but he was also the most handsome, charming man she had ever met — which included the many friends of her two elder brothers, the boys who often visited on holiday during the summers.

But none of them, even with their impeccable manners and distinguished titles, had ever caught her attention like Eddie.

"I only gave you a little advice," he said with a shrug and a wink that made Julia sigh inwardly. Were she not on a horse, she might swoon so that he would catch her — that's what her friend Caroline had recommended — but she had too much pride in her riding ability to do so. Instead, she simply sat there staring at him, her cheeks warming, which made her only blush all the more as she knew he must be aware of just how embarrassed she was.

He took pity on her, however, which was just one more thing she loved about him.

"Come, little one," he said, tilting his head back toward the expansive estate that loomed in the distance behind him. "We should get you home before someone comes looking for you. Wouldn't want anyone to find you riding the way you are, now would we?"

Julia furiously shook her head. No, if her family caught her in such a position, it would be the last of her days riding alone. They trusted Eddie as a chaperone for her rides through the woods, for he had long been with their family, as had his father before him. Julia's maid was supposed to be accompanying them as well, but she could never keep up. It didn't take much to convince Maybelle to pretend to be doing so, however. All Julia had to do was offer her some of Cook's best pastries and an hour alone to read in the shade of the trees. Although Julia did also wonder if part of Maybelle's agreement had to do with Eddie's request along with his charming smile, which had made Julia's stomach turn in jealousy. But if it gave her a few moments alone with Eddie, well, it was worth it.

Their return ride to the stables was much slower, and they fell into companionable conversation.

"So, you're back to the city tomorrow?" Eddie asked her, to which Julia nodded.

"I do not wish to go, but Mother loves the balls and the parties, you know, and despite the fact that Martin is but one and twenty, my parents are already pushing for him to find a girl who would suit him. You know Father, with his love of horse breeding? Well, I suppose that extends to our family line as well."

Eddie gave a bark of laughter and Julia immediately snapped her lips shut as she realized what she had just said. It was true her father cared of not much but breeding and racing his horses — and ensuring the happiness of his family — but it wasn't something she should be speaking of aloud, particularly not to a man. That she had said such to Eddie was the height of impropriety. Though he didn't seem to mind. He was so easy to talk to, he made her forget her reservations.

"And you?" he asked, looking at her in such a way it was as though he already knew the answer. "Are you looking forward to London?"

"Not particularly," she said, turning her gaze from his as she tapped her foot and when Princess started forward a bit, Julia had to remind herself to keep her feet still when on the horse. It was her one fault as a rider. "London is ever so... stifling. And it is not as though I can even attend any of the parties, so more often than not I am confined to our London home. Of course, Father allows me to go on rides, but one must be so careful in London."

"No riding astride there, I imagine," Eddie said with a twinkle in his eye.

"Of course not!" she said, turning wide, astonished eyes on him before she realized he was kidding.

They slowed as they neared the brush near the house, and Eddie dismounted in one smooth motion as Julia did the same, refusing to wait for any assistance. She had a fair drop due to her small stature, but any proficient rider could dismount on her own. She made to undo Princess's saddle, but Eddie brushed her hands aside before he quickly and expertly did so himself, exchanging the saddle with the wretched and hated sidesaddle that was hidden in the brush. He held out a hand once more to help her mount, but Julia gripped the stirrup iron steady, placed her left foot in, and then reached up, grasped the pommel, and hoisted herself into the seat, sitting up as straight and stiff as possible on Princess as they returned back to the stables.

She sensed Eddie watching her, and when she turned to look at him, she could see the approval in his eyes and pride filled her.

"I shall miss your company, little one," Eddie said, causing Julia to look sharply toward him.

"Whatever do you mean?" she asked, her heart beginning to beat rapidly. Eddie typically returned to London with the family in order to look after Papa's horses. It was not as though she ever saw him there — truly, this was the first summer she had paid much attention to him at all – but she was looking forward to knowing that he would be nearby should she have the urge to see him this winter. "Are you not returning to London?"

"Nay," he said with a shake of his head as he looked off into the distance, but when he turned back toward her, Julia caught the sparkle in his eye. "I'm leaving. I've found a new position."

"What?" Julia knew her mouth was wide open, and her mother would be horrified at her unladylike behavior, no matter what company she was in, but she could hardly believe what he was saying. "Wherever would you go?"

"I've found a position not far from here," he said, and while the grin that broke out on his face was larger than any she had ever seen before, he wouldn't provide her another word of information. "I cannot tell you much of it — not at the moment — but it's of what I've always dreamed."

"But… but…" Julia sputtered, unsure of what to say, how to keep him from leaving. "Will you not miss… our family?"

"Of course I will," he said, and Julia was bothered when his smile was pitying, as though he knew what she really meant to say. "But this is an opportunity on which I simply cannot pass."

Julia nodded stiffly, though found she couldn't think of anything else to say as they neared the house. She knew, deep down in her soul, that her dream of being with a man like Eddie would never come to be. Her parents, as much as they loved her and wanted her to be happy, would never allow it. And then there was the fact that Eddie himself saw her as nothing but a child. She could hardly help the way she felt, however, and knew it was more than the infatuation of a young girl, as Caroline — a year older and, therefore, according to her, much wiser — had told her.

"It will pass," her friend had said flippantly. "But have fun while you can!"

Once they reached the stables, Julia slid down from her horse, and Eddie began to release the saddle and look after Princess. She stood watching him until finally he turned toward her.

"Well, my lady," he said with a bow, his hazel eyes sparkling as they always did, his dark chestnut hair peeking out from under his cap, so long it nearly covered his eyes. "It has been a pleasure to teach you to ride astride, though I trust it will remain our little secret."

"Of course," she said with a nod. It would be worse for her were any to know of what they had been up to, now that Eddie was changing positions. At the beginning of the summer Julia had tried to race her brothers, but they flew from her sight as she remained stiff and restricted in her sidesaddle. She had snuck back to the stables and switched the saddle herself, hiking up her skirts as she attempted to ride astride as her brothers did. After a few minutes of riding in the field next to the yard, she had been mortified when she heard a slow clap from the fence beyond and looked up to find Eddie watching her. Despite her initial dismay, however, it had proven to be fortune smiling down upon her. For Eddie had felt compelled to provide a few tips on riding astride and before long she had convinced him to teach her to race.

He, himself, had been learning from a horse trainer who used to be a jockey, and he had seemed happy to pass on some of what he knew.

It hadn't taken long for her to fall madly in love with him, and she lived for the days he would take her riding, instructing her and sharing all of his expertise. Though much to her dismay, Eddie had been nothing but polite and proper, and it didn't take long to realize he looked upon her as a child.

"Well," he said now, reaching out a finger to chuck her under the chin. "Be well, little one, and look after Princess."

And with one last wink, he turned, picked up a brush, and re-focused on the horse.

Julia wanted to say more, to tell him how she felt, but tears began to burn the back of her eyes. Rather than allow Eddie to see her emotion, she turned and fled, running back to the house as though the stables were on fire and she had to escape. She took one look behind her but could see nothing but the door open to the depths of the stalls within.

She was so blinded by her tears that she stumbled up the front steps of her home and nearly tripped, only to feel soft hands reach out and grasp her upper arms.

"Julia? Heavens, child, what is the matter?" her mother's gentle voice was nearly too much to bear, and Julia stepped back from her.

"I'm not a child," she choked out, but her mother's response was only to put an arm around her shoulders and steer her into a drawing room before urging her to take a seat next to her on the sofa.

"Is this about Eddie Francis?" her mother asked, bringing a finger to Julia's chin to tip her face up to look at her.

Julia widened her eyes at her mother, astonished at how she could be aware of her feelings toward him.

"I— yes," she finally blurted out with a cry, and her mother smiled sadly at her.

"He is a handsome man, Julia, and I can see why you might hold a bit of a *tendre* for him. But Eddie is a groom, and you are the daughter of an earl. Besides that, you are but fourteen, darling, and there will be plenty of handsome young men who will catch your eye in the future. Never fear, I will not prevent you from marrying for love – with a nobleman. The day will come when you truly understand what love means."

Julia shook her head at her mother, tears beginning anew.

"I already do. There are none like him," she whispered, as her mother took her hand. "And he is only four years older than me," Julia continued. "That's not much at all."

"Unfortunately, love, that matters not. Eddie has his own life to live, as do you. Your lives have intersected only for a moment in time. You've been born in very different circumstances, and therefore will take very different paths. I know it hurts, but it will pass. Now, darling, dry those tears as we must begin our preparations for London. Just think what fun it will be!"

But despite her mother's cheerful countenance, nothing could console Julia. For she felt, deep within her soul, that despite her age, what she felt for Eddie was far greater than a passing infatuation. For otherwise, it wouldn't hurt so much to know that he thought of her only as a young girl of the house, now would it?

And nothing was more painful than the knowledge that she might never see him again.

Chapter 1
Eight years later ~ April, 1815 ~ London

"Would you care to dance?"

Julia, currently deep in thought regarding the selection of a jockey for her prized horse, Orianna, looked up in astonishment, for it seemed as though the man had appeared out of nowhere in the very air in front of her.

She knew full well that the dance card attached to her wrist was near-to-empty, save for two names — one space marked later on in the evening by her friend Phoebe's well-intentioned husband, and another by a friend of her brother. Therefore, Julia saw no recourse but to nod as she stood. The man standing before her towered above her, though that was not at all a surprise, for Julia spent her life craning her neck to look up at others.

But when her eyes reached his face, she had to keep herself from gasping aloud. The Duke of Clarence? He wished to dance with *her*? She looked around to see if there was any other woman nearby to whom he may be speaking, but no, it seemed he was, in truth, asking her. Using every bit of restraint within her to keep the shock from her face, Julia took his arm as he led her to the dance floor as the musicians played a quadrille — thank goodness. Julia wasn't sure she would be able to manage a full conversation or the body contact a waltz would involve.

"You are a friend of Lady Phoebe's, are you not?" the Duke asked, to which Julia nodded. Ah, so that was how this came about. The Duke was a good friend of Phoebe's husband, the Marquess of Berkley. They must have cajoled him into taking pity on her. Julia and the Duke lined up as the notes of the dance began, and when they came together, Julia summoned her courage.

"Your grace," Julia said quickly. "Please do not feel that you must spend time with me out of debt to your friends. I —"

The Duke's eyes hardened ever so slightly as they separated and Julia took the hand of her next partner before she and the Duke were circling again.

"I do nothing that is not of my choosing, Lady Julia," he said with a hard voice, and Julia could only nod before the dance separated them once more. It was the last they spoke through the set, as time together was limited. Julia studied the man as they came together and separated. He was certainly handsome; there was no denying that. His hair was the color of midnight, his eyes a blue so piercing it was difficult not to be caught within their spell. But there was something about him that made Julia feel uncomfortable. It was as though he was trying to see through her, attempting to assess her thoughts. And she didn't like it — not one bit.

When the dance finished, she curtsied to him, and he bent low over her hand, shocking her when he laid his lips upon it.

"Until we meet again, Lady Julia," was all he said until he released her, and Julia whirled away, relief flooding through her when she found two of her friends awaiting her on the side of the dance floor.

"Were you just dancing with the Duke of Clarence?" Elizabeth asked, the surprise in her tone accented by a fair dripping of disappointment — whether in Julia or the Duke, Julia wasn't entirely sure.

"I was," Julia responded, leaning in toward them as Sarah handed her a glass of lemonade. "I could hardly believe it myself. I figured Phoebe or Lord Berkley must have asked him to dance with me, but he assured me that was not the case."

"Well, he certainly is handsome," Sarah said with a slight sigh, assessing the man who was now striding back across the room, stopping to speak with many acquaintances along the way.

"Looks can be deceiving," Elizabeth said dryly, and her friends turned to look at her.

"What does that mean?" Julia asked, but Elizabeth shook her head.

"Nothing of any note. I am simply being my typical shrewish self."

"Oh, Elizabeth, do not speak of yourself so," Sarah admonished, but Elizabeth simply shrugged an elegant shoulder.

"It's true, and I am well aware of it. However, when one knows the truth of the realities of certain people's character, it is difficult to think otherwise."

"And what is it that you know of the Duke?" Julia asked with curiosity as Phoebe joined them.

"Nothing of any note. We were acquainted in our youth, that is all. I have known the Duke far too long to be taken in by his charms."

"He actually was not particularly charming," Julia said as she took a sip of her drink. "In fact, there wasn't anything about him that overly attracted me. Nor do any of the gentlemen here or at any other party, unfortunately, much to the dismay of my mother."

Julia looked across the room now, catching her mother's eye. She was beaming, of course, clearly having noticed Julia grace the dance floor with a duke. Julia sighed. If only she could have refused him, for now her mother's hopes would be high and Julia wouldn't hear the end of it for days.

When her eldest brother had married, both of her parents had been overcome with joy. Martin had always done precisely what was expected of him, and now he and his wife, the daughter of a marquess, no less, were expecting their first child to be born this very summer. Julia's other brother, Samuel, was known by all to be a rake who enjoyed the company of far too *many* women, so her mother had set her sights on Julia's prospects instead.

Since Julia's come out three years ago, her mother had suggested one eligible young man after another, but none suited Julia, nor caused any emotion to fill her but boredom or, in the odd case, a simple bit of friendly affection. Fortunately, her parents would never push her to accept a man she didn't want, having known perfect happiness through their own marriage, but she could tell they were becoming frustrated with her lack of interest in accepting any sort of courtship or interest from the gentlemen who did call upon her.

"Well, at least you have had your fair share of callers," said Sarah somewhat morosely, but Julia shook her head at her friend.

"Only because of who my father is," she responded. "Why, to the rest, I believe they think me to be a child — a boy, at that."

When Phoebe began to chuckle, Julia narrowed her eyes at her friend. "That may be entertaining, Phoebe, but you with your beautiful curves can hardly imagine what it must be like."

Phoebe laid a hand on Julia's arm. "I only laugh because you are one of the most beautiful creatures I have ever laid my eyes upon."

Julia rolled her eyes, though she couldn't help the smile that crossed her face at Phoebe's words. She could always rely on her friends to say what she needed to hear, though at the moment she wished for nothing but to be done with this party.

"Are any of you going to Newmarket at the end of the month?" she asked hopefully, but all except Elizabeth shook their heads at her.

"Not with the new babe at home, but I assume you will be

off?" Phoebe asked, and Julia nodded enthusiastically. With her father's love of horses, they attended all of the major races, of course, and it was one of the family traditions that Julia actually loved rather than lamented.

"I can hardly wait!" she said. "Father has given me full control over Orianna, for which I am ever so grateful, and I can hardly wait to race her. I've chosen a new jockey for her. He's young, but I wanted to give him a chance, and I think he will do admirably well."

She was about to continue to tell them of the competitors Orianna would be up against, but she could tell from the blank stares on her friends' faces that they were simply humoring her and had little interest in hearing all Julia wanted to share about Orianna's preparations. But oh, it had been such fun, training Orianna. The horse spent much of her time with the trainer, of course, but Julia attended nearly every session and often did much of the work herself. Orianna was everything to her, and if she had to spend the rest of her days alone with her horses, she would do so happily.

The Marquess soon came to collect her for their obligatory dance, though Julia wondered what the point of it was when he spent the whole time staring at his wife, Phoebe, waiting across the room.

A few dances later, Julia was blessedly able to leave to return to her family's own London home. It would be a night in which she would forfeit much sleep, but it would be well worth it.

For every morning, long before the rest of the *ton* was even awake, Julia would summon poor Maybelle and, with a groom along, would sneak out to Hyde Park, where, in the early hours of the morning, she could ride for as long and as fast as she wanted to. She couldn't ride astride, unfortunately — not here, where anyone could potentially see her — but it was still freedom of a sort. A smile turned up the edges of her lips as she thought of it while she waited for her cloak to be brought to her, and her mother, standing next to her, greatly misinterpreted her expression.

"Oh, Julia, I am ever so happy as well," Lady St. Albans said, clasping her hands together. "A duke, no less! And he is so handsome. The fact that he asked you to dance, well, my dear, I am not sure why you caught his attention just now, but perhaps it is simply that the Duke is ready to settle down and recognizes the eligible young woman you are. I do hope he will be attending the Newmarket races. Perhaps we can make arrangements for the two of you to get to know one another better, do you not think?"

Julia allowed her mother to prattle on without interrupting her. She should stop her and tell her that it was nothing but a dance, but it would be much easier to allow the Duke to quit his interest in her than for Julia herself to destroy her mother's dreams. When nothing came of the Duke's intentions, her mother would move on to the next potential suitor.

"Are we ready?" her father asked, joining them, and the two women nodded.

"Father, I've been thinking," said Julia as they approached their waiting carriage. "I have a new strategy for Orianna in Newmarket, though some will depend on what we see from the other horses at the race this weekend at Middlesex."

She began to outline her thoughts for an initial warmup race to introduce Orianna to the Newmarket track, followed by her entry into the great race on the Saturday ten days following, when all would be in attendance. Her father nodded thoughtfully, and Julia was grateful to have someone with whom she could speak of such things; someone who was actually interested in what she had to say.

"Are you sure this is wise?" her mother asked once they

had entered the carriage. "I'm not sure that Julia should have anything to do with such affairs, Garnet. It might mar her eligibility."

"Oh, I think not," her father said, and Julia could have reached across the carriage and hugged him. She would have, if her mother did not look so upset at his disagreement. "Any gentleman worthy of my Julia will understand the lure of horse racing, will he not?"

Lady St. Albans did not look as though she agreed, but rather than argue with her husband, she simply sighed and sat back against the squabs as she looked out the window. Julia was sure that her mother was envisioning wedding gowns and colorful bouquets as she relived Julia's dance with the Duke of Clarence.

Julia's own dreams would never match with those of her mother. For her thoughts were far away — they were in Newcastle, with Orianna, on the racecourse.

KEEP READING Lady of Fortune on Amazon or in Kindle Unlimited!

ALSO BY ELLIE ST. CLAIR

The Unconventional Ladies
Lady of Mystery
Lady of Fortune
Lady of Providence
Lady of Charade

The Unconventional Ladies Box Set

Reckless Rogues
The Earls's Secret
The Viscount's Code
Prequel, The Duke's Treasure, available in:
I Like Big Dukes and I Cannot Lie

The Remingtons of the Regency
The Mystery of the Debonair Duke
The Secret of the Dashing Detective
The Clue of the Brilliant Bastard
The Quest of the Reclusive Rogue

To the Time of the Highlanders
A Time to Wed
A Time to Love
A Time to Dream

Thieves of Desire

The Art of Stealing a Duke's Heart

A Jewel for the Taking

A Prize Worth Fighting For

Gambling for the Lost Lord's Love

Romance of a Robbery

Thieves of Desire Box Set

The Bluestocking Scandals

Designs on a Duke

Inventing the Viscount

Discovering the Baron

The Valet Experiment

Writing the Rake

Risking the Detective

A Noble Excavation

A Gentleman of Mystery

The Bluestocking Scandals Box Set: Books 1-4

The Bluestocking Scandals Box Set: Books 5-8

Blooming Brides

A Duke for Daisy

A Marquess for Marigold

An Earl for Iris

A Viscount for Violet

The Blooming Brides Box Set: Books 1-4

Happily Ever After

The Duke She Wished For

Someday Her Duke Will Come

Once Upon a Duke's Dream

He's a Duke, But I Love Him

Loved by the Viscount

Because the Earl Loved Me

Happily Ever After Box Set Books 1-3

Happily Ever After Box Set Books 4-6

The Victorian Highlanders

Duncan's Christmas - (prequel)

<u>Callum's Vow</u>

<u>Finlay's Duty</u>

<u>Adam's Call</u>

<u>Roderick's Purpose</u>

<u>Peggy's Love</u>

<u>The Victorian Highlanders Box Set Books 1-5</u>

Searching Hearts

Duke of Christmas (prequel)

Quest of Honor

Clue of Affection

Hearts of Trust

Hope of Romance

Promise of Redemption

Searching Hearts Box Set (Books 1-5)

Christmas

Christmastide with His Countess

Her Christmas Wish

Merry Misrule

A Match Made at Christmas

A Match Made in Winter

Standalones

Always Your Love

The Stormswept Stowaway

A Touch of Temptation

For a full list of all of Ellie's books, please see
www.elliestclair.com/books.

ABOUT THE AUTHOR

Ellie has always loved reading, writing, and history. For many years she has written short stories, non-fiction, and has worked on her true love and passion -- romance novels.

In every era there is the chance for romance, and Ellie enjoys exploring many different time periods, cultures, and geographic locations. No matter when or where, love can always prevail. She has a particular soft spot for the bad boys of history, and loves a strong heroine in her stories.

Ellie and her husband love nothing more than spending time at home with their children and Husky cross. Ellie can typically be found at the lake in the summer, pushing the stroller all year round, and, of course, with her computer in her lap or a book in hand.

She also loves corresponding with readers, so be sure to contact her!

www.elliestclair.com
ellie@elliestclair.com

Ellie St. Clair's Ever Afters Facebook Group

Printed in Great Britain
by Amazon

39816137R00182